T0197138

Quicksteel

Quicksee

Quicksteel

Mike McLaughlin

authorHOUSE

AuthorHouse™
1663 Liberty Drive
Bloomington, IN 47403
www.authorhouse.com
Phone: 1 (800) 839-8640

Published by AuthorHouse 01/25/2016

ISBN: 978-1-5049-2518-1 (sc)
ISBN: 978-1-5049-2517-4 (hc)
ISBN: 978-1-5049-2524-2 (e)

Library of Congress Control Number: 2015911844

Print information available on the last page.

Any people depicted in stock imagery provided by Thinkstock are models, and such images are being used for illustrative purposes only. Certain stock imagery © Thinkstock.

This book is printed on acid-free paper.

Dedication Page

To my mother, Betty. Four kids can't be easy to deal with, especially when one of them is me.

Prologue

Jason's head snapped up. He couldn't sleep now, not while he still had a mission to accomplish. His horse was still plodding along. Jason put his heels to the poor creature and urged it into a trot.

He had been riding for three days, barely sleeping except in small infrequent doses. He had to finish his mission, even if it killed him. His poor horse had been up the entire time, covering hundreds of miles with only a few stops for water. Jason knew the faithful steed wouldn't survive to the end, but this task was more important than a good horse.

He still had the box tucked under one arm. Jason guarded it like it was the most precious object in the world. And as far as he knew, it was.

The box was simple, made of strong oak, steel covered the corners and made up the lock. It was about two feet long, a foot wide, and half a foot deep.

Jason shivered as an autumn night's breeze blew over him. He pulled his thick wool cloak tighter around himself. He gave his cowl a tug to shield his face from the night air. Under the cloak, he wore wool breeches, a studded leather tunic, and leather riding gloves.

"Just a little further," he urged his horse. "Not too long now."

Suddenly, a soft whistling sound pierced the silence. His horse gave a strangled scream and pitched forward. Jason sailed over its head and landed heavily on his back. He groaned and struggled to his feet, turning to look back at the horse. Protruding from its neck was a long, white-feathered, black arrow shaft. Jason started running down the path as fast as he could. Another arrow sailed over his head.

He ran into the woods bordering the path and kept running. Even through his exhaustion, he was quick and sure-footed. Then, he heard a sound that filled him with dread.

Horses. They had horses! Jason stopped. He would never be able to out run them. He took a deep breath and walked to the middle of the path.

He still held the box. Had miraculously held onto it the entire time. His master had trusted him to keep it safe, and he did not plan on letting his master down.

As the horses drew close, Jason pulled back his cowl. His unruly, brown hair stuck up all over his head. A coarse beard had grown since he had begun his flight, his face was gaunt and he had deep circles under his eyes. But his jaw was set, his fierce, brown eyes glowed with determination. He would not fail. He could not.

The horses were bearing down. Jason could see three of them. One of the riders had a bow drawn and aimed at his head. The rider in the center was a huge, giant of a man with a massive, two-handed great sword slung across his back. The rider to Jason's right had a whip curled in one hand while he held the reins in his other. All three wore black cloaks with their cowls up, hiding their faces.

So they sent these three, he thought.

The one with the bow released his arrow. Jason held up his hand. Just before the arrow hit, he released a small *pulse* of energy. The arrow hit the blast and shattered.

Jason jumped out of the way as the riders thundered past. He let out another *pulse* that smashed into the archer's horse. The blast caved in the horse's ribcage and it ran into the giant's horse, sending both riders and mounts crashing to the ground in a tangled, bloody mess.

The man with the whip had turned and was galloping back towards Jason. He uncurled his lash and sent it flying towards Jason's face. The boy sent up another *pulse*, which deflected the whip and slammed into the rider's chest. He was sent flying from his horse to land on the ground in a broken pile. Jason could tell from the awkward position the man was in that he was most likely dead.

The giant had untangled himself from the carcasses on top of him. The archer lay motionless. The big man started forward. He drew his sword from its sheath. The blade was wider than Jason's neck at its widest point. The man held the sword easily, seeming very comfortable with it in his hands.

Jason held up his arm and sent a *pulse* straight at the giant's heart. The big man didn't even break his stride. Jason cursed, the giant was wearing a magic resistant cloak. They were very rare and very expensive. A sure sign that someone definitely wanted him dead.

Jason sent up a silent prayer of forgiveness for what he was about to do. He hoped his master would understand.

Jason took a deep breath. He was so very tired. The giant continued his slow steady stride towards him. The boy brought the box forward. The giant stopped and cocked his head. Jason balanced the box on his arm, and then he did what his master had strictly forbid him to do.

He opened the box.

Jason reached inside and grabbed the item that was the cause for so much trouble, letting the box itself fall to the ground. It was a blob of a silvery, gel-like substance about the size of a large orange. Jason let the box drop. The blob jiggled, then grew two tiny little arms. A crease opened and revealed a mouth. The blob stretched its arms up and gave out a yawn, blinking open its eyes. They were metallic blue. There was no pupil or white, just the blue.

"I was having the best dream." it said. It looked around and spotted the giant. It then swiveled itself to look back at Jason.

"Having a little trouble are we, Jace?" it asked.

"Now is not the time for jokes, Slik." said Jason sternly.

"Awe, come on man," said Slik. "You need to lighten up. If I never joked before we were about to go into a fight, I'd never joke at all. That's the only time you ever seem to pull me out."

"You are a living weapon." pointed out Jason.

"Who gets lonely." said Slik. "Would it kill you to bring me out every once in a while just to talk?"

The giant cleared his throat.

"Yeah, yeah," said Slik. "We'll get to you. Right now we're having a private discussion. Just calm down."

"Slik," said Jason. "Can we talk about this later? You know, when we're not in mortal danger?"

"Fine," sighed Slik. "I suppose you want a sword?"

"That would be helpful, yes." said Jason. Slik began to elongate. In a few seconds, he had gone from a jiggling ball of liquid metal, to a slim, but incredibly sturdy and sharp, short sword.

When Jason had first touched Slik, he had felt his fatigue slip away. Slik was a Quicksteel, a type of lesser monster. There were normal monsters, like trolls and ogres. But there were also lesser monsters. Living weapons that bonded to hosts to give them amazing powers. Quicksteels had the ability to change into almost any weapon, as long as it wasn't bigger than they were. Along with this, they gave their wielder amazing strength, agility, and endurance. Basically making the person into the perfect warrior, at least physically.

Jason slipped into a fighting stance. He knew that Slik was perfectly balanced to him. The giant walked forward and swung his great sword. Jason ducked, sidestepped, and swung Slik at the giant's stomach. The big man moved with surprising speed for one his size. His blade met Slik and Jason felt the vibrations almost numb his arm.

Jason leaped back. The giant held his sword in front of him with both of his large hands. He charged forward and Jason spun out of the way and slashed at the man's leg. The giant turned and caught the blow. Jason spun away to the left and slashed at the man's kidney. As the giant brought the sword to block, Jason spun again, this time to the right and cut the giant's left leg above the knee. The giant grunted in pain and took a step back. He may have been big and strong, but Jason was much faster.

The boy's mouth spread into a slow grin. He may yet be able to survive this night. The giant charged again. Jason took two steps, jumped as the giant slashed at him with his great sword, stabbed Slik into the ground, pushed off with his arm, spun in the air, and drove his foot into the giant's chest. The big man was forced off balance. Jason landed in a crouch behind Slik.

The giant managed to keep his footing and started forward again. Jason grabbed Slik in a reverse grip and pulled him from the ground. He laid the Quicksteel against his forearm as the giant brought down his sword. Jason went to one knee and caught the blow, and then he immediately jumped up and shoved the great sword away. Slik melted into a liquid and extended himself on the other side of Jason's hand. Now Jason was holding Slik in the standard grip. The boy yelled a battle cry and drove Slik into the giant's chest just as the behemoth was bringing up his sword. The big man grunted. Jason cried out as the great sword bit into his side. Jason yanked Slik out of the man's chest and swung at his neck.

The giant's head hit the ground with a thump. His body fell a couple of seconds later with a crash. Jason dropped Slik and grabbed onto the hilt of the great sword buried in his side. With a jerk and a grunt, he pulled the blade free and let it drop. Thankfully, the giant had only swung it with one arm while he had been wounded. And with his magically hardened muscles, Jason had managed to survive the blow.

Slik reformed into his normal blob shape.

"Hey kid, you okay?" he asked, concerned.

"Yeah," said Jason as he picked up the box. "I'm fine."

"Maybe we should get that taken care of." said Slik.

Jason picked him up. "No time." he said as he opened the lid.

"Wait, what are you doing?" cried Slik. "We have to get that gash looked after."

"I'll be fine." said Jason. "Getting you to safety is more important."

"Wait! Kid! No!" screamed Slik as Jason shoved him in the box.

"Don't you put me in he…" His shout was cut off as Jason closed the box. The spell cast on it took over and Slik was immediately put to sleep. The Quicksteel's magic was also cut off and Jason felt his energy drain out of him. The pain in his side almost made him collapse.

It would just be easier to die here, he thought. But his feet would have none of it. They began to move of their own accord, one foot in front of the other. Jason slowly made his way the last quarter of a mile.

Fifteen minutes later, he came to the steps of a small chapel. A priest came running out when he saw the boy stumble up.

"You have come at last." he said with relief heavy in his voice. Then Jason collapsed.

"What has happened to you child?" exclaimed the priest as he knelt down beside Jason.

"Bless me father for I have sinned." grunted Jason. He held the box to the priest. "I have killed three men to get this to you. Keep it safe."

"I will, my son." said the priest. Jason gave a shuttering breath and slowly let himself slip away into nothingness.

"I will, my son." repeated the priest.

Chapter 1

"Got to go. Got to go. Got to go."

Axel Matson was in a rush. He flew down the upper hall of his school. Ducking and dodging, he weaved his way through the flow of human traffic.

"Crap, crap, crap, crap."

His long black hair flew back from his face as he ran. His brilliant green eyes, normally calm and collected, looked like the eyes of a crazy person. They were wide and flicking in every direction. Unfortunately, they didn't see the teacher carrying a large stack of papers walking out of a classroom until it was too late.

Crash. A small storm of papers exploded into the air.

"Sorry!" Axel shouted back as he continued his head long dash for the exit. Why did his locker have to be on the other side of the school?

He raced down the stairs, taking them three at a time. He stumbled as he hit the bottom, but managed to keep his feet. He sprinted down the hall where his locker was.

Axel came to a skidding halt in front of his locker. His hand flew to the lock. Unfortunately, his hand flew a little too fast and he missed one of his numbers.

"Ah, come on!" Why did he have to be running late today? Today of all days he was running late. It could have been any other day, but no. It had to be today.

Axel finally managed to get his combination dialed and yanked the door open. He quickly ran through his classes in his head and grabbed the books he'd need and shoved them all in his bag, slung the bag over his shoulder, and slammed his locker shut and locked it all in one fluid, well-practiced motion.

"I really need to get a car," Axel muttered to himself as he flew towards the door, "And a license."

Axel burst through the doors just in time to watch all of the canary yellow buses pull away.

"God damn it!" he shouted, just as the principal walked out of the school.

"Watch your language, Mr. Matson."

"Sorry, sir," said Axel, grimacing.

"Use the phone in the office if you need a ride."

"Thanks, sir," said Axel dejectedly. He turned back into the school and walked slowly to the office. His mom was going to kill him. Axel breathed a heavy sigh. He was six-foot-two and weighed over two hundred pounds, most of which was muscle, but his tiny little mother could back Arnold Schwarzenegger into a corner when she got mad. And being late today was guaranteed to make her explode.

Axel's grandfather was coming to town.

His mom always got a little overdrawn whenever her father came to visit. Axel saw no reason why. Axel's grandfather had always been a little strange, but fun. Axel loved when he came over. He always told the most amazing stories. They were always about creatures he'd never heard of before. Tiny little beings he called Calla Lutai, or lesser monsters. His grandfather said that while the lesser monsters were immortal, they were almost defenseless on their own. They were impervious to disease and didn't age like humans, but they could be easily killed. Their entire existence depended upon other beings. Axel's grandfather said that the only way that a Calla Lutai could survive was to bond to another creature. Normally this was a Calla Meda, mid-monster, or a Calla Bas, greater monster. But they could also bond to humans. He said that in exchange for protection and care, a lesser monster granted it's wielder a special power. This could be anything from increased strength, to fire resistance, to rock-hard skin, depending on the Calla Lutai.

Every time his grandfather told one of his stories, his mother would shake her head in disapproval. Axel didn't get it. They were just stories. Awesome stories, but stories nonetheless. What harm could come of Axel hearing a few good fairy tales.

Axel walked into the office. He ran his fingers through his thick black hair as the secretary glanced up at him.

"Can I borrow your phone?" Axel asked awkwardly. "I missed my bus."

The secretary nodded to it and returned to typing on her computer. Axel picked up the receiver and dialed his number. There were three rings on the other end before his mother answered.

"Hello?" she asked.

"Hey, Mom," said Axel nervously.

"What's up?" asked his mother, suspicion audible in her voice.

"I kind of...," Axel sucked in a deep breath through is teeth then continued hesitantly, "...missed the bus."

"What?!" his mother screamed. Axel jerked the phone away from his ear.

"Okay, okay, Mom," Axel began.

"Do you know how important it was for you to get home on time today?" his mother asked angrily.

"Believe me," said Axel, "I tried everything I could to get on the bus. Nothing ended up working."

His mother sighed on the other end. "I'll be there in twenty minutes." she said and hung up. Axel set the phone back on the cradle. Tonight was not going to end well. He could tell that right now.

At least tomorrow was his birthday. Axel was turning sixteen. That was why his grandfather was coming to town.

Axel walked to the front steps and sat down. At least things couldn't get any worse.

"The one time I ask you to be on time and what do you do?"

"For the billionth time, Mom," said Axel, "I'm sorry, there was nothing I could do."

"Sorry doesn't cut it this time, kiddo," said his mom.

Alice Matson was a short woman with a short temper, and hair that was the same midnight black as her son's. Her brilliant green eyes were bright and intelligent, though the dark bags underneath them gave a hint to her stressful existence. She worked two jobs as a bartender and a cashier. Axel's dad had split when he'd found out his girlfriend was pregnant, leaving the young woman to support herself and the child alone. Axel had no idea how she did it, but she did. His mother could be short-tempered and ornery, but she was there, and that was the most important thing.

They rode in silence the rest of the drive. They pulled up in front of the apartment building where they lived.

It was a small, five floor building. It was made of ancient, crumbling brick held together with loose mortar. Axel was surprised it was even standing, but despite appearances, it was solid.

"Hey, Mom," said Axel as they climbed out of the car.

"What?" she asked.

"I really am sorry."

"I know." said his mother with a sigh. "Let's just get inside before it rains."

Axel looked up at the sky. There wasn't a cloud in sight. He shook his head. He'd be willing to bet that it'd be raining within the hour. His mom was never wrong when it came to predicting the weather.

Axel and Alice lived on the fourth floor. And because the elevator never worked, they always had to walk the entire way.

Alice opened the door to their apartment and immediately froze. All of the lights were on.

"That's not right." said Axel. His mom *never* forgot to turn off the lights. Axel could feel the adrenaline rising in his system. He stepped around his mother into the apartment.

"Axel," his mother hissed, "get behind me."

"I'm not five, Mom," he whispered back. "*You* get behind *me*."

"And where's my hello?"

Axel and Alice spun around. Standing in the middle of the room with his arms spread wide was Axel's grandfather.

"Grandpa!" shouted Axel, rushing forward to give the old man a hug. "It's good to see you."

"You too, kiddo," said Axel's grandfather. "You've gotten big, boy."

"Or maybe you just shrunk," Axel teased.

"Ah, you're probably right."

"Dad!" Alice's voice cut through their conversation. Her tone was not pleasant.

"There's my little sweetheart," said her father.

"Don't you 'sweetheart' me," said Alice. "Breaking into my apartment?"

"I know where you keep the spare key," said her father defensively. "Now is that any way to greet your father?"

Alice shook her head and gave her father a big hug. "Glad you could make it, Dad."

Grandpa was a big man. In his youth he had been broad-shouldered and strong. Age hadn't made his shoulders any less broad, and his arms still had the generous coating of muscle found on people who had worked hard all their lives, though a generous beer gut had replaced the thick abs he once had. His hair had faded to gray and his hairline was almost nonexistent. Liver spots dotted the top of his scalp and the back of his hands. He wore the type of trousers commonly worn in old mobster movies. He had on a white shirt tucked into them and brown loafers. A pair of bifocals rested on the bridge of his rather large nose. He peered through them with a pair of surprisingly youthful looking blue eyes.

"How 'bout I order us a pizza?" said Grandpa. "We can catch up while we wait."

"Sounds good to me," said Axel.

"Why not?" said Alice, closing the door.

Rain pattered against the window as they sat down to eat.

"So, Grandpa," said Axel through a mouthful of pizza. "How about one of those stories?"

"Aren't you getting a little too old for stories, Axel?" scolded Alice.

"Ah, leave the boy alone, Alice," said Grandpa. "It's good for him to get a little magic in his life."

"Yeah, come on, Mom," said Axel. "What's the harm?"

"Fine," relented Alice. "One story."

"Better make it a good one, then," said Grandpa. He sat back and scratched his chin in thought.

"Let's see, here," he said. "Did I ever tell you the reason why we don't see too much magic nowadays?"

Axel shook his head. "Nope."

"Well, get comfortable," said Grandpa. "This one's a long one."

Axel smiled. He always loved the way his grandpa told stories. It didn't matter that he was almost sixteen, Axel always had time for a good story. He didn't care what other people thought, magic was always interesting. He didn't care too much for the stage magic that guys in tuxes did in Vegas. That was all fake and stupid. It was good for a cheap laugh and not much else. No, what Axel was really interested in was actual magic. The real stuff. People throwing fire from their hands, or turning invisible. That was real magic.

"Nearly five-thousand years ago," Grandpa began, "All manner of monsters and magical beasts ran freely through the world. They lived side by side with humans. I won't say it was peaceful; many wars were fought before and after this era. But humans and monsters somehow managed to get along. Then man, as he always does, got greedy.

"You see, monsters built their own cities. Gigantic, magical places full of mystery and wonder. Humans were jealous. At this time we were still living in what were basically holes dug into the ground. We were dirty and poor and grew sick and died easily. But, monsters were strong and healthy. Some were even immortal."

"Like the Calla Lutai," said Axel.

Grandpa nodded. "In a way, yes. Calla Lutai do not age or get sick, but they can be killed."

"That's why they needed to bond to hosts in the first place," said Axel, "for protection."

"Who's telling the story here?" Grandpa laughed.

Axel blushed. "Sorry."

"Now where was I?" muttered Grandpa. "Oh, yes. Man was fed up with being weaker than monsters. They wanted to be fit and healthy and well fed. But the monsters didn't think man could be trusted with magic. Humans grew to resent the monsters who looked down on them. Some of the more powerful ones even took us as slaves."

"If monsters were so much more powerful than us, then how could we come as far as we have?

"People don't like being looked down on and mistreated," Grandpa explained. "After a while they begin to get angry. They begin to get desperate. The most dangerous enemy is one with nothing to lose and everything to gain. Eventually the humans began to strike back. It started as a few riots, then monsters began to show up dead. Humans started banding together, little pockets of resistance here or there.

"But one man stood above all the rest. You would know him as Achilles. He was strong, fierce, as good a fighter as any, and he had something that even the monsters feared."

"What?" asked Axel.

"Magic," said his grandfather with a wink. "It was said that his magic rivaled that of even the Calla Magus, the most powerful of all monsters.

"And so the humans united under Achilles and marched on the Calla's capital of Trohara. Or as we remember it, Troy. For ten years, the humans held the city under siege, but the defenses were too great. And the Monsters couldn't fight the humans directly for we had great numbers. Finally it was a trick that won the war. You've probably heard of the Trojan horse."

"Of course," said Axel.

"Well Achilles and a small band of warriors he trusted hid inside the horse and the rest of the army retreated. The Monsters took the gift thinking the humans had finally realized the siege was futile. They performed magic to see if it was a trick, but Achilles managed to hide his band from even the best of the monster's mages. When night fell, Achilles's band opened the gates to let the rest of the army in, while Achilles himself went to go confront the Magus.

"As he entered their chambers, he found not swords and spells waiting for him but a large pool of completely still water. He looked into the depths of the pool and saw himself reflected there, but then his reflection faded and showed him images of the world. Images of before and during the war. The pain and suffering felt on both sides. Achilles collapsed to his knees and wept, all fight gone from him.

"And then the Magus appeared. They told Achilles that he could end the fighting and suffering. He asked how. They told him to give up his sword."

"His sword?"

"It wasn't a normal sword. It was a Calla Lutai. A Quicksteel. It was the source of Achilles magic and fighting prowess. He gave it up willingly, to end the bloodshed. The Magus had gathered one of each of the hundred types of Calla Lutai, including the Quicksteel. They then used them to perform the most powerful spell ever heard of. They wiped all magic from the minds of mortals and all remnants of their civilization fell into myth. They made every monster appear as human or animals to us mortals. And then they themselves hid from existence.

"But there was still the problem of the Calla Lutai. The ones used in the spell had been touched by the souls of the Magus. Now they were much more powerful than they had any right to be. Achilles ordered them scattered and hidden. Vowing that such valiant creatures should never be used for evil. Then he also faded into legend."

Axel sat back and nodded his head in contemplation. "What would happen if someone were to bond with one of the One Hundred?"

"They would experience power beyond imagination," said Grandpa, "but power always comes at a price. Magic is not an easy thing to control. It takes a lot of energy to wield. Use it too much, and the result is not pleasant."

"You say that like magic is real," said Axel.

"And who said it's not?" asked Grandpa.

"Gramps, I love you, but that is the craziest thing I've ever heard."

Grandpa shook his head. "You'll learn soon enough just how real magic is."

Axel cocked his head and furrowed his brow. "What?"

Grandpa heaved a big sigh. "Nothing, kiddo, just a crazy old man's mutterings."

Axel glanced at the clock on the wall. It was already eleven-thirty. Grandpa looked at the clock too.

"Whoa," he said. "Time for this old codger to hit the hay."

"I think you should go to bed too, Axel," said Alice.

"But I'm not even tired," complained Axel, attempting to stifle a yawn and failing.

"Bed," commanded Alice. "Now."

"Fine." relented Axel. He walked away grumbling.

Alice turned to look at her father.

"Are you insane?" she asked as soon as Axel was out of earshot.

"The boy asked for a story," Grandpa said defensively.

"Don't mix my son up in the same shit you got me into." said Alice sternly.

"He has to learn some time." said Grandpa.

"I have worked for sixteen years to make sure that he has stayed safe." Alice replied.

"By keeping him ignorant?" asked Grandpa incredulously.

"Ignorance is bliss." Alice stated.

"Not when the monsters show up at your door." Grandpa pointed out.

"I've made sure that that won't happen."

Grandpa shook his head sadly. "I thought I raised you better than that, Alice. There's no escape, especially with someone with Axel's potential. Every time I come near the boy, I can feel the energy coming off him. It's stifling. And I'm just a human. Imagine what kind of beacon that is to a monster."

"My son is not going to learn magic." said Alice. Her tone brooked no argument. "And he sure as hell is not going to wield your little toy."

"There will come a day when Axel will realize what he is. When that happens, I want to be sure he's prepared."

"No, Dad," said Alice. "He's my son, not your little warrior."

"You think I'm doing this for me?" asked Grandpa.

"Are you?" asked Alice.

"For my piece of mind, yes," said Grandpa. "I would like to not have to worry whether or not I'll live to see it passed on to its rightful owner. And I worry about Axel's safety. This will kill two birds with one stone."

"No," said Alice.

"Listen, Alice," said Grandpa, "I know how you feel. I know what its like to want to make sure your child is safe from every potential danger. But what happens when you're gone? You can't protect him forever. He's my grandson, and I love him, but he's not a child anymore."

"Yes he is," said Alice. "He's my child."

"And he always will be." said Grandpa. "But while you were busy trying to protect him, he was busy turning into a very fine young man. I'm going to tell him, whether you like it or not."

"Not if I have anything to say about it," said Alice.

"He turns sixteen tomorrow," said Grandpa, "His magical energies will become too strong to stay hidden without training. He needs this."

Alice shook her head. "I don't want to argue with you, Dad. We'll discuss it tomorrow."

"Very well," said Grandpa. "Now I'm going to bed. Good night."

"Good night."

Chapter 2

Axel stifled a yawn as he walked into the living room the next morning.

"Good morning," said Grandpa raising a cup of coffee in acknowledgment. He was sitting at the kitchen table reading the morning newspaper.

"Hey, Gramps," said Axel. He walked over to the cupboard and pulled out a box of cereal. He got down a bowl and poured some of the cereal into it. He went to the fridge and pulled out a can of Mountain Dew and emptied it into the bowl. He grabbed a spoon sat down and started eating. Grandpa shook his head.

"Happy birthday, by the way," said Grandpa.

"Thanks," said Axel, through a mouthful of cereal.

"So what are your plans for today?" asked Grandpa.

"I was going to see a movie with Richie then come back here for cake."

"Sounds fun," said Grandpa.

"That's the idea," said Axel. He shoveled down the rest of his cereal and drained the bowl. "See ya later, Grandpa."

"Have a good time," Grandpa called as Axel rushed out the door. Axel gave a wave as he left. Grandpa shook his head and went back to reading the paper.

"Teenagers," he muttered.

"I. Am. Iron Man. Something, something, something, something, Iron Man," Axel's best friend Richie sang as they were riding the subway out of Queens on their way to the movie theater in Manhattan.

"We're not even going to see Iron Man," said Axel. "It's the Avengers."

"It has Iron Man in it," said Richie, waving his hand in a dismissive gesture. Axel shook his head.

Richie was built like stretched taffy. He was close to Axel in height, but where as Axel was filled out from all the weightlifting he did for sports,

Richie was incredibly thin. There was barely a scrap of fat or muscle to be found anywhere on his body. Richie was your classic Sci-Fi nerd. He could name every single member of the X-Men, along with their powers and secret identities. He was currently wearing a Hulk T-shirt and old worn out jeans. They hung loosely from his waist, but every pair of pants he wore hung loosely on him. He had wild, mousy-brown hair that stuck up in every direction. His blue eyes always had a little sparkle and the corner of his mouth was always a little crooked, like he was privy to some cosmic joke.

Axel looked up and glanced around at the other people in the subway car. There were a few business men chatting on cell phones. A few tourists snapped pictures at the tunnel walls, because a concrete tube was apparently interesting to people who had never seen it before.

On the other side of the car, a homeless man sat slouched in a corner covering up with a threadbare blanket. Axel scanned around some more. He was surprised to spot a girl leaning against the side of the train, staring at him.

She had hair that was so black it was obviously dyed with brilliant, ruby-red streaks running through it. It fell just past her shoulders. Her eyes were a brown so dark, they appeared black. Her lips matched the streaks in her hair. She was tall and willowy, yet very statuesque. Her curves were complemented by a tight halter top that was a deep scarlet color. She wore very tight black jeans that simultaneously covered and emphasized her long, shapely legs. She wore open-toed red sandals with two inch heels, adding to her already impressive height. Each long, elegant finger ended with a blood-red nail, and her skin was a soft pale white.

The girl's dark eyes met Axel's and she smiled, revealing beautiful teeth, even whiter than her skin. She stopped leaning against the wall and walked over to Axel. She stopped a couple of inches away and leaned down, placing her hands on either side of Axel, and giving him a peak down her shirt. He quickly glanced up so as not to look like a perv.

"You smell nice," said the girl, taking a deep whiff. "Very nice."

"Um, thank you?" Axel said, confused.

"How old are you?" the girl asked.

"Sixteen." said Axel, still not understanding.

"I thought so" she said. "You feel sixteen, but your looks had me a little confused. You look a bit older than you are."

"Cool, I guess?" said Axel, more than a little bewildered. This was every guy's dream, right? A beautiful girl walks up to him and starts complimenting him. So why was Axel acting like an idiot? He'd talked to pretty girls before, though none quite like this one. She was strange, to be sure, but in a way that Axel found surprisingly intriguing.

"Might I ask your name?" said Axel.

"You might," said the girl, raising her eyebrows.

"Will you tell me?" asked Axel.

"Ask and find out."

"What's your name?" asked Axel.

"Clara," said the girl. "And yours?"

"Axel."

"And I'm Richie," his friend chimed in.

The girl glanced in Richie's direction, and then turned her attention immediately back to Axel. "I have a feeling we will be seeing a lot more of each other," she said.

Axel grinned. "I'd like that."

"Maybe," said Clara. "But, then again, you might not."

"Let's hope it's option A," said Axel. "That sounds a lot more pleasurable."

"We can always hope, can't we?" Clara raised her eyebrows again. The subway came to a stop and the doors opened. Clara stepped off the subway, with a glance back at Axel. Axel glanced at the station number. He still had two more stops before the theater. He glanced at Richie, who was staring at him in amazement, then he did something he never did before. He changed his mind.

"Do you still want to go to the movie?" asked Axel.

"No," said Richie.

"Me neither."

"Then what are we doing here?"

They jumped off the subway just as the doors closed.

They caught up to her just as they came to the top of the stairs leading out of the subway. Richie was about to walk up to her when Axel caught his arm.

"What the…?" Richie began, spinning around.

Axel put his finger to his lips. He slowly shook his head. Richie nodded in understanding. The two guys began to walk casually, but kept their eyes trained on Clara.

At the end of the block, she turned left. Axel and Richie followed her. She walked past a couple of buildings before slipping into a side alley.

Axel stopped just before the alleyway and motioned for Richie to stop too. He cautiously peered around the corner.

Clara stood in the middle of the alley with her back to him.

"I know you're there," she called out.

Axel grimaced. He walked into the alley.

"How did you know we were following you?" he asked.

Clara tapped the end of her small, straight nose with one elegant finger. "Like I said, you smell nice."

"Ha-ha," Richie laughed. "You reek."

"She said I smell nice, genius," said Axel.

"You still reek enough for a girl to tell when you're near."

"If I could interject?" said Clara, "Would you mind telling me why you were following me?"

Axel shrugged his shoulders. "Felt like I was supposed too."

Clara gave him a critical stare, and then broke out into a huge grin. "My, my. Aren't you full of surprises?"

"I followed you too," protested Richie.

Clara turned her gaze to him. "I guess you did."

She walked up to Richie. She was almost to eye level with him. She gently put a hand on his cheek. Richie smiled a big, stupid grin. Axel's mouth dropped in amazement. Then Clara slapped Richie with a resounding smack.

"Ow, what the hell?" he cried, rubbing his rapidly reddening cheek.

"Don't stalk me," said Clara coolly. "It's not very polite."

Axel burst out laughing. Clara turned her icy stare onto him.

"And don't laugh at your friend's pain," she said. "That's even ruder."

Axel immediately sobered up.

Clara walked further down the alley. Axel and Richie watched her go. She stopped and turned around. She put her hands on her hips.

"Well what are you waiting for?" she asked. "Follow me."

Axel and Richie glanced at each other. Richie shrugged his shoulders and started walking after Clara. Axel stood there for a second. His face creased into a frown. Then he shook his head and started walking after his friend.

"I just know I'm going to regret this," he muttered.

Clara walked up to a metal door at the end of the alley. She knocked on the door. A slot retracted, revealing a pair of blue eyes. They regarded Clara critically, and then glanced at Axel and Richie.

"Who are they?" their owner asked.

"John asked me to pick them up." said Clara. The stranger grunted and closed the slot. Axel heard a bunch of whirring and clicking noises and then the door opened. A small man stood on the other side. He looked to be in his forties, with a few grey streaks running through his long, dirty looking hair. He had a scraggly beard that made it look like he hadn't shaved for a few days. He wore a beat up leather jacket over a stained white T-shirt. His jeans looked like they had seen better days. They had two huge holes in the knees. Strangely, the man didn't have on any shoes or socks. And his feet looked like they had also seen better days.

He fixed his icy blue eyes on the group before zeroing in on Clara.

"You better know what you're doing, girl," he said.

"When don't I, Jensen?" asked Clara, walking through the door. "And don't call me girl."

Jensen chuckled. "I will when you stop acting like one." He waved for Axel and Richie to enter.

Axel felt a strange sensation run down his spine. "What are we going to find in there?" he asked.

Jensen's mouth split into a wolfish grin. "Gonna have to come in to find out."

Axel took a deep breath…then walked inside. Richie followed closely behind. Jensen nodded and closed the door sealing them in blackness.

Chapter 3

"So what is this place?" asked Axel.

A light clicked on. Axel and Richie blinked their eyes.

"Why were you standing around with the light off?" Richie asked Jensen.

The man shrugged. "Didn't see a reason to have it on."

"Are you going to stand there chatting all day, or what?" asked Clara.

Axel and Richie followed her as she led them down a long dark hallway. They stopped when they reached another door, this one made of sturdy wood. Clara produced a set of keys from her pocket. She unlocked the door. Before she opened it she turned around and faced the two boys.

"If you tell anyone what is behind this door, or where this place is, or that it even exists, I will hunt you down and make sure you die a slow and *very* painful death," she said sternly. Her face suddenly broke out into a delighted grin. "Shall we then?"

Axel and Richie stared at her, dumbfounded. Richie closed his hanging jaw and shook his head to clear it. "You are one crazy-ass chick."

"Thank you," said Clara brightly.

"So," began Axel. "What exactly *is* behind that door?"

"This is your last chance," warned Clara. "Once you go through this door, there is no turning back."

"So we either see what's behind that door and have our lives changed dramatically, and probably not safely, or turn around, go home, and wonder exactly what we missed out on," said Richie. "Well that choice is obvious."

Axel stared at his friend. He wanted to protest, but he knew that Richie was right. If he walked away now, he would spend his life regretting it. On the other hand, he could end up regretting it anyway. But, he'd take a possible regret over a for-sure one any day.

"Glad that's settled," said Clara. "Now let's go."

With an elegant flourish, she opened the door and bowed, extending her arm as she did so in a gesture of invitation. Richie walked through the door without any hesitation. Axel, however, paused. He still wasn't absolutely sure whether or not he should go. He had no idea what he was getting into.

"Time's a wasting," said Clara, raising her eyebrows and nodding her head towards the doorway.

"Hurry up, kid," came Jensen's gruff voice from behind them. "Can't leave that door open too long."

Axel took a deep sigh. "All right, all right. I'm going."

After Axel stepped through the doorway, Clara followed him in and shut the door behind them. Like the previous room, the one they were currently in was pitch-black. Axel heard a small click and the room was suddenly bathed in light.

Axel and Richie blinked as their retinas were seared once again.

"Could you maybe warn us the next time you turn the lights on in a pitch-black room?" Richie complained.

"You'll get used to it," said Clara impatiently.

"I don't think that's how it works," said Axel.

"Then you thought wrong." said Clara.

"But…"

"Can we just get a move on?" said Clara, cutting of Axel's response.

Axel took a look at the room they were currently in. It was large and circular. There were four doors, including the one they had entered through. Judging by the mural on the floor, the doors were placed at each of the compass points. They had entered through the south door. Long, blood-red curtains hung down over the pillars spaced evenly, making the room seem to, somehow, be at the same time regal yet simple.

A pedestal stood in the middle of the room. It was roughly three feet in diameter at its base and tapered to about a foot before rapidly expanding out again at the top. A black stain cloth was draped over it.

To Axel, it felt as if they had stepped back in time. He glanced up at the ceiling and was surprised to see that the room was lit by large glowing balls of light that drifted lazily around the room.

"I thought I heard you flick a light switch." he said.

"I did," said Clara, stepping to the side so that he could see it.

"Then how…?" Axel began, but then shook his head deciding it was better for his sanity not to know.

"So, what are we doing here?" he asked.

"I was told to find you for the ceremony," said Clara.

"What ceremony?" asked Axel.

"The ceremony that will reveal who you truly are."

Axel jumped in surprise at the voice. It was strangely familiar.

"Grandpa?"

"That's right, kiddo." said Grandpa, stepping out of the shadows. He was carrying a large wooden box. He walked up to the pedestal and set the box on top.

Axel was dumbstruck. "But...How...When?" he stumbled. "I left the apartment before you. How the hell did you get here before me?"

"Oh, I have my ways," said Grandpa mysteriously.

"This just got very interesting," said Richie.

"Richie Carson," said Grandpa with an amused look on his face. "I thought you'd end up here. Always did have the spark. Not as much as Axel, but it was definitely there."

"Thank you, I guess?" said Richie hesitantly.

"What spark are you talking about, Gramps?" asked Axel.

"Show him, Clara."

Clara reached into her front pocket and pulled out what looked like a tiny piece of bright blue fuzz. It easily fit in the center of her palm.

"Time to wake up now, Farad." she cooed.

The little ball of fuzz suddenly puffed up to almost twice its size. Thin little hairs stood on end as if statically charged. Two small emerald spots appeared on the ball. It took Axel a couple of seconds to realize that the spots were eyes. That led to the realization that the fuzz ball was alive. He wondered how it got such fine hairs to stick out so straight, until he noticed tiny green sparks running between some of them. They were actually charged with electricity. The little blue puff ball was actually generating electricity!

"Good morning, Sleeping Beauty," said Clara lovingly. "Have a nice nap?"

The fuzz ball swiveled to look at Clara and gave her a high pitched chirping noise. It sounded like the charging sound that every high-tech weapon in movies and video games made right before they melted something into a pile of steaming muck.

Clara ran her free hand through Farad's hair. When she pulled her hand away, little green sparks were running across her palm and between her fingers. After a few seconds, they winked out.

"Whoa," said Axel in awe.

"What the hell is that thing?" asked Richie.

"Ask Axel," said Grandpa.

"Why me?" asked Axel.

"Because I've been telling you about Farad and his kind since before you could walk."

"What?" asked Axel. "Are you telling me that that thing is a Calla Lutai?"

"Exactly," said Grandpa.

"What's a Calla Lutai?" asked Richie.

"A lesser monster," said Axel. "They are tiny little beings that can't exist on their own, so they bond to a wielder and grant them powers."

"What kind of powers?" asked Richie.

"Depends on the monster," said Axel. "I'm guessing Farad here is a Stormpuff."

"Stormpuff?" asked Richie.

"Don't let the name fool you," said Axel. "If the stories Grandpa told me are true, then that little fluff ball is currently generating a few thousand volts of electricity."

"Really?" asked Richie. "That cute little thing?"

"Yes," said Axel.

"Wait a minute," said Richie holding up his hands and shaking his head. "If that thing can generate a few thousand volts, then how come it needs a wielder?"

"He's generating the electricity," said Axel, "but he can't release it."

"Wouldn't he eventually overload?" asked Richie.

Axel tilted his head. "I never thought of it like that. Never really thought I'd be meeting a Stormpuff face-to-face."

"That's where I come in." said Clara, gathering a few more sparks from Farad. "As long as he's physically in my possession, I can control electricity and I'm immune to electric shocks. I take all of his excess and disperse it into the air. But I find it also makes a pretty good weapon."

With that, she gathered a few more sparks. But instead of letting them dissipate, she concentrated them into her pointer finger and aimed it at the wall. A brilliant green flash lit up the room and blinded the two boys.

When the spots cleared from their vision, there was a distinctive black scorch mark on the wall next to Clara.

"Holy crap!" shouted Richie. Axel's jaw was set in a line. He may not have been as vocal as Richie, but he was just as surprised.

"Are all the stories you told me true, Grandpa?" asked Axel.

"More or less."

"Then that makes Clara a mage." Although Axel didn't phrase it like a question, Grandpa still nodded his head in the affirmative.

"Correct," he said. "Clara is a mage. So am I. And so is your mother."

"Mom?" asked Axel shocked.

"She's been trying to shield you from all of this, but you would have figured out eventually."

"That's why she always gets uncomfortable when you tell me stories," said Axel, suddenly making the connection.

Grandpa nodded. "She was afraid that you would believe me. I knew you were smart enough to not buy into them without proof."

"But you also had to figure out some way of passing on the knowledge without me knowing you were doing it."

Grandpa smiled. "You always were quick on the uptake. Yes, I've been subtly preparing you for this day."

"Why not just tell me? Or follow along with Mom and pretend none of this exists?" asked Axel.

"Your mother wouldn't let me outright tell you before now," said Grandpa. "But, I knew that no matter how hard she tried, she could never hide you forever. Before today, I was willing to follow along, but now your magic is too powerful to be hidden."

"Why now?" asked Axel. "Why is today so special?"

"You are now sixteen," said Grandpa. "Your magic is finally starting to mature. It's acting like a beacon to the magical community. Normal people don't normally have enough magic to cast even the simplest of spells. But you, you come from a long line of mages. Our family's magic potential has always been great, but you have more power than either your mother or I ever did. If we don't train you soon, every monster and evil mage will be drawn to you like moths to a flame."

Axel shook his head. "Are you kidding me!" he shouted.

"I know this is a lot to take in…" said Grandpa.

"Ya think?" asked Axel sarcastically. "First I learn that the bedtime stories I've been told as a kid were real. Then I figure out that my entire family is magical. And on top of that I seem to be even more powerful than most people ever dream. Oh, and let's not forget that I have no idea how to use that power and that it will draw every bloodthirsty monster from every horror story ever told to try and take a bite out of me. Am I forgetting anything?"

"The weird girl with the fuzz ball that can shoot lightning," Richie added helpfully.

Axel gave him a withering stare and the skinny kid shut his mouth.

"I do have something that will help you," said Grandpa.

"What?" asked Axel a little vehemently. "What could possibly help me now?"

Grandpa patted the chest. "Your birthday present."

Axel gave him a disapproving look. "Really? A birthday present?"

"Open it," said Grandpa. "You may be surprised at how appropriate it is."

Axel sighed. "At least I get to do something normal today."

"That's the spirit," said Clara enthusiastically. "Even if that statement is completely wrong on so many levels."

Axel sighed heavily again. "Way to cheer me up."

"Glad to help," said Clara.

Axel shook his head and walked up to the podium. He started to reach for the box, but hesitated.

"Is this going to be painful?" he asked.

"Depends on how you look at it," said Grandpa.

"That's…so reassuring," said Axel sarcastically, shaking his head.

He reached for the box again. He tentatively put his hand on the lock. He glanced at his grandfather. The old man nodded his head in encouragement. Axel turned to Richie. His best friend gave him a thumbs-up. Axel looked back at Clara. She rolled her eyes in impatience.

"Would you get on with it already?" she complained.

Axel turned back to the box. He took a deep breath to calm his nerves…then slowly lifted the lid.

Chapter 4

Axel peered inside the box. He immediately jumped back as a silver flash leaped toward him.

"Jason!" it screamed. The silver object landed on Axel's shirt and clung on. It was a blob the size of a grapefruit. Its metallic blue eyes were darting around the room. Suddenly, it fixed its gaze on Axel.

"Where is he?" it demanded.

Axel blinked in surprise. The tone was so forceful he found himself intimidated despite the creature's small size.

"Wh-who?" Axel stammered.

"Jason," said the blob. "Maybe you've seen him? Tall, kinda scrawny, brown hair, gaping wound in his side that your people put there."

"I have no idea what the hell you're talking about," said Axel.

"Don't lie to me!" shouted the blob.

"I'm serious," said Axel. "I have no idea what you're talking about or who this Jason guy is."

The blob blinked. Then it looked closely at Axel. Its eyes widened in surprise and it drew its head back. "You really don't know."

Axel shook his head. "No, sorry."

"I should be the one apologizing," said the blob. "I'm just a little disoriented. Can you tell me what the date is?"

"March sixteenth, two-thousand-twelve," said Axel.

"Two-thousand-twelve?!" exclaimed the blob. "I've been trapped in that box for seven hundred years?"

"I guess so." said Axel with a shrug.

"And who are you?" asked the blob.

"Axel."

"Nice to meet you Axel," said the blob. "My name is Slik."

"I'm Richie," said Richie.

"Nobody cares," said Clara.

"Clara," admonished Grandpa.

"Well it's true."

"And who are you people?" asked Slik.

"I'm John Matson," said Grandpa. "I'm Axel's grandfather. The young woman is Clara, her Stormpuff is Farad and you've already met Richie."

Slik nodded to each of them in turn.

"So what's the situation?" he asked.

"Excuse me?" said Axel.

"Well If I've been in the box for seven hundred years without so much as a hello to pass the centuries and you decide to take me out now, I'm assuming something bad happened for you to risk using me."

"What's so dangerous about using you?" asked Richie.

"You mean besides the fact that I'm the Quicksteel?" asked Slik.

"What's so dangerous about Quicksteels?"

"I have the ability to become almost any weapon," said Slik.

"How 'bout an AK-47?" asked Richie.

"A what?" asked Slik confused.

"You idiot, Richie," said Axel. "He's been asleep for seven hundred years. Guns weren't even invented back then."

"What's a gun?" asked Slik.

"Remind me to show you a picture off the internet later," said Axel.

"Okay," said Slik. "I'm assuming you'll also explain what a picture and the internet are too."

"There is a definite technological gap here," said Axel.

"I've only been asleep for seven hundred years," said Slik. "How much could have changed?"

"You have no idea," said Richie. "Let's just say that when we leave this room, you might have a mental breakdown from all the things that were invented since you were put in the box."

"That much, huh?" asked Slik.

"'Fraid so," said Grandpa. "Technology started on a rapid increase a few centuries ago. Even now there are probably hundreds of new inventions on their way to the general public."

"So what weapons can you turn into?" asked Axel.

"Swords, maces, axes, things like that," said Slik. "There are some limitations. It has to be size appropriate. I can't become a great sword, but a short sword is do-able."

"So, nothing too big is what you're saying?" asked Axel.

"Pretty much," said Slik. "You're stuck with one handed weapons."

"That's cool and all," said Richie, "but I don't see how that makes you so dangerous that something bad has to happen for you to be taken out."

"I'm a Calla Lutai," said Slik. "We have to bond to someone or we get killed."

"So?"

"So, if I don't have someone to wield me, I'm just a useless sword on the ground."

"You can still be useless if the person wielding you has no training or skill."

"I can't do anything about the training," said Slik, "But skill is a moot point when you're holding me."

"How so?" asked Richie.

"Whoever holds me immediately gains amazing physical abilities. Much stronger, faster, and more agile than normal."

"That happens to all mages," said Clara. "The raw magic coursing through their veins makes them more physically capable."

"I make my wielders stronger than most mages," said Slik.

"Cool," said Axel.

"It's actually kind of warm in here," said Slik.

"That word has a new meaning nowadays," said Richie.

"It doesn't just mean that something's cold," explained Axel, "It is also a synonym for awesome."

"Oh, I see," said Slik. "So when you said 'cool' you were commenting on my Gift, not the temperature."

"Precisely," said Axel.

"Now that we have that settled," said Grandpa, "I think it's time to start Axel's training."

"What about me?" asked Richie.

Grandpa shook his head. "Your magic isn't awakened yet. I'll find you a partner as soon as possible, but for now you're going to have to be careful."

"Wait, what?" asked Richie. "Axel gets an awesome sword-blob…"

"Quicksteel," corrected Slik.

"…but I have to go out in a world filled with monsters with nothing to defend myself?"

"You did that before," Axel pointed out.

"That was before I knew that monsters actually existed," said Richie.

"Why should that make any difference?"

"He's right, Axel," said Clara. "Now that he's been near the Calla Lutai and seen what they can do, the Veil has been broken."

"Veil?" asked Richie and Axel simultaneously.

"The magical covering placed here by the Calla Magus," explained Clara. "It's how they kept monsters secret for so long. The only downside is that it isn't very strong. If you see a monster, then the illusions it makes are broken."

"Two questions," said Richie. "One: if it's so weak, then how does it work so well? And two: what happens if a bunch of people see magic?"

"You have to actually see a monster for what it is," said Grandpa. "Once you do then the illusion is broken, but up until that point you could be best friends or even married to a monster without realizing it. They would have to actively try to expose themselves before you figured out what they actually are. Which brings us to your next question. Unless a bunch of people see a public display of magic that can't be rationalized in any other way, the Veil remains intact. And thanks to Vegas and Hollywood, almost all magic can be rationalized as either pyrotechnics or some other form of special effect."

"What do we do now?" asked Axel.

"We have to get you to a safe place where you'll be protected while we train you," said Grandpa.

"Right," said Axel. "'Cause apparently I have a lot of magic potential."

"You don't believe us?" asked Clara.

"No I don't," said Axel. "I don't believe that there's anything special about me. I'm just some kid from Queens. I get average grades. And nothing strange has ever happened to me until today."

"I know it's a lot to take in," said Grandpa.

"That's an understatement," said Axel.

"But you're going to have to trust us," Grandpa continued as if he hadn't been interrupted.

"What would happen if I walked out of here right now?" asked Axel.

"You'd probably die," said Clara.

"What?!" screamed Axel.

"Some monster would smell you for sure," explained Clara, "and with your current skill level, which is pretty much zero, you'll get killed in about five seconds."

Axel turned his bulging eyes to his grandfather.

"Is she serious?"

Grandpa nodded his head solemnly. "I'm afraid so."

"Great birthday gift, Gramps," said Axel sarcastically. "I get a very out of the loop blob-thing…"

"Quicksteel," said Slik.

"Like it matters!" shouted Axel. "I get a very out of the loop blob-thing and a very good chance of dying. Thank you so much."

"If you stick with us," said Grandpa calmly, "then there is a very good chance that you'll not only survive this day, but you'll also become strong enough to scare away almost any monster."

"And how long will that take?' asked Axel.

"About ten years," said Clara with an angelic smile.

Axel clenched his left hand into a fist and distorted his face like he was trying very hard not to explode. He took a deep breath and unclenched his fist.

"And how long do we have before something tries to kill me?"

BAM!

The door that they came through shook in its frame like something heavy had been thrown against it.

Axel gave a huge defeated sigh. "Of course."

BAM!

"I was afraid of this," said Grandpa. "We have to get out of here now."

"What is that?" asked Richie.

"I was being followed," said Grandpa. "I thought I lost them but I guess they found me.

BAM!

"What was following you?" asked Axel.

BAM!

"No time," said Grandpa. "You have to leave now."

BAM!

The door shook again and a large crack appeared in the middle. They could here the sounds of an intense struggle.

Then the door exploded.

Chapter 5

Jensen flew through the now shattered door. Axel figured that he had been the heavy thing that was thrown against it.

Through the broken door frame walked a man from a nightmare. He was almost eight feet tall and seemed to be built entirely of muscle. He was wearing a black cloak that dragged on the floor and completely covered his body. He even had a cowl hanging over his head, hiding his face in shadow.

"That's impossible," Slik whispered.

"What is?" asked Axel.

"Kid, I have some advice for you," said Slik. "Run."

"But…"

"Now!" ordered Slik.

"Do as he says," commanded Grandpa. "I'll hold him off. Clara, take the boys out of here. You know where to go."

"Right," said Clara, nodding her head. She rushed forward and helped a dazed Jensen to his feet.

"You two, follow me," she barked.

Richie obeyed without hesitation, but Axel froze. He glanced between his grandfather and the newcomer. Grandpa caught his eye and gave a wink.

"Go, Axel," said Grandpa, "I still have a few tricks up my sleeve."

Grandpa raised his hand toward the giant. A huge blast of energy rippled out from his hand and slammed into the giant's chest. The big man took a step back from the blow. The giant flung his cloak back and revealed a huge sword clutched in his right hand. It had to weigh at least seventy pounds, but the man held it as if it was barely seven.

The giant began advancing toward Grandpa slowly. Richie ran up to Axel and grabbed his arm, tugging him toward the door Clara had just helped Jensen through.

"Come on, Axel," screamed Richie, "we gotta go."

"But Grandpa," said Axel worriedly.

"He can take care of himself. Now come on!"

Axel allowed himself to be dragged out of the room, but the last image he saw before he and Richie took off running after Clara was of the giant raising his sword above Grandpa's head.

Clara lead the boys down a short hallway and out through a door that lead to a back alley like the one they had used to enter the building.

"Can you walk?" she asked Jensen.

The short man nodded his head.

"Then let's go," commanded Clara. She ran over to a nearby fire escape attached to the right-hand building and jumped eight feet to catch the lowest rung. She quickly swarmed up the ladder and lowered it for the boys.

"Wow," breathed Richie.

"Yeah," said an equally stunned Axel.

"Are you going to stand there gawping at me or what?" yelled Clara.

Both boys shook their heads and ran to the ladder. Jensen was already at the top with Clara. Richie reached the ladder before Axel and began his rapid assent. He was about half way up when the door behind them burst open.

Axel whirled around, expecting to see the giant. Instead, two smaller, but still fairly large men stood in the doorway. They both had on cloaks that looked similar to the giant's, but one had a quiver of arrows slung over one shoulder. He opened his cloak to reveal the bow that went with them.

Axel glanced down at the blob in his hands. Slik was literally quivering with fear. Something about these strangers deeply terrified the Quicksteel. That seemed to make up Axel's mind.

"Richie," he said, "meet me at the theater."

"What?" asked Richie, shocked, but Axel had already started sprinting for the alleyway.

An arrow whistled past Axel's head. He reflexively ducked but kept running for the end of the alley way. He made it and turned left. He barreled past pedestrians who cursed and swore at him as he ran past.

Axel looked at Slik again. The blob had regained its composure.

"We need a plan here," said Axel.

"Why are you looking at me?" asked Slik.

"You are useless," shouted Axel.

"Oh yeah?" asked Slik. "Well you're a coward."

"Why, because I'm running away from guys who are better trained and have less aversion to killing than I do?"

"I still say turn and fight."

"Even if I was totally insane," said Axel, "there are still too many innocent people around. Someone besides me could get hurt."

"Do you know a place where you could fight without anyone getting hurt?"

"In New York?" asked Axel incredulously. "This is the most populated city in the world. Everywhere you go, there's guaranteed to be at least fifty other people."

"I've never even heard of New York," said Slik.

"Right," said Axel, "seven-hundred year lapse. Are they even behind us?"

Slik slid up Axel's arm and glanced over his shoulder. One of the men in dark cloaks was shoving his way past pedestrians.

"The archer is still following us," said Slik.

"At least one of them took the bait," said Axel.

"What weapons training do you have?" asked Slik.

"None."

"You'll never beat him in a fair fight."

"That's what I've been trying to tell you!" shouted Axel, getting strange stares from the people he was shoving past.

"You'll have to catch him off guard."

Axel spied an alley up ahead. He glanced back. The Archer seemed to be having trouble getting past people. This guy definitely wasn't used to walking through crowded cities.

Axel dove into the alley.

"What's the best weapon for this situation?" asked Axel.

"Due to your lack of training, we're going to have to use a weapon that archer won't be used to fighting. It's very simple to use, so you'll have no trouble mastering it. Punch to stab, move your arm back and forth to slash. If he fires an arrow, try and move your arm in front of it, and keep moving and make yourself as difficult a target as possible."

"What are you talking about?" asked Axel, but Slik was melting.

At least it looked like he was melting. The Quicksteel slid underneath the sleeve of Axel's jacket. Axel could feel Slik's cold metal body wrap itself around his arm from the wrist to about half way down his forearm. Then,

Slik extended his body out of the jacket and about half a foot past Axel's hand. This part flattened out and curved slightly.

Axel was now wearing a large bracelet with a short, yet very sharp double sided blade attached that ended in an extremely sharp point. Axel turned his arm to get a good look at the weapon he now wielded.

"Cool," he breathed. Just then, the archer barreled around the corner and flashed past Axel.

Before the cloaked man could turn around, Axel leaped forward and aimed a punch at his back. But the man was fast. He rolled out of the way and turned around, raising and drawing his bow as he did so, landing on one knee with an arrow pointed at Axel's heart. It was all done in one very fluid, well rehearsed motion.

Axel barely had time to move his arm before the arrow was released. It punched a hole through his jacket, but deflected harmlessly off the metal cuff underneath. Now it was the archer's turn to be surprised.

Unfortunately, Axel had surprised himself. He had never moved so fast before. He and the archer recovered at about the same time. The archer had an arrow nocked and drawn before Axel could draw in a breath. Axel jumped out of the way of the next arrow and began zigzagging toward the archer who was firing arrow after arrow at Axel and missing every one. This caught the man off-guard. He had been expecting the boy to be docile and helpless. He was about to regret that mistake.

Axel felt the adrenaline rush he got during football. As soon as he said 'hike' and the ball was in his hands, everything would slow down. His mind would find all the opportunities to pass, asses the outcome of each, and determine the best course of action all in a few seconds, then it would tell him exactly where to put the ball and how much force and the angle needed to hit the target.

Now he could see every arrow. Knew exactly where and how to dodge. His arm moving faster than he thought he was capable of. Not just blocking, but actually cutting the arrows in half.

Axel rolled under the last arrow the archer fired and came up on one knee, plunging the arm-blade into the man's chest. Axel heard a groan and a startled gasp. He yanked the blade out and the archer toppled over.

Axel stood up and stared open mouthed at what he had just done. He had actually killed a man! Not only was he surprised at the sheer act of him taking another's life, but it was the way he had done it that also shocked him. He had never moved like that before, even in his football games he hadn't been quite this coordinated. Every muscle in his body felt perfectly tuned to his mind. He was full of anxious energy, all of his senses on alert. He felt powerful. And it scared him.

Slik returned to his blob form. He slid up to Axel's shoulder and looked down at the man he had just been stabbed through.

"Not to be insensitive here," he said, "I mean, I know the first kill is hard, but we gotta go. Now."

Axel just stared at the body.

"I killed somebody," he breathed.

"Kid, we really don't have time for this," said Slik. "It was either him or you. You just did what you had to do to survive. We can worry about your damaged psyche later. Right now, we have to keep moving before somebody else comes after us."

"Like the cops?" asked Axel, suddenly coming out of his stupor.

"Who?" asked Slik.

"Law enforcement," explained Axel. "If they find me here with this body they'll throw me in jail."

"I take it jail's not a good place," said Slik.

"Under normal circumstances, no," said Axel. "But if they throw me in there I'll be trapped and you'll be easy pickings for whoever sent these guys."

"So jail is bad and we should avoid cops, got it."

"Let's go," said Axel. With one last look at the archer's crumpled corpse, Axel took off running down the streets of Manhattan.

Chapter 6

Richie watched Axel race down the alley and onto the street with the archer close behind.

"We have to go after him," he said to Clara.

"We can't," she replied.

"Why not?" Richie asked angrily.

The man below him uncurled a whip and sent it snaking up towards them. Richie jumped back and narrowly avoided getting hit.

"That's why," said Clara. She began pushing him and Jensen further up the fire escape. The man with the whip began to quickly climb the ladder after them.

They reached the top of the building and climbed onto the roof.

"Nice," said Richie, "now we're stuck up here."

Clara raced across the roof with Jensen close on her heels.

"Come on."

Richie watched them hit the edge of the roof and then his mouth hung open as they jumped across. They flew over the gap to land gracefully onto the next roof.

"This crazy bitch is going to get me killed," He muttered to himself.

"Come on," shouted Clara.

"I can't jump that far!" exclaimed Richie.

"You're going to have to," she shouted back.

The cloaked man 's head appeared over the edge of the roof.

Richie swore and took off running towards the edge of the roof. He reached the edge and propelled himself forward. He felt a moment of weightlessness. He had never jumped so far in his life. He saw the edge of the next roof drawing closer. He was going to make it.

Then he felt the whip snake around his ankle. He slammed into the roof's edge just and managed to get a grip before he felt the cloaked man give a tug. He could feel his hold slipping. Just before he fell he felt two strong pairs of hands grab his arms and pull him back from oblivion.

The man with the whip wasn't done yet. He braced himself and pulled, but it was two against one. Jensen and Clara both strained as hard as they could. Richie felt like he was being pulled in two. Then the whip came undone. They all collapsed on the roof in a jumbled heap. They scrambled to their feet and Richie started laughing with relief.

"Take that!" he shouted at the cloaked man. "Try getting at us now."

The man backed up a few steps then ran toward the edge and flew over the gap.

The grin dropped from Richie's face. He turned and ran.

"Don't taunt the enemy." Clara shouted as she scrambled over the opposite side of the roof and onto that fire escape. They raced down. They didn't even bother to extend the ladder, just simply jumped from the bottom rung with the cloaked man close on their heels.

"This way," said Clara. She went through a side door. Jensen and Richie were close behind. Richie noticed that Jensen seemed to be favoring his right leg.

"Are you okay?" Richie asked concerned. He glanced over his shoulder to see the cloaked man still following them.

"I'm fine," said Jensen. "But being thrown through a door and then jumping over a roof probably wasn't the brightest idea. I am getting way too old for this shit."

Clara began taking a very confusing path through the apartment building they had ended up in. After a few twists and turns the cloaked man seemed to have lost site of them. They came out of another side door, and ran towards the street. They came out right next to a bus stop which conveniently had a bus parked there. Richie was the first on board and swiped his bus pass three times.

They found seats just as the bus pulled away. Richie glanced out the window and saw the whip man burst through the front door of the building they were just in. Richie sighed as they left him behind.

"Well, glad that's over," said Jensen. "Now, if you don't mind, I'm going to get some rest."

With that he closed his eyes and within a few seconds was snoring softly.

"How the hell can he do that?" asked Richie.

"When you live like we do you get very used to grabbing sleep when you can."

"Will he be alright?"

"Mages heal much faster than normal people," Clara explained. "He should be fine in a few days."

Speaking of mages," said Richie, "Why the hell didn't you just blast that guy back there?"

"Because shooting a guy from the top of a roof in New York City would be a very public and stupid display of magic."

"I get that magic should be hidden," said Richie, "But what about when your life is in danger, there has to be exceptions."

"There is, but I knew we could lose him without using magic."

"But I almost died."

"But you didn't."

"Almost is enough to piss me off and beg for an explanation."

"Some people view magic as a gift," said Clara. "But I think of it as more of a tool. And like any tool, if not used properly it can have very unpleasant consequences."

"John said I have the spark. What does that mean?"

"It means that you can be a mage," Clara answered. "But you are untrained and highly inexperienced. Which is why I'm explaining this to you. You need to know what kind of effect your actions can have."

"So I'm supposed to learn magic."

"Whether you are supposed to or not is debatable. You have the spark, but it is not nearly as potent as Axel's and you don't come from a family of mages. You could have lived your entire life without knowing about magic and been perfectly happy. But your involved now, so you are going to have to learn how to harness your power."

"So I had a choice, but Axel didn't."

"Not everybody does."

"Did you?"

Her face creased into a frown. "I'd rather not talk about my past," she said. "The concern right now is finding Axel and making sure he's okay. He said to meet him at the theater?"

"We were going to see a movie when we ran into you. But I still want to know whether or not you had a choice."

"It's complicated," she said.

"That's not an answer."

"Just drop it!" she shouted, eliciting stares from the people around them.

"Sorry," said Richie holding his hands up in surrender. "I just wanted to get a feel of the person who I would probably be traveling with."

"Everybody has their secrets," she said sternly. "Remember that the next time you try to pry into somebody's personal life."

"I'm sorry," said Richie.

"It's okay," said Clara calming down a little bit. "Let's just focus on the task at hand."

"Then we might want to get off this bus, unless that guy was following us."

"We should have bought ourselves a little time, let's go get Axel."

Chapter 7

Axel paced restlessly in front of the theater. As people passed they gave strange stares to the kid frantically walking back and forth and muttering to himself. Axel noticed a few people had actually stopped to gawk at his strange behavior.

"What are you looking at?" he snarled. The people jumped and scurried away like frightened rabbits.

"Kid, you really need to calm down," said Slik from inside of Axel's jacket.

"I left my best friend with a chick who I barely know, but who also doesn't seem to be completely sane. A weird guy in a cloak is after them, and let's not forget that I just murdered someone ten minutes ago," said Axel. "Tell me again why I should be calm."

Slik opened his mouth as if to reply, but closed it and shook his head in resignation. "I got nothing."

Axel glanced around. He stood on tiptoe to see over the heads of the people walking by. He let out a sigh of relief as he saw Richie's lanky form walking through the press of people. Clara and Jensen were with him. The short man was walking on his own, but he still had a noticeable limp.

"I am so glad you guys are okay," said Axel when he got to them. "What happened to the other guy with the cloak?"

"Don't know," said Richie. "Clara had us jump across to the next building, climb down that fire escape, go through a few doors and take a bus to Midtown before she let us come here. The creepy dude never even caught up to us. How 'bout you?"

"I have some news that I'll have to explain better later, but long story short, the guy with the bow is dead."

"What?" His companions shouted simultaneously.

"I said I'll explain later," said Axel, glancing around nervously, "But right now we have to get moving."

Axel turned to Clara. "Grandpa said that you knew someplace to take us, someplace safe. We should probably head there as soon as possible."

"'Kay," said Clara slowly, "There's just one problem."

"What?" asked Axel.

"You're not going to like this," said Clara.

"Just tell me," said Axel.

"Alright, but don't say I didn't warn you."

"Out with it!" shouted Axel eliciting a few more stares. He rounded on the onlookers. "Keep moving or so help me God…"

Turning back to Clara, Axel waved his hands in a circle in the classic "go on" gesture.

"The safe place is a school," she said.

"That's not so bad," said Richie.

Axel held up his hand. "Wait for it."

"The school is in New Mexico," Clara finished.

Axel smiled a defeated smile and heaved a huge sigh. "Of course it is."

"Why New Mexico?" asked Richie.

"Think about it," said Jensen, "most of it's a desert and there are thousands of miles between most of the cities. Natural defense and not a whole lot of people to accidentally stumble upon a school for magic. It's the best location in the U.S. for a safe haven."

Axel nodded. "Okay, that makes sense," he said, "But before we go, we have to make one little stop."

"You said yourself that we have to get moving," Clara pointed out.

"I still think we do," replied Axel, "but we have to pick up my mom first."

"What about my parents?" asked Richie. "And my sister?"

"They should be safe," said Clara, "If they have no idea that monsters exist, then they won't be attacked. And since you were a completely normal human an hour ago, whoever sent the cloaked men probably didn't even realize that you existed. They still probably don't."

"Thanks," said Richie sardonically, "I feel so important."

"No problem," said Clara with an angelic smile that was completely incongruous with her devilish look.

"But we still have to get my mother," said Axel.

"Weren't you just listening to me?" asked Clara, impatiently

"She's my grandpa's daughter," said Axel, "Grandpa even said that she knew magic. If she's by herself, she probably will be attacked. And if she's with us, she'll be able to help defend us until we get to the school."

"Fine," said Clara conceding to Axel's logic. "But then we have to leave as soon as possible afterward."

"Fine by me," said Axel. "So we all okay with the plan? Get my mom and then get the hell out of Dodge."

"I thought we were in New York," said Slik.

"It's an expression," said an exasperated Axel.

"This time is very peculiar," said the blob, looking curiously at passing cars.

"I'll try to get you up to speed as soon as I can," said Axel.

"If we're all okay with the plan, then let's get moving," said Richie.

Axel hailed a cab and they all piled in.

"Greta's Bar on eighty-sixth," he said. The cabbie flipped the meter and started driving.

"Ain't you a little young to be goin' to a bar, especially this time of day?" asked the cabby.

"My mom works there," Axel explained.

"So that's where she's been hidin' all this time. Never would have thought Alice'd be the type to be a bartender."

A cold fear gripped Axel. "How do you know my mom?" asked Axel.

The cabbie let out a chilling laugh. "Kinda hard to kill somebody without knowing where they are."

There was a loud *thunk* as the doors locked. The cabbie glanced in the mirror. As he did Axel caught a glimpse of his eyes. They were glowing a hateful, blood-red.

"They've been lookin' for you and your mom for sixteen years," said the cabbie in a guttural growl. "And I find the both of you in under five minutes."

The cabbie let out another chuckle, this one was far more frightening. It reminded Axel of the nightmares that made him wake up screaming as a child. It stirred the deepest, darkest fears in his soul. Fears so deep that they were written in his DNA.

"c-c-c-Clara?" he stammered. Axel was so frozen by fear that he couldn't take his eyes off the cabbie. But out of the peripheral of his vision, he saw a brilliant green glow, then a gigantic *Boom* erupted in the car and the light moved into his field of vision and left startling afterimages.

The cabbie screamed, shaking Axel out of his stupor. He grabbed Slik out of his jacket.

"Blade! Now!" he screamed.

Slik didn't hesitate. He slid around Axel's arm and morphed into the arm blade. Axel jammed it into the hinge of the door and jerked his arm up as forcefully as he could. The metal screeched as Slik tore through it like paper. The door flew off the cab and bounced in the street. The car was swerving as the cabbie continued to spasm from the massive amount of electricity still racing through his body.

"Everybody out!" Axel yelled over the screams of terrified people, the blaring of horns, and the rush of wind through the door. Axel tucked himself into a ball as he jumped out of the car. He hit the ground and rolled, avoiding getting seriously injured.

Clara followed immediately afterward, then Jensen. Richie stared at them dumbstruck.

"Jump, Richie!" shouted Axel.

"Are you crazy?!"

The cab slid to a halt and the driver roared. Richie swore and jumped out of the car and sprinted towards the others.

"Run, run, *run*!!!" he screamed as he flew past.

The driver's door suddenly went sailing over their heads. The cabbie crawled out of the car and bellowed at the sky.

Axel's jaw dropped open. "Aw, son of a…"

The cabbie roared again and charged towards them. He was now well over ten feet tall and rippling with muscle. His clothes were in shreds that barely managed to cling to his massive body. Shaggy brown fur that was thick and matted covered most of it. His eyes glowed red and his nose had fused with the upper part of his mouth which jutted forward to give him a short, but obvious muzzle. When he opened his mouth to roar, Axel noticed that his canines were like miniature spears sprouting from his gums. His ears were now elongated and pointed like an elf's, but had huge tufts of fur billowing out of them.

The cabbie's arms, which were now long enough to swing past his knees, fell to the ground as he started running on all fours. His massive bounds rocketed him toward Axel and his friends.

Axel took Richie's advice. He ran as fast as he could, which is pretty easy to do when you have a hulking gorilla-man trying to eat you.

"Shit, shit, shit, shit," he cursed as he ducked and weaved in between cars.

"Duck!" shouted Slik, once again in blob form.

Axel bent almost double but continued running as fast as he could in that position. The ruined taxi slammed down on the hoods of both of the cars on either side of Axel and continued rolling down the street.

"Aw, come on!" shouted Axel. "He can throw a car? Really? Why is this happening?"

Axel caught up with Richie.

"Dude, what the hell is that thing?" asked the skinny boy.

"How the hell should I know?"

"You seemed to know a lot about the lesser monsters," Richie pointed out.

"Those were just some stories my grandpa told me. I'm not even sure how much of them are true."

"He's a lycanthrope," said Slik.

"A what?" asked Richie.

"A werewolf," said Clara, coming up on Richie's other side.

"Holy…" Richie swerved and almost ran in front of a car. He managed to dodge out of the way before it clipped him.

"Don't do that!"

"Clara," Axel shouted. "How do you kill a lycanthrope?"

"Silver or beheading."

"That makes our job a lot harder than I thought," said Axel

Another car landed right next to him.

"And It was still kinda hard before." Axel cursed again. He swore even more when they hit a very large traffic jam. The cars that the demon cab driver had been hurling at them had caused several cars to swerve and crash, effectively blocking their path.

"That's it!" shouted Richie. "I've done everything I could. I'd say that this is definitely the straw that breaks this camel's back. Now if you don't mind, I'm going to curl up in the fetal position and hope to God the giant monster man doesn't literally break my back. At least not before he kills me."

"We can't give up now," protested Clara.

"Watch me," said Richie.

The cab driver slowed to a walk and raised himself onto his legs. His giant feet left little spider cracks in the asphalt as he stomped laboriously over to them.

Clara held up her arm. It slowly started to glow green as little sparks of electricity flashed over it. The glowing intensified until Axel, Richie, and the werewolf all shielded their eyes from its brilliance.

With an earth-shattering *Boom* loud enough to drown out the Daytona Five-hundred, a giant bolt of green lighting flashed from Clara's arm and smashed the lycanthrope square in the chest. The monstrosity staggered back as the acrid smell of burnt hair and scorched flesh assaulted their nostrils.

Instead of falling down, the cab driver shook his head and patted out the few sparks that smoldered in the remains of his chest hair. A low grumble sounded from deep within his throat and he resumed his slow advance.

He stopped a few feet from them and lifted his arms. All three of the teenagers cowered, waiting for the final crushing blow.

"Hey, Ugly," Jensen shouted as he suddenly appeared on top of the werewolf's back. "Looks like you need a time out." The lycanthrope and Jensen flickered for a moment, and then disappeared. The short man reappeared a couple of seconds later without the monster. On his shoulder sat a small lizard-like creature with brown scales and enormous eyes that seemed to flicker like interference on a television. Its tail ended in a small round ball that distorted the air around it.

"Guys, meet Clip," said Jensen, gesturing towards the lizard. "He's my partner. And he just so happens to be a Teleporter. Now let's go before the behemoth comes back."

Chapter 8

"You can teleport?!" asked Richie incredulously.

"Yes," said Jensen. "Clip gathers energy and channels it into the ball on the end of his tail. Then he uses the energy to bring two points that are usually far apart much closer together. Technically, they start to occupy the same position in space. When he separates them, he goes with the new spot and the world reorients itself."

"That's awesome," said Richie excitedly

"There is a slight problem," said Jensen. "Clip can't control where the energy puts him or even how much is used. If he uses too much energy, it could create a miniature black hole. If he doesn't use enough, half of him will be teleported and the other half will stay where he's at."

"Okay," said Axel with a disgusted look on his face, "that sounds unpleasant."

"That's where I come in," said Jensen as he started herding them away from the accident site before the cops started pulling in. "I can regulate the flow of energy from Clip's body and direct it to a particular spot and make sure that only the correct amount of energy is used."

"How far can you teleport?" asked Axel.

"Depends," said Jensen. "The farther I go the more energy it takes to move the two spots on top of each other. Plus if I'm taking something else with me, like our hairy friend back there, that also takes more energy. I also need to be sure that I know where I'm going. I need to be able to see it in my mind or I could end up inside of a wall, which I can tell you from experience is very unpleasant. If I had to guess I'd say I could comfortably and easily jump at least one hundred feet. Too much more than that or if I'm carrying cargo, and the energy required could exhaust, or even kill, me and Clip."

"Sounds dangerous and kinda touchy," said Richie. "I'd rather just take the bus."

"I normally don't teleport unless I absolutely have to," said Jensen, "As you just pointed out, it's very tricky and potentially fatal. But, it's very handy to be able to teleport yourself out of a sticky situation."

"This is all very interesting," said Axel, "and I'm glad you saved our asses back there, thank you, but now we really need to get to my mom."

"Hey," said Slik, "Where'd the weird girl go?"

A cherry red Mercedes Benz screeched to a stop beside them, its engine purring like an entire pride of lions. Clara waved from the driver's seat and motioned for them to get in.

Axel took shotgun while Jensen and Richie crawled in the back.

"This is awesome," said Axel. "How the hell did you afford a Mercedes?"

"It was free," said Clara jovially. "I just needed to give it my magic touch." She wiggled her fingers while static jumped and danced between them.

"You stole it?!" asked Axel incredulously.

"Well you committed a murder already so I figured that whatever illegal things we do now aren't going to make much of a difference to the cops."

"She does have a point," said Richie.

Axel turned around to glare at his best friend.

"What?" asked the skinny kid. "She does."

Axel burst through the door of Greta's Bar. He spotted his mom behind the bar serving a few customers. It was almost noon and the lunch rush was in full swing. Axel took a deep breath; she was going to kill him for this. Then again, it *was* his birthday so she might at least wait until tomorrow before she strangled him. Axel sighed and shook his head in despair. He wasn't that lucky.

Steeling himself, Axel walked up to the bar. "Hey, Mom."

"Axel?" said Alice, surprised. "I thought you and Richie were seeing a movie. What are you doing here? And why are you so filthy? Is that a hole in your jacket? I can't afford to buy you a new one, and look how big it is."

Axel glanced down at himself. The hole in his jacket was from the arrow he had deflected right before he had killed the archer. As for him being filthy, bits and pieces of debris clung to his clothes, his shirt had a few singe marks, and there was a fine layer of dust covering most of his body.

"The reason I'm so filthy is actually why I'm here," he said, shouting to be heard over the noise of people and music. "Can we talk somewhere a bit more private?"

"Sheila," Alice shouted to the other bartender, "I'm going on break."

"Now?" asked Sheila, horrified, as she was trying to mix six drinks at the same time.

"I need to talk to my son," said Alice in a tone that brooked no argument. She motioned to Axel and walked through the back door into the kitchen, her son close behind.

"So what's going on?" asked Alice, crossing her arms.

"Grandpa gave me my birthday gift," said Axel.

His mother tilted her head and gave him a quizzical look. "And why is that so bad?"

"It's not bad, just very valuable," said Axel, "and kind of dangerous."

"What did he give you?" Alice's tone was severe. She looked like she was going to explode.

"Well, you see…" began Axel hesitantly.

"Me," said Slik, sliding out of Axel's jacket pocket and onto his shoulder. Alice's mouth opened in shock.

"Oh, Dad," she groaned in despair, "What have you done?"

"That's what I'd like to know," said Axel. "Unfortunately, we were attacked about thirty seconds after I let Slik out of the chest and Grandpa stayed behind to try and hold them off."

"I'm guessing the Quicksteel is Slik," Alice said.

"Ma'am," said Slik giving a quick bob of his silvery head.

"Grandpa took on a giant with a broadsword," said Axel. "He was amazing. He kept firing some kind of shock wave from his hands. It looked kind of like he was using the force or something."

"That's a good way of describing it," said Alice.

"That's not even the worst part," said Axel.

"There's more?" asked his mother incredulously.

"Two more guys showed up and chased us," said Axel. "I managed to get one to follow me while the others escaped."

"Others? What others?"

"Richie, the guy that was guarding the door to the place where Grandpa gave me Slik, and the girl who led me there," explained Axel.

"What happened after you led the guy away?"

"Um… you see, he had this bow, and he was firing arrows, and I… well…you see…"

"Axel," said his mother sternly, "What happened?"

"I …" Axel sucked in a breath through his teeth. "I killed him."

Axel didn't think there was any way that his mom could possibly be more surprised at that moment.

"Really?" asked Alice. "You actually killed someone?"

"In self-defense, Mom, I swear. If I didn't have to I never would have. And why do you have that strange look on your face that you only get when I win a game or get an A on my report card?"

"It's called pride," said Alice. "You actually handled yourself in a fight. I'm guessing the hole in your jacket was from an arrow, though you'll have to explain where the singe marks and dust came from."

"Can I tell you on the way to New Mexico?" asked Axel.

"New Mexico?" Alice asked sternly. "Why would we be going to New Mexico?"

"Clara said there was some kind of school for magic there," Axel explained.

A look of understanding washed over Alice's face. "Mortimer's. Of course."

"Mortimer's?"

"I'll explain later," said Alice, "But if we're going to New Mexico we better leave fast, especially while you're carrying him." She nodded towards Slik.

"Right," said Axel. "Don't want him falling into the wrong hands."

"You know, I'm right here," said Slik. "You don't have to talk about me like I'm a dog. I *can* understand what you're saying."

"Sorry," said Axel. "So we better get going."

"Right behind you," said Alice.

They left through the backdoor and ran over to the Mercedes. Alice jumped in the front while Axel climbed in the back.

"Drive," commanded Alice.

"Hey," said Clara, "I'm driving, so I'm in charge. Who do you think you are, anyway? Climbing in and telling me what to do."

Alice raised her hand and curled her fingers into a fist. The air around it began to distort noticeably.

"Listen, girl." said Alice threateningly, "We don't have time to argue. So either you start driving, or I throw you out of this car and leave you behind for the monsters to chow down on. Do I make myself clear?"

"Damn," said Jensen.

"Watch your mouth," snapped Alice.

"Yes ma'am."

Richie chuckled as Clara pulled away from the curb. "You know Miss Matson; I love it when you do that."

"Thank you, Richie. Now quit kissing my ass."

Jensen grumbled something about not being able to swear.

"What was that?"

"Nothing," he said quickly.

"I thought so."

"So what's our plan, Mom?" asked Axel.

"Get to New Mexico as fast as possible," said his mother. "But first we need to make a quick stop at our apartment to grab some things."

"I don't think we have time for that," said Clara.

"Then make time."

They manged to get to Axel's and Alice's apartment without too much trouble. They entered the apartment and Alice ran into her room. It sounded as if a tornado was making its way through it as she began to pack what she needed.

Axel took one last look around the apartment that had been his home for his entire life. Glancing at the pictures of himself when he was little. One was of his mom holding a baby Axel and standing next to her father in front of the apartment building. She looked so much more vibrant and carefree than the woman she was now. But even back then she still had a fierce glint in her eyes as if daring the world to try and get her baby.

"Hey what's this?" asked Richie. He picked up a note from the kitchen table. Axel walked over and took it from his hands. As he read the hurried handwriting he could feel a weight being lifted off of his heart.

Dear Axel and Alice,

I am hoping you find this letter before you leave. Hopefully I held off the cloaked man long enough for you to get away. If you do find this, then don't come looking for me. Your job now is to get to the school safely as soon as possible. And don't worry, this old man still has a few tricks up his sleeve.

Love,
Grandpa

Alice came out of her bedroom with a bag over her shoulder. Axel handed her the note. She nodded and tore it to pieces. "Your Grandfather is right. We need to get you to the school. He can take care of himself. Let's go."

"So how are we getting to New Mexico?" asked Richie. As they climbed back into the car. Clara was once again in the driver's seat

"Plane's out of the question," said Jensen. "They've probably got a few agents in security. Fake a drug bust and pull us out of the way to kill us all nice and quiet. Simple, clean, and highly effective."

"Then it looks like we're driving," said Alice.

"That's going to take awhile," said Richie.

"Thank you, Captain Obvious," said Axel.

"Now that we've got that settled," said Clara, "Let's go."

With that, she began to weave in and out of traffic. That rumor about traffic in New York being almost impossible to get through at rush hour is completely false. It is actually extremely easy if you ignore most signs, rules, regulations, other vehicles, pedestrians, and the laws of physics. People scattered and cars swerved as Clara swung around the corner and drove straight into oncoming traffic. Everyone in the car screamed as Clara drove the Mercedes into gaps that it shouldn't have been able to fit through. Clara herself laughed maniacally as she smoothly shifted gears and turned the wheel. As dangerous as her driving was, she remained cool, confident, and completely in control.

Of course, when you run through red lights, stop signs, and drive the wrong way down the middle of the road in a cherry red Mercedes the cops tend to notice.

"Clara, there's like ten police cars behind us," yelled Axel.

"Oh, don't worry about them," said Clara idly waving away Axel's comment.

"Why do I have a sudden strange urge to try and wake myself up?" asked Richie.

"Because that's the normal reaction to living out nightmares," said Jensen.

"I'm new to the whole concept of motor vehicles, and well motors," said Slik, "But I'm assuming driving the opposite way of all the other cars is not a good thing."

"It is a very, *very,* bad thing," said Axel. "Not only does it immediately draw every cop within three miles, it tends to end very abruptly and violently."

"In that case, I'm going to hide inside your coat now."

"Probably a good idea."

"We're almost to the highway," said Clara.

"And there's a blockade," Alice pointed out.

Sure enough, a line of police cars stretched out in front of them.

"A little help please?" Clara asked sweetly.

Alice sighed and unclipped her seat belt.

"MOM!" shouted Axel. "What the hell are you doing?"

"Clearing a path," said Alice as she leaned out the window. She raised her arm. The air around her hand began to distort noticeably even at the speed they were traveling. With a huge *BOOM* a gigantic *pulse* blasted from Alice's hand and flung a couple of the police cars aside. Alice let out two more *pulses* and the barricade crumpled. Cars and people were scattered along the road. Clara dodged them carefully, but was soon speeding away down the highway leaving a bunch of confused police officers wondering what had just happened.

"That wasn't so bad," said Clara.

"New rule," said Alice. "No more drawing attention to ourselves. And we have to ditch this car in the next town."

"Aww, but why?" whined Clara.

"Because thanks to you, it's now plastered all over the news. Plus it sticks out way too much."

"Still don't see why we have to get rid of it," Clara mumbled.

"What was that?" asked Alice sternly.

"Nothing."

"Thought so."

"It is going to be a long drive to New Mexico," said Axel.

"You're telling me," said Slik from inside of his jacket pocket.

Chapter 9

"I'm hungry," said Richie.

"Too bad," said Alice.

"I'm kinda hungry too," said Axel.

"I could eat," said Jensen.

"So where are we going to get some chow?" asked Clara.

"We are on the run from monsters, evil mages, and the cops," said Alice, "We don't have time to stop."

"Mom, we're starving. It's going to take us a couple days to get to New Mexico. We have to eat or we're never going to be able to make it."

"It's only noon," said Alice. "Can't we wait a little bit longer?"

"The last thing I had to eat was a bowl of cereal for breakfast. And that was at least four hours ago."

Axel furrowed his brow at this. Had it really only been four hours since he had left home that morning? So much had happened that it seemed like a life time ago. He shook his head. Nothing he could do about it now.

"Fine," his mother said. "We'll get something to eat at the next town. And while we're at it, we can find a different car."

"It took me forever to find one this nice," Clara complained.

"You were only gone like five minutes," said Richie.

"Yeah, in New York City. Imagine how hard it will be to find a car like this in some tiny, backwoods hickville."

"We aren't looking for a car like this," said Alice. "We find some nice, average looking car that will be almost impossible to track."

"Fine," said Clara, "we'll do it your way, you boring old lady."

"You have no idea how wrong that statement is," said Axel.

"There's a town coming up." said Richie. "Whatever happens here, I better end up with something delicious in my stomach."

"'Cause the world's gonna end if the kid with no magic doesn't get a pizza," said Clara.

"Hey, just cause I can't shoot lightning doesn't mean I'm useless."

"It sure doesn't make you use*ful*."

"You know what…"

"Probably."

"Shut up, both of you," said Axel, cutting off their argument. "We'll debate Richie's usefulness later."

"Ouch."

"Right now we have to focus on getting food and a new car."

"You got a plan, kid?" asked Jensen.

"As a matter of fact I do."

"Okay so it's very simple," said Axel. "Mom and Jensen go into the gas station here and get us some food while we find a car."

"Why are you repeating the plan?" asked Richie, "we already found the car."

"Shut up," said Axel. "It helps me if I can think out loud."

"That inspires so much confidence," said Clara.

"Screw you."

"You wish."

"Whatever," said Axel, taking Slik out of his pocket. "Okay, little guy, since we don't have any tools, you're going to have to become a wrench."

"That thing you showed me a picture of on the weird glowing brick?"

"You mean my cell phone?" asked Axel, "Yes, that thing. And just to save a little time, I need to ask, can you split yourself up."

"Yes, but it's tricky to hold my shape like that."

"You'll just have to hold out as long as possible," said Axel. "So, Richie and I will switch plates with the car next to us so that it's going to be a lot harder for the police to track us. After we do that, then Clara just has to do her thing and we pick up Mom and Jensen and get the hell out of this town."

"Sounds good," said Richie.

"Nice, simple, to the point, good plan," said Clara.

"Then let's get started." Axel sank his fingers into Slik's body and pulled. The silvery blob split with a soft squelching sound. He handed one half to Richie even as it turned into a wrench. Richie hurried over to the other car and began unscrewing the front license plate while Axel began to do the same with the car they were going to steal.

It was an old, black car with multiple rust spots, a few dents, and obvious wear-and-tear. It would be impossible to distinguish from any other car.

Richie finished taking off his plate just a couple seconds before Axel. They traded and began screwing the new plates back on. Clara calmly stood guard, making sure that no one spotted them.

With the front plates finished, Axel and Richie hurried to do the back. In a few minutes, the back plates were switched out and they hurriedly tried to get into the car. They quickly hit a problem, however.

"It's locked," said Richie.

Axel swore. He held out his hand and Richie gave him his half of Slik. The two blobs quickly melted back into one. Slik shook himself off.

"You have no idea how weird it is to be in two places at once."

"Slik, can you turn into a key?" asked Axel.

"Yeah, why?"

"Because the door's locked and my trick will only work on the electrical parts of the car," said Clara.

"I'll see what I can do," said Slik.

Axel held him down to the door and Slik extended a small tendril of himself towards the lock. It slithered inside and began to shift around.

"Hmm," said Slik. "Locks have gotten a lot more complicated."

"Can you unlock it?"

"Yes, but it's going to take me a few minutes to find the right shape."

"Hey, what are you doing to my car?" shouted an angry voice from behind them.

"I don't think we have a few minutes." said Axel.

"I've almost got it," said Slik.

"Hurry, hurry, hurry," said Richie as a red-faced fat guy waddled towards them. Whether he was red-faced from running or anger Axel could not tell, though he suspected it was probably both.

"I can take care of this," said Clara, Farad sitting on her shoulder.

"No lightning," said Axel.

"Aww, come on."

"If he get's too close, we run away and try again at some other gas station," said Axel. "But if you shock him the sorcerers after us will find out."

"You give them far too much credit," said Clara.

"They had a cabbie pick us up from a movie theater that I never said the name to. Who knows how far into the system they've gotten. I'm not taking any chances."

"Got it," said Slik, sliding his makeshift appendage out of the key hole. Axel opened up the door and jumped into the driver's seat while unlocking the other doors.

"Get in," he shouted.

Richie hopped into the back while Clara slid over the hood and climbed in the passenger seat.

"Start the car. Start the car. Start the car!" Axel shouted.

Electricity crackled between Clara's fingers as she began to focus the energy.

"Clear!" she shouted as she placed her hands on the dash board. She sent out a pulse of energy and the car roared to life.

"I so love you right now," said Axel as he threw the car in reverse and backed it out of the parking space.

"Richie, open the door."

The skinny kid did as he was told and Axel came to a stop in front of the gas station just as Alice and Jensen came out.

"Get in," screamed Richie.

They wasted no time and crammed into the back seat with Richie. Axel didn't even wait for them to close the door as he sped out of the parking lot. Richie looked out the back window to see the fat guy waving his arms and attempting to run after them.

"Well that went better than I expected."

"Shut up and eat," said Alice handing him a small personal pizza and a hamburger.

"Awesome," said Richie. He then began to shove as much food as he could into his mouth.

"You okay to drive, Axel?" asked Alice.

"Yeah, I'm fine, why?"

"Because you're holding onto the steering wheel like it's the only thing holding you to Earth."

Axel looked down and was surprised to see that his knuckles were white from tension. He took a deep breath and loosened his grip.

"I'm fine," he said, "Just don't ever ask me to steal a car again."

"I can't make that promise," said Alice.

"That is something you never want your mother to say."

"This is what happens when you discover magic."

"Still not reassuring," said Axel.

"Oh you'll be fine," said Clara.

"You really think so?"

"Yeah," said Clara, "Just don't ever be alone."

"Thanks, that makes me feel so much better."

"No problem."

"You really need to learn when someone's being sarcastic."

"I do," replied Clara, "I just choose to ignore it."

Chapter 10

"Higher, hold it steady," said Alice.

"I need to ask, though I probably don't want to know," said Axel as his mom instructed him on basic sword fighting positions. "Where the hell did you get swords?"

"I grabbed them when we went back to the apartment. Plus, I always keep a few blades on me for protection," said Alice. "Now shift your weight to your back foot and stop slouching."

After they had stolen the car they had driven the rest of the day. They switched drivers every couple of hours and only stopped to get gas and food, which wasn't nearly as hectic as the first time. They had bought a couple of tents at a sporting goods store and were now camping on the side of the road. Alice had decided it was a good time to start teaching Axel how to properly fight.

"You mean to tell me you've been carrying weapons on you and you somehow kept that a secret from me?" asked Axel.

"There are a lot of things you don't know about me."

"I've noticed."

"Good, just hold that position for as long as you can."

"How long would be good?" asked Axel.

"When you can hold that position for about an hour without the tip of your sword wavering you'll be ready to actually learn how to use a sword."

"You're joking right?" Axel could already feel the tension in his forearm. He didn't think he would be able to last much longer.

"It takes most people years to master the art of sword-fighting," said Alice. "A good portion of that is just building up your endurance. If you get into a long, drawn out fight, it helps if you can hold your sword up longer than your opponent."

"So you really kept swords on you while I was growing up?"

"Especially when you were growing up," said Alice. "I didn't know who was magic and who was just some ordinary human."

"So you took the blades everywhere?" asked Axel.

"Pretty much."

"When you dropped me off for school when I was little?"

"Yep."

"That one parent-teacher conference when I thought you were going to rip the teacher's head off?"

"I was stroking the handle of a dirk the entire time. That prick was lucky I have good self control. He tried to convince me you had some kind of learning disability"

"I'm almost positive I have A.D.H.D." said Axel.

"If you do, that'll help you in a fight."

"Really?"

"People with A.D.H.D. have trouble focusing on one point. Their eyes are constantly moving. In today's world where we need to read and pay attention this is a problem, but back when we had to fight for everything, being able to divide your attention effectively was a very useful advantage. It helped you anticipate an enemy's moves by watching all of them, not just their weapon."

"That actually makes sense," said Axel. "It also explains why so many people seem to have trouble sitting still."

"It's very hard to break thousands of years of conditioning and habit," Alice agreed.

"I still can't believe you managed to hide all of this from me."

"It was for your protection."

"I could understand that when I was little it was better to hide all of this from me," said Axel, "but I'm sixteen. I think I have a right to know who my mother is."

"I am the woman who protected you since the day you were born," said Alice. "And I plan to keep protecting you for as long as I can. But things have gotten hectic now and you need to learn how to fight properly."

You gonna teach me how to shoot a gun too?" asked Axel sarcastically.

"If we can find some, yes," replied his mother calmly.

Axel shook his head. "That is not something most kids expect to hear from their mother."

"Well you don't have a typical mother. And you're putting too much weight on your back leg, shift forward a little bit."

"Definitely not a typical mother," said Axel, shifting his stance.

"Not bad," said Slik, crawling out of Axel's pocket. "A few more years and you may actually be able to use me properly."

"A few years that we don't have right now."

"That's the spirit kid," said Slik, "always stay positive."

"This whole everybody trying to maintain a cheery attitude thing is getting really annoying," said Axel. "We are being chased by monsters and demons and mages, not to mention the giant guy with the freaking claymore. What have we got to be so happy about?"

"The fact that you're still alive should be enough," said Alice.

"Sorry if being on the run has made me a little testy, Mother, but I think I'm having a perfectly normal reaction to this particular situation."

"Okay we're done for the night," said Alice.

"What?" asked Axel, startled. "But we just started."

"Yes, but you're not in the proper frame of mind. You must be calm and steady when holding a sword." Alice gestured for Axel to return her blade. As she sheathed it she motioned for him to sit down.

"Let's work on meditation."

"Meditation? Really?"

"You must learn to calm yourself," said Alice, sitting in a cross-legged position. "Cross your legs and straighten your spine."

Axel did as he was told.

"Now close your eyes and breathe in through your nose and out through your mouth, counting to ten between each inhale and exhale."

Axel rested his hands on his knees and took a slow inward breath through his nose. He counted to ten and breathed out through is mouth.

"Good," said Alice. "When you feel that your mind is clear, come talk to me."

Axel could hear her as she walked past. He opened his eyes to see her walking towards the fire the others had set up.

"Oh, well that's just beautiful teaching mom," he complained.

"What do you want her to do?" asked Slik, "Sit and watch you breathe?"

"How the hell am I supposed to clear my mind when there's so much going on?"

"Clearing your mind doesn't necessarily mean having no thoughts," Slik pointed out. "You just have to be calm."

"This is the same fight we had outside the theater," said Axel. "How the hell am I supposed to calm myself when everything is happening?"

"True calm happens when everything goes to hell," said Slik.

"Thank you, Confucius. I completely understand everything now."

"This is what meditation is for," said Slik. "Don't try to empty your mind, focus it."

"Okay," said Axel. "Any advice on how to do that?"

"What is your main problem right now?" asked Slik.

"Making sure you stay safe," said Axel.

"Right," said Slik, "And how do you know that?"

"Because all the bad things started happening when I bonded to you," said Axel. "You're right, my mind does feel clearer."

"No," said Slik, "you think this is stupid and don't want to do it anymore so you're saying anything that will get you out of it."

Axel blinked in surprise. "How did you...?"

"We're bonded, remember," said Slik. "I can feel what you're feeling and I can assure you that your mind is far from clear."

"Fine," said Axel. "Please continue, Oh Wise One."

Slik gave him a disapproving glare. "You figured out the problem. Now we just need to focus on how to solve it."

"Best thing is to get you somewhere highly defended and well hidden."

"Like this school we're going to?"

"Good point."

"So now that you have a goal in mind," Slik continued, "you can focus all of your energy into achieving it."

"What if something happens?" asked Axel. "What if we're ambushed or attacked or something else gets in our way?"

"Then we deal with them as they come."

"So we just walk right into any trap we find?"

"We can plan ahead," said Slik, "but there's no way for us to predict every little thing that's going to happen to us between here and New Mexico."

"So we plan for the things we expect to happen and cover for the things we don't?"

"Pretty much."

"So then how do we do that?"

"We meditate."

"Wonderful."

"One thing that meditation brings is the ability to use magic."

This caught Axel's attention. "So I can do that energy blast that Grandpa and Mom were doing?"

"Actually, yes," said Slik.

"Will I be able to shoot lightning like Clara?"

"No," said Slik. "Clara can only do that because of Farad. When people bond to Calla Lutai, their magic changes on a very fundamental level. Quicksteels are unique in the fact that we don't do this. Instead we amplify how much magic is able to be used. Even now your magic is seeping into your body and changing it on a cellular level. You are much stronger and faster than the average human."

"Does this also mean I can use stronger bursts of magic."

"Yes," said Slik. "But I don't increase the amount of magic you possess, meaning that you will run through your supply of it faster."

"So where as mom is like a revolver, I'm like a cannon."

"I have no idea what either of those things are," said Slik.

Axel sighed. Then a thought occurred to him. "You said you could feel what I do, right?"

"Yes," said Slik.

"Does that mean that we could read each other's minds too?"

"That would require a very strong connection between us."

"Have you ever had that with one of your wielders before?"

"A few," said Slik.

"How do I rank with them?" asked Axel.

"What do you mean?"

"How do I compare with your other wielders?"

"You are young and we haven't had time to properly get to know one another yet. So it's hard to say. But so far you seem like you'll make a fine partner. You do seem to have a large natural supply of magic though."

"Can we try that link I was talking about."

"Then we will have to meditate."

"I think it's worth a shot."

Axel closed his eyes and began to use the meditation technique that his mom had taught him. He tried to focus his mind on Slik. He could feel the Quicksteel's energy sitting just outside of his mind, but every time he tried to reach for it it seemed to move away or disappear entirely.

"It doesn't seem to be working."

"Focus on finding your own energies for now," said Slik. "This is a very advanced ability. You are going to have to work up to it."

For the rest of the night Axel tried to look inward. He thought he could feel the energy that everybody was talking about, but it wasn't as strong as Slik's, certainly not enough to make such a fuss about. And every time he tried to reach it, like Slik's, he would seem to lose it. But Axel was determined and stubborn and continued to try.

Slik watched with approval. The boy was not easily deterred. That strength of will was going to be very important soon.

"I wish you were here to see this, Jason," he said to himself. "This boy might even be stronger than you. But only time will tell."

"Axel, wake up!" shouted Richie.

"Huh, what?" Axel jerked awake. It was still night out and he had fallen asleep in his cross-legged position. He scrambled onto feet that were still asleep and almost fell down again.

"What's going on?" he asked.

A whip snaked around his ankles and sent him plummeting towards the ground.

"Slik!" Axel screamed.

The silvery blob jumped into his hand and morphed into a sword. Axel slashed at the whip, but before Slik made contact it recoiled.

Its owner stood a few feet away. Axel had trouble distinguishing the man from the rest of his surroundings because of the black cloak he wore.

"Ah, shit," Axel cursed. It was one of the men who had attacked them earlier. Axel guessed it was the one who had followed Richie, Clara, and Jensen. Axel managed to get his feet under him and lurched into a standing position. He then began to dash wildly towards the camp.

The whip cracked next to his ear. Axel flinched away but kept running.

"Holy..."

Axel had reached to camp, but failed to notice where he was running. He tripped over one of the support lines for one of the tents and for the second time in less than five minutes, Axel Matson face-planted into the dirt.

"Damn it," he groaned. "That's going to hurt tomorrow."

The whip cracked again.

"If you have a tomorrow," said Slik.

The cloaked man flung the whip out straight behind him. He raised his arm to bring it forward. Axel closed his eyes and tried to hide his face. He waited for the sting of the lash, for the sound of the whip biting into his skin. But what he heard next was much more reassuring.

He heard the sound of leather hitting steel.

Axel opened his eyes to see his mother standing over him, the whip wrapped around one of the two blades she held in her hands, the right one to be exact.

"You alright?"

"Uh… yeah," Axel managed to stammer.

"Good, then get to the car," commanded Alice.

"What about you?"

A slow smile spread across her face. "I'll be just fine."

The man yanked on the whip and unwound it from Alice's sword. In doing so, he also pulled Alice a step forward. He quickly sent the whip back towards Alice, but he didn't wind up properly. Instead of going for her neck as the man intended, the whip went for her left side.

Alice quickly slashed at the whip with her left-hand blade. The whip bounced harmlessly off, giving Alice enough time to regain her footing. The man kept the whip in motion and began to send it at Alice from all sides faster than Axel could track. The blades in her hands seemed to come alive as they blurred around her body. The whip was deflected every single time.

Alice began to slowly move forward, her short-swords carving deadly arcs in the air. The lash-bearer was still flinging his whip as fast as he could, but none of his attacks came close to penetrating Alice's defense. Soon she was only a few paces away. At that distance she was able to crowd out the man so that he wasn't able to use his whip effectively.

"All right," cheered Axel. "Go Mom."

It looked as if Alice would defeat the cloaked man. She was on the verge of closing the distance and finishing him off when the giant appeared out of nowhere. His Claymore was already free of its sheath.

"Mom, look out," screamed Axel.

The giant swung his sword. Luckily, Alice had seen him just in time and managed to roll herself out of the way. The claymore cleaved the air where her waist had been only a split-second earlier.

The car pulled up behind Axel with Clara in the driver's seat and Richie riding shotgun. He didn't see any sign of Jensen.

"Get in," shouted Richie through the open window. Axel scrambled to his feet and quickly got in the back.

"Where's Jensen?" he asked.

"Getting your mom," said Clara.

Sure enough, Axel saw Jensen appear behind Alice and grab onto her waist just as the giant was about to bring down his sword in a crushing blow. The blade sank into the ground a second later.

Alice and Jensen materialized in the back seat with Alice sitting in Jensen's lap. Clara slammed down on the gas and the car took off down the highway.

"Just had to grab my waist didn't you?" Alice scolded. "Couldn't have grabbed my shoulder or my arm, no it had to be my waist."

"I was moving fast and preparing the next jump even as I grabbed you. I didn't really have much time to think."

"Of course you didn't," said Alice sliding onto the seat next to him. "Thank you for getting me out of there, anyway. That giant would have probably ended up killing me. The cheap bastard. Waits until I'm worn out from blocking the guy with the whip then jumps in to finish the job."

"I'm glad you're okay, Miss Matson," said Richie, "But we lost the tents. Where the hell are we going to sleep now?"

"Tonight," said Alice. "We sleep while we drive. I'll take over for Clara in a couple of hours so she can get some rest, then we'll start a rotation. From now on the only times we're going to stop is to get something to eat and fill up the tank."

"That sounds delightful," said Axel. "Spending the entire drive to New Mexico in a very cramped car. I can't think of a better way to end my birthday."

"Dude, it's like three in the morning," said Richie, "Your birthday was over a few hours ago."

"It was your birthday yesterday?" asked Clara. "You know what that means."

"Please not now," begged Axel.

"Happy birthday to you," sang Clara happily. Axel started to keep the beat by banging his head repeatedly against the window.

Chapter 11

Axel woke to a very unusual sound. Silence.

"Whoa, what the hell, why are we stopping?" he asked.

"We need gas, Numbnuts," said Clara. "And it's your turn to drive."

"If you have to go do it now," said Alice.

"I call it first," said Richie, jumping from the car and running for the station.

"I need some coffee," said Jensen.

"I'll come with you," said Axel. "I could really use something to wake me up."

"Wait for me," said Clara, "I'll pick us out some breakfast."

They entered the store and Axel spotted the row of coffee machines.

"Hey, I just thought of something," said Axel as he filled his cup.

"What?" asked Jensen.

"How the hell have we been paying for everything?"

In answer, Jensen handed him his wallet. Axel opened it up to find five different credit cards. Axel took one out.

"Kurt Wagner?" asked Axel.

"What?' asked Jensen.

"You went with Nightcrawler, really?"

"So I like X-men. What of it?"

"You went with the guy who could teleport," said Axel. "Isn't that a little cliché?"

"Hey it's my credit card," said Jensen defensively, "I can put whatever name I want on it."

"Mine says Ororo Monroe," said Clara from behind them. She had a stack of breakfast sandwiches in her arms.

"Storm, nice," said Axel, "Why don't I get one with James Howlett on it."

"I don't think you're much of a Wolverine, kid."

"Hey," said Axel. "I could totally be Wolverine, minus the whole metal skeleton thing."

"I really needed that," said Richie walking up to them.

"We better be hitting the road before those guys who attacked us last night find us," said Jensen.

"We just drove for like six hours straight," said Richie, "I doubt they could catch up to us."

"We drove longer than that before last night and it didn't seem to be much of a problem for them then," Axel pointed out.

"Do I at least have enough time to call my parents?" asked Richie.

"I thought we said that it's better to not talk to them." said Clara.

"I can't just up and leave," Richie pointed out. "I need to let them know I'm okay."

"What part about no contact..." Jensen raised an arm to cut Clara off. "Make it quick."

Clara looked as if she was about to protest but Jensen shook his head. Richie dug a few quarters out of his pocket and ran over to the pay phone.

He quickly dialed his number. His father picked up on the first ring.

"Hello?"

"Hey, Dad."

"Where have you been?"

"I'm sorry," said Richie. "Something happened with Axel's grandfather and I completely forgot about you until now."

"Oh my god, is he okay?"

"Kinda. He's in a coma." Richie winced. This lie was getting very huge very fast. Alice crooked an eyebrow at him. Richie hadn't even noticed her walk up. He shrugged his shoulders.

"Send my condolences to the Matson's. Now you need to get home right now."

"Well you see, they are sending his grandfather to a specialist in New Mexico, and I was kind of hoping to go with them."

"No," said his father in a tone that brooked no argument.

"But..." Richie began.

"I said no." Richie was about to respond when Alice yanked the phone from his hand.

"Hi Mr. Carson, this is Alice."

"Hello Miss Matson, I am very sorry to here about your father."

"Thank you for your concern. But that's not why I'm talking Peter."

"Oh?"

"You remember that thing I told about when we first met?"

"Of course," said Richie's father.

"Well it's happened." There was an audible intake of breath on the other end of line. "I'm sorry to say that Richie got involved and we had to take him with us. He will be perfectly safe with me."

"I see. Take care of Richie then. And tell him I love him."

"I will, and good luck."

"Same to you."

Alice hung up the phone and turned to Richie. "Well your parents are okay with you going and your dad says he loves you.

Richie's mouth dropped. "What just like that?"

"Just like that."

"But...I don't even...What?"

"Just come on."

"Where are we?" asked Axel. He was riding shotgun while Clara was driving. He was starting to feel a little cramped from being in a car for almost five hours with very infrequent breaks to stretch his legs.

"Just outside Hershey, Pennsylvania," said Richie reading the road signs.

"Hershey as in chocolate?" asked Axel.

"Yeah," said Jensen. "Got a big amusement park here and everything."

"Maybe we should go there for a few hours," suggested Axel.

"No," said Alice immediately.

"But, Mom," said Axel.

"I said no," snapped Alice.

"But, *Mom*," said Axel in his best Cartman impersonation.

"For the last time, no,"

"But it's right there," said Richie pointing.

"No, and that's final!"

"And over here is where the coca beans are split open so that we can harvest their rich cocoa, the main ingredient in chocolate."

"You people really need to learn the meaning of 'that's final,'" said Alice.

"We did know that," said Richie. "What we didn't know is to never mention the prospect of free chocolate around Clara, especially when she's driving."

"Mommy, can we get some chocolate now?" asked a little girl whose family was also taking the tour.

"Can we Alice, can we?" asked Clara, excitedly mimicking the girl.

"Okay Clara, I have a deal for you," said Axel taking her gently by the shoulders to calm her down. "I'll buy you one chocolate bar right now."

"Really?"

"*Or*, if you're good, I'll buy you as much chocolate as you want at the end of the tour."

"Okay," said Clara. She let out an excited squeal and started hopping up and down. Farad mimicked the sound from Clara's shoulder and snuggled into her cheek.

"But you got to pay attention to the guide, okay?"

Clara nodded so enthusiastically that Axel thought her neck might snap. She rushed off to listen to the tour guide while Axel shook his head in amazement.

"You know," he said to Richie, "When we first met Clara, I thought she was really hot. Pretty weird, but hot."

"Yeah," said Richie, nodding his head in agreement. "She is pretty hot."

"And now that I've gotten to know her, she's just crazy as hell," said Axel.

"Yeah," said Richie, "I'd still tap that."

Axel stared at his friend, shocked. "Dude, she's insane."

"I know," said Richie, "But for some reason that just makes her hotter."

"Okay," said Axel. "As your friend and someone who genuinely cares about your well-being, I'm going to say this once. Don't try to sleep with Clara. It will not end well."

"I think you're exaggerating there."

"Richie, if you try this, when, and this is a when not an if, when Clara goes ballistic, I will not help you," said Axel. "I'm going to laugh my ass off while hiding in a bush saying I told you so and praying to any deity I can think of to not let her find me."

"But she's just so damn hot," said Richie.

Axel pinched the bridge of his nose. "Richie, quit thinking with your dick before someone cuts it off. And knowing Clara, that's a strong possibility."

Richie glanced down at his pants. "You may be right here."

"May? What do you mean may? I'm definitely right here."

"Yeah, I'm still going to go for it."

Axel slammed his forehead into the heel of his palm. "Fine, just promise me two things first."

"Okay, shoot."

"One," said Axel, "Use a condom. 'Cause I am *not* babysitting a lightning-wielding psycho kid. I've got Clara for that."

"Fair enough," said Richie. "Don't plan on being a dad yet."

"And two," said Axel, "give me a head's up before you try anything. I want a good head start before she erupts into a storm cloud of anger and rage."

"Yeah, okay," said Richie. "I see your point."

"No you don't," said Axel, "Or we wouldn't be having this conversation."

"I still think you're overreacting."

"And I still think you're a dumbass."

"Come on, you two," said Clara. She grabbed their hands and started dragging them back into the tour. It was interesting to watch. They saw exactly how chocolate was made. Watched how all of the ingredients were melted and stirred together in a giant vat. The way the chocolate became all frothy and creamy set everybody's mouth watering.

At one part of the tour they actually got to make a candy bar of their own. This candy bar filled the large container they supplied to help to keep its shape while the entire thing cooled. They could put what ever they wanted in it. Axel chose to put a few almonds in. Richie went for a marbled one. Jensen made his with dark chocolate and a few peanuts. Alice put some caramel in the center of hers. And Clara, of course, tried to put everything they had to offer into one gigantic, beautiful, diabetes-causing masterpiece. And one could never be enough with her. She wouldn't stop until she had completed five different versions of her coma-inducing concoction. She walked out of the tour with her arms full of chocolate. One little boy heading in saw her and immediately started begging his mother to buy him that much candy. This started his mother whispering at her son to shut up and behave and giving the group very disapproving stares.

"See this wasn't so bad," said Axel to Alice as they were walking.

"I just want to get back on the road before anything shows up to kill us."

"Mom, would you relax," said Axel. "This stop was to show you something."

"And what would that be?"

"That no matter how fucked up our life becomes, just because we stop to enjoy ourselves for a few hours doesn't mean that something bad is going to happen."

"Kreeeeeah!!"

"Why do I talk!" shouted Axel as a screeching cry split the air. He turned around and swore obscenely. A few mothers nearby gasped and covered their children's ears. Then they looked in the direction that Axel was staring and screamed.

"Car! Now!" shouted Jensen. His instructions were redundant. The other four were already sprinting towards the parking lot, Clara still trying to keep a hold of her chocolate. The others had already dropped their candy as they began to pull weapons out. Even Richie had a couple of daggers that Alice had given him so that he would have something to protect himself with.

Axel pulled Slik out of his pocket.

"What's a good weapon for a flock of birds?" asked Axel.

"What kind of birds we talking about here?" asked Slik. Axel raised him up so that the silvery blob could look behind them. His metallic-blue eyes grew widened farther than Axel would have thought possible.

Behind them was a cloud of angry, screeching, and very, very large birds of prey. There were hawks and eagles, falcons and ravens, and even a few crows thrown into the mix. But riding inside of the oversized flock of normally-solitary predators was something even worse.

They had the wings, legs, and tail feathers of birds, but their heads and torsos were completely human. They were screeching as loudly as the birds around them and seemed just as intent on killing everything they could find.

"Kid," said Slik, "You have neither the skill nor the experience to fight what is after us. No weapon I can turn into would be overly helpful and if you don't find some way of getting out of here, and fast, you will die."

"Thanks for that very positive outlook on our situation," said Axel. "Now what's after us?"

"Harpies," came the answer. "A lot of harpies."

"Which are?" asked Richie, coming up beside them.

"Bird men," said Slik. "Foul, disgusting creatures. They behave like raptors and carrion birds. They have no problem hunting and killing, but will not shy away from dead carcasses either."

Richie looked like he was about to throw up from that ghastly image. "That sounds wonderful."

"What are they doing here?" asked Axel.

"My guess," said Slik, "Looking for us. The men that have been chasing us serve some very powerful warlocks. Warlocks who would have no problems convincing a flock of harpies to attack in broad daylight in a very populated area."

"That sounds just beautiful," said Axel. "Any sure fire way to kill a harpy?"

"They can die like any other creature," said Slik. "Stab them, beat them, light them on fire, you name it and it will probably work. The problem isn't with killing them. It's with not letting them kill you. They are vicious, strong and above all, cowardly. They will not attack unless they are sure they can win. This makes them crafty and they tend to avoid no-win situations. When a harpy attacks, you better have something up your sleeve that they can't see, 'cause if you don't you're dead."

Clara sent a bolt of lightning into the onrushing cloud. A few normal birds burst into flames and one of the harpies dropped out of the sky as the electricity caused its muscles to seize up. It hit the ground with a very audible thud.

"Well at least we know lightning works," said Richie.

"Yeah," said Axel. "Five or six down, about a billion more to go. Keep running."

"Don't need to tell me. Preaching to the choir."

They reached the parking lot and made straight for the car. Clara jumped in the driver's seat, Richie took shotgun, and the other three piled into the back with Jensen in the middle and Axel behind Clara.

Clara dumped her chocolate in the middle of the front seat and slammed her hand on the dash. The car instantly roared to life.

"Hold on to your lunch," she shouted as she backed up and peeled out of the parking lot.

The flock was now over them. The birds started dive-bombing onto the roof and the hood of the car. They could hear them pecking and scratching as they tried to break into the car.

"We need to do something about that," said Axel.

"I'm on it," Clara shouted back. She rolled down the window and reached up. She placed her hand on the roof and sent a pulse of electricity through the metal. All of the birds on the car either burst into flames or collapsed unconscious and rolled off the car. Clara quickly brought her hand in and rolled up her window.

"Good work," said Alice. "Now it's my turn."

Chapter 12

Alice rolled down her window and crawled on top of the car.

"If anybody has any nukes, now's the time to use them," she shouted.

"I don't have any nukes," said Clara. "But I do have a neat little trick."

"Then get on with it!"

"I'm kind of busy right now!"

"I can fix that," said Jensen. He reached forward and grabbed onto Richie and Clara's shoulders. Their forms flickered, then re-solidified, with Richie now in the driver's seat and Clara riding shotgun.

"Jesus," Richie exclaimed as he grabbed the wheel. The car swerved as he fought to get it under control.

"Watch it!" Alice screamed.

"Sorry," Richie shouted back. "Could you maybe warn me next time you do something like that?"

Jensen shrugged. "I figured you being the only person without magic that you'd probably be most useful driving."

"I get why you did it, just give me a little heads-up from now on."

Clara took Farad out and held him in her hands. "We're going to need a big one, sweetling."

Farad cooed and seemed to scrunch his eyes shut in concentration. He almost seemed to double in size as all of his hair stood straight out.

"Jensen, get me on the roof." Clara commanded. Jensen grabbed her shoulder again and teleported her and himself onto the roof of the car.

"What should I do?" asked Axel.

"Try and find your magic," said Slik.

"How am I supposed to do that now?"

"You're going to have to meditate."

"You want me to meditate in the middle of a battle?" asked Axel incredulously.

Slik moved his body in a gesture that could only be described as a shrug.

"You're not serious."

"You think you'll be able to kill that entire flock with just a sword?"

"Well, no, but the idea of meditating right now just seems kind of weird."

"Just shut up and do it."

"Fine."

Clara sat down on top of the roof with Farad in her lap. She held her hands in front of her a few inches apart. Sparks began to dance back and forth between them. The energy began to grow at a steady rate. A bitter metallic taste began to grow in the back of Alice's throat as the energy began to produce ozone.

Alice drew her swords and turned to look at Jensen. "We need to buy her some time." she said.

Jensen gave her a nod. He looked at the flock. A few of the birds had detached themselves and were dive bombing the car. Jensen focused on them. They disappeared and reappeared above the flock. The startled birds gave a shriek as they collided with each other and other members of the flock.

Alice whirled her blades and sent out long scythes of energy. They cut through the flock, killing dozens of birds and even a few harpies. Both of them smiled as they surveyed their handy work. Then they gazed up at the rest of the flock and their hopes sank. They had killed maybe fifty or sixty birds and a dozen harpies, but there were still thousands more to take their place.

"We may be screwed here," said Alice.

Axel centered himself and focused on his breathing. "What am I looking for?"

"It's going to feel like a tiny trickle of energy." said Slik.

"What?" asked Axel confused. "You guys keep saying that I have this gigantic well inside of me."

"That trickle is the magic seeping into your body. Everybody has magic to some degree, but most people don't have much more than the amount necessary to survive."

"And I'm guessing that I have more."

"So much more."

"So why am I looking for the energy that's already in my body?"

"Your going to have to follow it like a river to it's source."

"That sounds like its going to take a while," said Axel.

"Then you better get started."

Axel refocused himself. He could sense the energy, but like the night before every time he tried to grab a hold it slipped through his fingers.

"I can't catch it."

"You're going to need to try harder, man," said Richie from the driver's seat.

"I'm trying," said Axel bending his will towards the flighty energy.

Slik looked on with concern. He could here the battle raging on the roof.

Hurry, Axel, he thought, *We're going to need you to survive this.*

"You almost ready, Clara?" asked Alice decapitating a harpy that had landed on the trunk.

"If you know any shielding spells you might want to put them up right about now," said Clara opening her eyes. They were glowing green with electricity. The energy between her hands had formed a crackling ball of lightning. It was about six inches across and so condensed that Alice was surprised that the girl was able to contain it without passing out.

This girl has some talent, she thought.

Clara stood. Both of the adults threw up walls of energy to shield themselves.

Clara raised the ball towards the flock.

"Cover your ears and close your eyes," she said. "And make sure you don't clench your jaw. This is going to be loud."

The ball of energy exploded, sending a large lightning bolt directly into the heart of the flock.

BOOM!

The thunder that came with the lightning was so loud that all of the windows on the car exploded. The lightning bolt hit the flock and began to jump and arc from bird to bird and harpy to harpy. Alice opened her eyes, her ears still ringing to see hundreds of bodies dropping out of the sky. Clara herself was thrown off of the car by the sheer force of the energy she had just released. Jensen teleported and caught her. He teleported back onto the roof. Clara was unconscious in his arms.

"You boys alright in there?" asked Alice.

"Fine," said Richie. "Could have warned us though."

"I'm sending Clara down," said Jensen. "She used a lot of energy in that blast."

"At least she took care of the flock," said Alice.

Kreeeah!!

Alice glanced back. A large portion of the flock had been killed in Clara's blast. But there were still thousands more.

"Hurry up, Axel."

"I can't get it!" Axel shouted in frustration. "I can feel it, but every time I try to grab it it either moves away or disappears."

"Don't try to grab it," said Slik. "That energy is already in your body. If you try to use that you'll burn through the magic that's keeping you alive. Follow it. Find the source. That is where most of your magic is being stored."

Axel nodded. He tried to follow the energy, running straight into it. He felt a sudden adrenaline rush which quickly faded leaving him tired. He shook his head. The energy had disappeared again. He found the energy and tried again and again he felt a sudden burst of adrenaline that quickly faded leaving him even more tired than before. And again the energy was gone.

"If I keep running through it I'm going to collapse from exhaustion."

"Don't chase, follow," said Slik. "You're not trying to catch it."

Axel clenched his jaw. "One more try."

Alice could feel herself tiring. She had already vastly depleted her stores of magic. And fighting the ones that came too close was quickly wearing her body down.

"I don't know how long I can keep this up," she said turning to Jensen. The older man looked about to fall down where he was standing.

A harpy dive bombed them. Jensen quickly teleported it behind the car about a foot off the road. Without enough time to slow or change direction, the startled harpy slammed into the road and didn't get back up.

"I don't have too many of those left," he said.

Alice set her jaw. She could almost sense her death before her.

"If we die here today, then I'm taking as many of these bastards with me as I can."

Jensen nodded and turned back to the still sizable flock. "Still, if we can prevent it I would rather if we didn't die today."

Axel slowly, agonizingly followed the trickle of energy. He could feel it getting gradually bigger.

"I've got to be getting close."

"Go slow," said Slik. "We may not have time for another attempt."

Axel nodded and continued on his journey into the depths of his soul. The energy was growing much faster now. The trickle soon became a stream, then a river. He began to increase his pace as much as he dared. It was getting harder to move forward now.

"I have come too far to stop now. This energy is mine." He screamed a battle cry and surged forward. The energy resisted. Axel gave one final push and suddenly he broke through the wall of his mind. He was swimming in an ocean of energy. Little tendrils snaked away from the source.

"I wonder where those go," he said.

"Axel, focus!" screamed Slik. "Your mother and Jensen are in danger."

"But it's so beautiful," said Axel. "So much energy."

He felt it overcome him. It was like when he had jumped through the stream, but a thousand times stronger. He kept waiting for it to fade, but there was too much energy this time.

"It's too much, I can't hold it."

"Jensen," Slik screamed, "Get him up top now."

Axel landed on the roof with a thump but barely noticed.

"Slik, help me," he pleaded, "it's too much."

"Don't hold it," said Alice. "Let it go."

"But it's mine."

"Axel," screamed Slik. "Your body can't hold that much energy."

"Yes I can."

"You'll overload. If you don't let it go your atoms will pull apart and you'll die."

"But It's mine."

"Axel let it go."

Axel's eyes snapped open. A silver light burned through them. "No," he said in a voice charged with energy.

"It's mine."

"Axel," said Slik desperately. "Come back to me, boy. Let it go."

"IT'S MINE!!"

An explosion erupted through Axel. His voice was supercharged with magic. The harpies and birds screeched in pain as the noise assaulted there sensitive ears and the raw, uncontrolled magic crashed over there bodies.

Jensen teleported Axel before the energy erupting from every pore of his body destroyed the car and it's occupants. Axel appeared in the center of the flock. Suspended in one place by the forces exploding from his core.

Richie stopped the car and jumped out. He watched in horror and amazement as the beings closest to his friend were literally tórn apart. Their atoms breaking turning them to dust. The ones who weren't de-atomized were no luckier. The torn and crumpled remains were completely unrecognizable. The entire flock was dead within a span of a few short seconds. But still Axel roared, still the energy was erupting from him.

Finally, after an eternity, the magic faded and Axel began to plummet out of the sky. Jensen teleported and caught him. He warped them safely to the ground.

They collapsed in a heap. Alice scooped up Slik, jumped down from the car, and rushed over to her son. Jensen was breathing heavily and clearly exhausted, but except for a few cuts and bruises from the fight he was otherwise unharmed.

She nodded her thanks and crouched down to examine her son. He was unconscious. She placed two fingers on his neck and was relieved to feel a pulse.

"Thank the Magus. He's alive." Slik let out a breath he didn't realize he was holding

Jensen shook his head. He had a look of awe touched with fear on his face. "Now I see what all the fuss is about."

Chapter 13

"I always thought motels would be worse," said Richie. They had stopped at the first place they could find to rest up. Axel and Clara were still passed out on the two beds while Jensen and Alice were resting on the couch. Richie had been the only one who had any kind of energy left after the battle, so he ended up with the job of nursemaid. The only time they left was for him and Jensen to steal a car. Apparently the old man had learned a few tricks over the years, including lock-picking and hot-wiring.

"Just don't bring a black light in here," said Jensen. "You might not like what you find."

"Fair enough. So how long are we staying here?"

"Until those two can walk," said Jensen, nodding towards the two prone teenagers. "Or something tries to attack us."

"I'm hoping for option A."

"We all are Richie," said Alice.

"Well if we're going to be here for a while I might as well go get some supplies."

Alice nodded. "I'll come with you."

"No," said Richie.

Alice blinked in shock. "What was that?"

"You heard me. No."

"What do you mean no?"

"Just that, no."

"You are not going out by yourself."

"Alice, I don't have any magic and therefore am the least likely to be attacked by myself. If you go with me, then if something tries to attack, all Clara and Axel have to defend them is Jensen. And he can barely walk. They are going to need you here too to have any sort of chance."

"You are my responsibility young man."

"If I'm a young man then you're going to have stop treating me like a child. I don't have any magic or way of contributing if something attacks. In this way I can at least be useful."

"Richie, you are so much more useful than you realize."

"So then let me prove it."

"The boy will be fine," said Jensen. "And he's right. I can't defend these two by myself."

Alice closed her eyes and breathed deeply. "Fine, but be quick."

"Thank you," said Richie.

"Just go before I change my mind."

Richie nodded and took the credit card that Jensen extended towards him. Alice heard the door open and close. She opened her eyes. They had a look of concern on them.

"He'll be fine," said Jensen.

"I know," said Alice. "But I've known that boy since he was little. He's been like a second son to me."

"And like any parent, surrogate or otherwise, you're going to have to learn to let him go and figure some things out for himself."

"I just wish I could help him. I think seeing what we can do has got him thinking about why he's even here in the first place."

"That kid will end up being a powerful mage. I can feel his magic. He's definitely not Axel, but he might be even more powerful than me someday."

"That's what I'm afraid of."

"I love gas stations" said Richie. He knew that they were some of the few places where you could get groceries, gas, and a few extra supplies that you're not entirely sure you'll need but don't want to risk going without. He picked up some bread and sandwich meat and even found a jar of mayo to make them a little more appetizing. He got some milk, bottled water, and just for the hell of it three six-packs of energy drinks. He decided to pick up a couple of lighters, a couple of books of matches and a couple of gas jugs too.

"That seems like quite a load you've got there."

Richie turned away from the oil he was thinking about getting for the car to see a stranger standing next to them. He was a little on the tall side with dark brown hair that was neatly combed and slicked back. He wore a dark green button-down shirt tucked into black dress pants. His dark brown eyes had a little twinkle and a little amused smile decorated his face.

"I'm going a road trip and thought I could use a few things."

"New Mexico's still a long way off, do you think that will be enough?"

Richie's heart skipped a beat. "How did you know I was going to New Mexico?"

"I know a lot about your little group Richie Carson. How must it feel seeing Axel do all of these amazing things. To see Clara shoot lightning like it's nothing. Alice has her swords, even Jensen can be anywhere he wants. But what can you do? You even have to beg to pick up the groceries."

The twinkle in the man's eyes seemed to be less of joy and more of cold brilliance. His smile seemed suddenly more sinister.

"Who are you?" Richie breathed.

"The person with the answers to all your problems. All I ask in return is a small favor."

"What kind of favor."

The man took a large gold coin out of his pocket.

"Just hold on to this for me."

"What is it?"

"That's not important."

"What do I get in return for keeping that safe."

The man grinned and held up a small orb. It was orange, red, and yellow, but the colors didn't seem to want to stay still. They swirled and mixed together like gasses in a jar. Richie stared at it entranced. It felt like it was calling out to him.

"This is the egg of a Calla Lutai. When it hatches you can bond to the creature inside. Think of it as a way to even the playing field between you and your peers."

Richie hesitated. It all seemed too good to be true. A Calla Lutai of his own. But was it worth making a deal with this man, who Richie was sure was one of the warlocks that was trying to steal Slik from Axel, for the creature inside of the egg.

"So what do you say?"

"I'm back."

"How's it going," said Jensen. He was reclining on the couch reading a magazine from the pile the motel left in the room. Alice was nowhere to be seen.

"Pretty good. Where's Alice?" Richie asked setting the bags of supplies on the counter.

"Right here," she walked out of the bathroom toweling off her hair.

Richie nodded towards Axel and Clara. "Any change?"

Jensen shook his head. "They both used a lot of energy in that fight. But they'll survive."

Richie nodded his head.

"Anything happen while you were out?" asked Alice.

"Yes, actually." Richie dug the egg out of his pocket and tossed it to her.

"I found this while I was out. Thought it was magical so I picked it up."

"Smart move, kid," Jensen scolded. "You could have found a bomb for all you know."

"It hasn't exploded yet."

Jensen shook his head. "Alice help me out here."

Alice remained silent.

"Alice?" Jensen looked at her and realized she was staring at the object in her hand with her mouth hanging open.

"What's..." he glanced at what she was holding and did a double take. "What the hell?"

"I think Richie just solved his magic problem," Alice said slowly.

"What?" asked Richie in fake surprise.

"Th-that's the egg of a Calla Lutai," Jensen stammered.

"Specifically a Brimflare," said Alice.

"What's a Brimflare," Richie asked confused.

"It's a Calla Lutai that generates massive amounts of heat," said Jensen.

"Sweet!"

"But it can't release it," Alice explained, handing it back to him. "So it gives it's wielder the ability to control heat and it also makes them heat proof."

"So I'll be like a pyromancer?" asked Richie.

"Effectively, yes."

"Awesome."

"Are you sure you just found this and nobody just gave it to you?" asked Jensen.

"I think I would remember someone just handing me a monster egg," said Richie.

Jensen held up his hands defensively. "Just trying to make sure this was legit."

"So how do I make sure it hatches?" asked Richie.

"It's like a chicken's egg," said Alice. "Just got to keep it warm."

"How warm are we talking here."

"About ninety-eight point six degrees Fahrenheit."

"That's the temperature of the human body."

"Which is why the most common way of keeping it at temp is to eat it," said Jensen.

Richie laughed nervously. "That's a good one, try to get me to eat an egg the size of a golf ball."

Jensen stared at him seriously."

"Aw, come on. Are you serious?" he looked desperately between the two of them.

"Is this really the only way to keep it warm enough."

"The best way would actually to be to get an incubator," said Alice. "But since those are expensive and need to stay plugged in and there's not really much chance of that..."

Richie stared at the egg apprehensively. He gave up too much to just let it die. He could already feel the bond growing between him and the creature inside.

"Well here goes nothing." He put the egg in his mouth and swallowed as hard as he could. It slipped into the back of his throat and lodged there. He gasped and started choking. He swallowed again and again. Finally the egg slid passed the opening to his wind pipe and he could breathe again. Richie sucked in deep gulps of air.

"That was painful," he said when he could talk again. "So I'm not going to crap this out again in a couple of days am I? Cause I don't want to do that again. Especially after it already went through me once."

"It'll stay inside your stomach until it hatches," said Alice. "And after it hatches it'll stay in your digestive tract for a couple of weeks and then you'll regurgitate it."

"You mean I have to puke this thing up?"

"How else do you plan on getting it out of your body?"

"Good point. So how long until it hatches."

"I'd say a couple of days," said Jensen. "It looked pretty close to hatching."

"You mean someone else had it inside of them?" asked Richie horrified.

"I'm guessing it was kept in an incubator until recently, which is why I found it strange that you were able to just find it."

"But now that your bonded to it you have to make sure you never lose it," Alice warned.

"What happens if a Calla Lutai is separated from it's wielder?" asked Richie.

"It feels like your heart's being ripped out," said Jensen. "Trust me when I tell you it's not a pleasant experience."

"Then I better make sure to never let this little guy out of my sight," said Richie patting his stomach protectively.

"Be sure you don't," Jensen warned gravely.

Chapter 14

Axel groaned and sat up. "Why does my head hurt so much. And why am I so hungry."

Alice tossed him a bottle of aspirin Richie had picked up at the gas station.

"You let off a massive amount of magic. Your body is severely depleted. The headache and weak feeling is a direct side effect of that. Also the hunger is a result of you burning a huge portion of your stored calories."

Axel took a couple of aspirin from the bottle and swallowed them.

"I hate having to swallow these dry."

"We have water you idiot," said Alice tossing him a bottle.

"And don't get me started on things that are hard to swallow," said Richie, handing him a sandwich and sitting down on the edge of his bed.

Clara groaned. "What did Axel shove it in too hard?"

Axel tossed her the bottle of aspirin. "Take a couple of these."

"I'll be okay," said Clara setting the bottle on the nightstand. "After awhile the magic drain doesn't affect you as much."

Her stomach grumbled. "Though the hunger is something that can only be fixed by one thing."

"Your chocolate is on the nightstand," said Jensen.

Clara grabbed the first tin and yanked it open. Farad climbed out of her pocket saw the chocolate and let out a high pitched chirp. He jumped onto the already half-eaten bar of chocolate and began to help Clara devour it. Axel leaned over to Richie.

"Still want to do her?" he asked.

"Somehow even more so."

Axel shook his head. "Get help."

"No one is doing anyone," said Alice.

"And like I'd ever have sex with someone who can't even do magic."

"That's not exactly a problem anymore," said Richie.

Slik crawled out of Axel's pocket and stretched. "What's going on? What's not a problem anymore?"

"Richie solved his problem of not having magic," said Jensen

"I was getting supplies when I found a Calla Lutai egg and swallowed it to keep it warm."

Axel paused in taking a bite from his sandwich. "What the...? When did you...? How long was I out?"

"About a day," said Richie.

Axel looked like he was about to say something, but wasn't sure how to respond. Finally he just shook his head and let out a defeated sigh.

"What kind of Calla Lutai was it?" asked Slik.

"A Brimflare."

"Pyromancy," said Clara scrutinizing Richie closely. "Nope can't see it."

"What?" asked Richie confused.

"I can't see you being a pyromancer. I just keep getting the image of you trying to throw a fire ball and setting yourself on fire."

"How incompetent do you think I am?"

Axel drove the heel of his hand into his forehead. "You have got to stop leaving yourself so open like that."

"Like what?"

"Let's just say your arguing skills need work," said Slik.

"Why?"

"Because you're an idiot," said Clara.

"I will cut you in your sleep."

"Bring it on, Dick."

"Don't call me that," said Richie.

"But I thought that was your name."

Richie drew in a deep breath to try and calm himself. "I prefer Richie."

"But you seem like such a Dick."

"Enough!" shouted Alice. "Clara shut up and eat your chocolate. Richie, start meditating, you're going to have to try to find your magic. And Axel..."

She reached behind her and pulled out one of her swords and threw it end over end at her son. He snatched it out of the air.

"...practice your stance."

"Are you insane?" Axel screamed. "You could have killed me."

"Get up and practice. We don't have much time before we get to the school and you're never going to survive if you don't know how to use a weapon."

"I'll never be able to learn if you keep chucking swords at me."

"Nice catch," said Alice. Axel looked perplexed until he realized he was holding her sword. His eyes bulged in amazement.

"How did I...?"

"You awakened your magic," said Slik. "My gift changes the form a humans magic takes. It makes you more inclined towards the physical side of it. Your reflexes were sharpened the moment you bonded with me. Now they are overcharged. Unrefined, but very good."

"Dude, you'd be so awesome at video games," said Richie.

"What are video games?" asked Slik.

"A form of entertainment for blood-thirsty and socially repressed teenagers," said Jensen.

"Hey, I'm not that blood-thirsty," said Richie.

"Get into your stance," said Alice. "And Richie start meditating."

"Do I have to?"

"Yes," said Alice in a tone that brooked no argument. "You are now bonded to a Calla Lutai. That means to use the powers it gives you, you will need to unlock your magic."

Clara smiled through a mouthful of her third chocolate bar.

"And what are you grinning at?" said Alice giving her a stern glare.

"Nothing," said Clara and stared down at her chocolate and began shoving as much of it into her mouth as she could.

Jensen chuckled.

"And what's so funny?" she asked sternly.

"I wish I could do that. Every time I would tell my kids to do something they would backtalk me."

"It works on adults too," said Alice with a glare.

The grin dropped from Jensen's face. "I think I'll go for a bit of a walk."

"You do that," said Alice. "And get us something to eat besides sandwiches."

Jensen hurried out as fast as he could.

When the door closed behind him Alice turned her attention back to Axel who was now standing in the proper stance. She walked around him looking over his form with a practiced eye.

"Very good. Now hold it as long as possible."

She then walked out of the room.

Axel took a deep breath to focus, trying to shut out the sound of Clara gorging herself on her final chocolate bar.

"What is the point of this?" he mumbled to himself.

"The point is to build your strength." said Slik. "When you first started that sword would start shaking after about five seconds. You've been holding it rock steady for about five minutes now."

"I kind of see the point to that," said Axel. "I mean it's like my mom said, if you can hold your sword up longer than your enemy than you have an advantage, but is a sword fight going to last long enough for me to actually get tired. I always thought they were quick."

"They normally are," said Slik. "But think of what would happen if you were ever in a battle. You would have so many enemies to fight that it wouldn't matter how quick each individual sword fight was. You could be fighting dozens of enemies over the course of a few hours and still be expected to be swinging at full force."

"Okay, but how many battles am I going to end up in?" asked Axel critically.

"You never know," said Slik. "Plus what if you end up fighting an enemy like the man with the claymore. He is not going to tire easily and will not die quickly. Plus the only real advantage you have over him is speed and agility. You would need to be constantly moving and dodging while he has the luxury of pretty much swinging at you from one spot."

"Alright I think I get what your trying to say. It makes no difference if I can beat a normal average human if I can't beat what's actually coming after us."

"Precisely," said Slik. "Now I suggest you stop questioning your mother's teachings. She may be demanding, but she definitely knows how to work a sword."

"Thank you, Slik."

They were surprised by the sound of Alice's voice. They hadn't even heard her enter the room.

"No problem. I've been around for a very long time and I've seen many people try to teach the art of sword fighting. Most were good, some were just terrible, and a very few actually knew exactly what to do to make sure their students didn't get themselves killed. You seem to fall into the last category."

"Now if only Axel would see that and stop complaining."

"Hey, I haven't complained that much."

"Yes, you have," said Richie. "Now if everybody could please shut up I'm trying to focus. It's very hard to find my inner self with everybody talking."

Jensen took a breath of the fresh spring air.

"What have we got ourselves into little buddy?" he asked Clip, who was currently riding on his shoulder. The Teleporter burbled and clicked in response.

"I know he needs protection, but I am getting way too old for this shit."

"On that we can agree."

Jensen spun around to confront the voice that spoke from behind him. The man was leaning casually against the tree. He looked like the snow made flesh. His skin was almost pure white, and his unruly platinum hair stuck out underneath a snow cap. He wore a thick white winter coat even though it was about fifty degrees. His white snow-pants and heavy white, fur-lined snow boots gave the impression he was about to head somewhere very cold, very soon. The only spot of color on him were his chilling, dark blue eyes.

"Alexei," said Jensen, inclining his head. "It's been a long time."

"That it has old friend." The man had a Russian accent but spoke English surprisingly well.

"What are you doing here?"

"What, we can't just have a nice pleasant chat?"

"We aren't actually friends, so don't even try to act like you're just trying to catch up with an old acquaintance."

"You know, for a man who's spent his life running and dodging trouble, you're surprisingly blunt," said Alexei getting off of the tree. "I see you still have that annoying little instigator." He gestured toward Clip.

"And judging by your attire, you still have that charming little devil."

"Hey now, words hurt," said a voice that sounded like ice cracking and snow sliding. More surprising than the voice itself was the creature it came from. A small, snow-white monkey crawled onto Alexei's shoulder. It's eyes matched it's partner's. It smiled, baring it's large fangs.

"I never was a huge fan of Permafangs," sad Jensen.

"And I was never fond of Teleporters," said Alexei. "But we're not here to debate the usefulness of our respective Calla Lutai."

"Which brings me back to my original question," said Jensen. "Why are you here?"

"I'm here to give you some friendly advice, for old time's sake."

"Which is?"

"You should be very careful with your new little protege. My mistress very much wants him dead. So much so that she sent your brother after him."

"Mordechai?" Jensen said skeptically.

Alexei smiled evilly. "The one and only."

"I figured as much when I saw those three goons of his show up. Which begs the question of why you are telling me things I already know."

"Like I said, old times sake. I feel my former teacher should have a fighting chance. And to warn you that my mistress has instructed him to intervene personally."

"So why hasn't he shown his ugly mug."

"Oh you know Morty. He likes to take his time, save a few tricks for later. It's not too often he actually attacks at his full strength."

"It has more to do with cowardice than caution," said Jensen. "Even though he'll never admit it, he is most afraid of that which he thinks he controls."

"That statement is true on more levels than you think."

"So what's in this for you, cause I'm positive that you aren't doing this out of the kindness of your heart."

"I am shocked, Master. How could you think I have ulterior motives?"

"Because I'm not stupid and I know you better than that."

"Fair enough," said Alexei with a grin. "But that's not your concern right now. Just remember what I said and keep the boy safe. He's more important than even you realize. And I'd leave this town as soon as possible. Mordechai is here. I've thrown his goons off your trail for now, but I suspect he's getting impatient. He might try something himself."

A gust of cold wind blew and a swirl of snow covered Alexei. When it had cleared he was gone.

"Little bastard was always so dramatic," said Jensen shaking his head. "Come on little buddy, he said to Clip. "I could really use a pizza right now."

Chapter 15

Clara groaned in agony.

"That's what you get for eating about five pounds of chocolate in less then ten minutes," said Richie without opening his eyes.

"Shut up," said Clara. She groaned again and hugged her stomach.

"Did you at least learn a lesson?" asked Axel, still holding his sword-fighting stance.

"Yeah," said Clara. "I learned that you're a sanctimonious bastard who insists on people bettering themselves."

"You know I've got an extra Hershey's Kiss in my pocket."

Clara gagged. Axel grinned.

"I don't care that you didn't learn not to eat that much chocolate in one sitting. It's funnier this way."

"Jackass."

"Dumbass."

"Douche bag."

"Bitch."

"Enough with the name calling," said Richie. "It is very hard to find the center of my being with you two shouting at each other like a dysfunctional pair of siblings."

"Aww," said Axel. "You mean to tell me that Clara's the stupid, bitchy, sister I never wanted?"

"And that Axel's the uptight jackass of a brother I wouldn't wish on my worst enemy?"

"Okay, now you guys are starting to sound like a broken record," said Richie. "You didn't even come up with any new insults for each other."

He got up and started walking towards the door.

"Where are you going?" asked Axel, dropping his stance.

"To find somewhere quiet so that I can focus."

There was a knock on the door. Alice came out of the bathroom in fresh clothes. She was running a towel through her still damp hair.

She snatched the sword from Axel's hand and replaced it in its sheath. "Don't want to freak anybody out."

"Last thing we need is a maid running off and telling everybody that we've got weapons in here," Axel agreed.

Alice opened the door and Jensen walked in carrying a couple of pizza boxes.

"That smells delicious," said Richie following the aroma of the pizzas inside. "Pepperoni and sausage and a bacon cheeseburger."

Jensen stared at him impressed. "How the hell did you do that?"

"Richie may be skinny as hell but he lives for food," said Axel.

"Well he's gonna to have to eat on the go," said Jensen. "We gotta get outta this town as soon as possible."

"Something happen?" asked Alice.

"Yeah, you could say that," said Jensen. "My brother's here."

"Cool," said Axel. "Invite him in."

"Not something I would recommend." said Jensen. "My brother is a very powerful, very evil sorcerer named Mordechai."

"Mordechai?" asked Alice, appalled

"I see you've heard of him."

"Heard of him? He's one of the most powerful sorcerers alive. And his reputation for cruelty is almost legendary."

"Yep," said Jensen, "That'd be Morty."

"I've heard of him," said Clara, easing herself into a sitting position. "But isn't he like nine-hundred years old?"

"Nine-hundred-thirty-eight."

"And this dude is your brother?" asked Richie.

"Unfortunately."

"Then how old does that make you?"

"Nine-hundred-forty-two," said Jensen seriously.

"Huh," said Axel. "You look pretty good for your age."

"I try," said Jensen with a cocky grin.

"How the hell are you so old?" asked Richie.

"Magic is one hell of a miracle cure," said Alice. "I'm not exactly as old as I look either."

"How old are you?" asked Axel.

"Never ask a lady her age," snapped Alice.

"When I meet one I'll be sure to remember that," said Axel.

She slapped him in the back of the head. "Mind your elders, boy."

"Which brings us back to the original question," said Richie, "How much of an elder to us are you?"

Alice gave him a death stare.

"Just tell us how old you are so we can get moving," said Richie, completely unfazed.

"Ninety-seven," said Alice.

Axel's jaw dropped. "That certainly explains a lot."

Richie turned to Clara. "And how old are you?"

"Sixteen," said Clara. "People who look like teenagers tend to be teenagers."

"Magic doesn't stop the aging process," said Jensen. "It just slows it down a lot."

"But what about vampires?" asked Richie.

"What about them?" asked Clara.

"Aren't they immortal?"

"I can actually answer this one for you," said Axel. "Vampires are immortal, but they do not look like humans or even come from humans."

"You lost me."

"The actual name for them is Nosferatu," Axel explained. "I believe they fall under the level of Calla Meda, they are a species of mid-level monster."

"How the hell do you know so much about monsters?" asked Richie.

"My Grandpa used to tell me monster lore as bed-time stories."

"But what the hell is a Calla Meda?"

"It's one of the three classifications of monsters. They are classified by their power. There is Calla Lutai, who are all pretty much powerless and most of them have some kind of genetic defect that can be potentially fatal."

"So then why do people seem to be freaking out over them?"

"Because they all grant a special ability to whoever possesses them. This ability normally fixes the fatal flaw they have."

"Like Fared building up massive amounts of electricity but being unable to release it, so he gives Clara the ability to control lightning."

"Exactly, they compliment each other."

"Okay, what are the other two levels?"

"Let's discuss this in the car," said Alice shepherding them out the door.

"The next level is Calla Meda," said Axel. "These are your typical movie monsters, like vampires and harpies. They have some kind of special ability and for the most part no genetic flaws, at least no fatal ones."

"So these ones can live by themselves?" asked Richie.

"And normally they do," said Axel. "There was a big war between humans and monsters a few millennia ago and now most of them prefer to stay away from humans except to eat a few of us, of course."

"Oh that's a pleasant thought."

"There have been myths and legends about monsters for thousands of years. I'm guessing little bits of our genetic memory floating to the surface. And in almost every monster legend, they end up eating a few villagers."

"So what's the last level?" asked Richie, getting into the car.

"Calla Bas," said Axel. "These are the biggest, fastest and most powerful monsters you will ever come across. These are things like dragons, werewolves, giants, stuff like that."

"All the really big, destructive monsters you hear about."

"Yep," said Axel. "But there is one more level of classification for monsters. It's not really counted because there are only seven monsters in it."

"What is it?"

"The Calla Magus," said Slik. "They are the closest things we monsters have to deities. As a matter of fact some of your ancient cultures based their gods off of the Calla Magus."

"So insanely powerful?" asked Richie.

"That war I mentioned," said Axel. "They stopped it by erasing the memories of monsters from human's minds and setting up the Veil so that we couldn't even see them."

"I had no trouble seeing those harpies yesterday."

"That's because you've had monsters shoved in front of your face," said Clara. "It's kind of hard to ignore that. And once you've seen through the Veil, you can't get the illusion again."

"So this Veil is weak in that you see through it once and it's broken," said Richie, "But unless you have monsters forced in front of your eyes you can live without knowing that they actually exist."

"Pretty much," said Jensen from the driver's seat, "The Veil works on your memories. It changes them even as you experience them. But once you know about monsters and that they walk among us, your mind starts to reject the Veil completely. After two days you may start to see some people's forms start to flicker like bad TV reception. Those people are actually monsters, but you won't be able to fully discern their true forms for another few days."

"So by the time we get to New Mexico?" said Richie.

"Yeah about then," said Alice. "But we need to pick up the pace. We've been driving for two days and we've just hit Ohio."

"Hey can we stop at the Rock 'n' Roll hall of fame?" asked Axel.

"What the hell did I just say?" asked Alice sternly. "We are not taking unnecessary side-trips."

"But I've always wanted to see the Rock 'n' Roll hall of fame."

"Too bad," said Alice. "I'm putting my foot down on this one."

"You let Clara go to Hershyland," Axel pointed out.

"Clara was driving and I said no to that too." said Alice.

"Oh yeah. So, can I drive sometime soon?"

"Sure," said Alice, "just as soon as we get out of Ohio."

"Ah, you're no fun."

"Not my job to entertain you," said Alice.

"Still uncool."

Chapter 16

"I can't believe we're tenting it again."

Richie skewered a hotdog with one of the metal cooking sticks they had bought and held it over the fire he had started.

"Shut up and stop complaining, Axel, it's not that bad," he said.

Axel broke the stance he had been holding for an hour and sat down next to Richie. "I kind of miss having a bed."

"We all do," said Clara, finishing off her tenth smore. "Now shut the hell up."

"You all suck."

"Axel!" came his mother's cry. "How long were you supposed to hold that stance for?"

"An hour, which I did."

"Good," said Alice. "Then it's time to move onto the next part of your training."

Alice tossed him one of the wooden practice swords she was holding.

"This feels heavier than it should."

"That's because the center is filled with lead," said Alice. "You have to get used to the weight of a real sword."

"So why use these anyway?" asked Axel.

"Because they don't have an edge and you're going to be getting hit a lot."

"Oh," said Axel, suddenly less enthused about his next sword fighting lesson. "That sounds fantastic."

"Get into your stance," commanded Alice. She walked around her son and nodded approvingly. "Good, very good."

"What, no corrections?"

"Oh, you'll get corrected soon enough," said Alice with a mischievous smile.

"Why do I not like the sound of that?"

Alice took up a position in front of him. "You've gotten past the hard part. Now the rest is simple."

She lunged forward. Axel quickly brought up his sword and parried her thrust. But Alice didn't stop there. She spun around to her left and aimed her sword at the right side of Axel's head. He managed to block that blow, but the follow-up she sent at his ribs made him double over and gasp for breath.

"You've got the gist of it," said Alice. "Try and block your opponent's blows as much as you can. But that's only half of it. Again."

Axel got back into his stance. Alice came at him low and from the left this time. Axel caught her blow with the flat of his blade, but then she whipped her blade up remarkably fast. He managed to lean back just as the wooden blade whistled through the space where his head had been. Axel danced back a little further to get out of her reach.

"No," said Alice. "You should have attacked me."

"What?" asked Axel.

"When I missed your head, your blade was perfectly positioned to hit my ribs. You should have attacked instead of backing off like a coward."

She came at him again with a series of lightning-fast blows. Axel managed to block or dodge every one. But Alice kept coming. She kept up a relentless onslaught. She attacked him from the left. Axel blocked and she spun around and attacked from the right. Axel jumped back and her blade sliced through the air where he had been standing. Axel lunged forward and thrust his sword at her exposed chest. Alice barely managed to get her blade in the way of his. They stood with their blades locked together.

"Good," said Alice. "Get your opponent off balance and attack their weak spot."

"But what if they just block like you did?" asked Axel.

"Then use your strength," said Alice. "You've got at least fifty pounds on me and that Quicksteel of yours makes you much stronger than you should be."

Axel took her advice and leaned his weight onto the sword. Alice fell to one knee. Axel backed off and Alice sprang up a little more violently than she wanted. Axel brought his sword around and swung at her side. She caught the blow and sent her sword into his stomach. He doubled over and gasped for breath.

Alice swung her leg up and kicked Axel in the side of the head. He landed heavily on his side and rolled onto his back. Alice stood over him, her sword hanging over his throat.

"It's going to take some work, but you definitely have some potential."

"Thanks," groaned Axel as he sat up. "So when are we going to get to the point where I can hit you?"

"That might take you awhile," said Alice with a grin. "We're done for the day. Go and rest by the fire."

Axel climbed to his feet and handed Alice the practice sword. He walked over to the fire and sat down next to Richie. His best friend stared at him wide-eyed.

"What?" asked Axel.

"Where'd you learn to move so fast?"

"What?"

"I could barely follow you two. I didn't know who was winning until your mom actually took you down. And for a bit there, it looked like you were actually going to beat her."

"I got lucky at that part," said Axel. "And the rest was just my mom being the badass she is."

"I wouldn't count yourself out just yet," said Slik. "I saw that lunge. Most people wouldn't have been able to see that break in Alice's defenses. And if you had just been able to spot it a split second earlier you would have had it."

"You think so?"

"Yes," said Slik. "I have to say, at first you didn't seem like much for a wielder. But now, I definitely see potential. Given time and proper training you could be a force to be reckoned with."

Clara laughed. "Now that I'd like to see. Mother monsters telling their children about Axel to get them to behave."

"I bet they already do that with you," said Axel. "Hell I plan on doing it to my children."

"That would be funny if it weren't true," said Clara. She raised her eyebrows and her eyes sparkled green.

They all laughed. They laughed until their sides hurt and tears ran down their faces. They didn't know why they were laughing so hard, after all it wasn't that funny. But it felt good to laugh. They hadn't had much to be happy about in the last few days and it felt good to release all of their pent-up emotions in a few glorious minutes.

Unfortunately, it didn't last.

The greatsword came crashing down on the fire. All of them jumped in surprise and scrambled to their feet.

The cloaked men were back. The giant hefted his sword out of the fire pit. The man with the whip stepped out of the shadows and let his weapon unfurl behind him.

"Every fucking time we get comfortable," shouted Axel even as Slik morphed into a sword in his hands."

"It's two against five," said Richie. "I think we'll be okay."

"It's two against four, Genius," said Clara. "Your egg hasn't hatched yet."

The giant cocked his head. He held up his hand and motioned towards the whip-bearer. The smaller man snapped his lash and the ground began to tremble.

"Did they get some kind of earth magic or something?" asked Richie.

"I've never heard of a Calla Lutai that does that," said Clara.

"Then what the hell is going on?!" Axel shouted over the rising din.

Barks and howls joined the sound of thundering paws, for what was making the earth shake wasn't magic, it was a particularly ferocious breed of monster.

One of them leaped into the circle of light made by the fire. It stood on its four gigantic paws and growled, bearing fearsome teeth as it did so.

"Dire wolves?!" shouted Axel incredulously. "They have dire wolves?"

"What the hell are dire wolves," asked Richie.

"You're looking at one," said Axel. "Wolves the size of horses. No real magic, but still not something you'd want to see up close."

"I see your point," said Richie.

Four more wolves stalked out of the darkness. They all stood glaring at the group. Alice drew her two shortswords and spun them around. She glared at the alpha male.

"You going to stand there all night, bitch?" she taunted.

"Hey Mom, I don't think it's a good idea to mock the giant wolf. Normal sized wolves are known for being savage when threatened. I'm pretty sure the super-sized versions would be too."

"Just be ready," said Alice. "We aren't going to be able to outrun these things and Jensen won't be able to get all of us in the car fast enough. We have no real choice here."

"Sure we do," said Axel. "With what you just explained to us, we have the choice of fight or die."

"And which one are you choosing?"

"I have been through way too much to just give up and die now," said Axel, getting into a fighting stance. Slik thrummed with excitement at the prospect of battle. Fighting was what he was made to do.

"That's the spirit, Axel," said Clara. Lightning sparked and crackled in her hands, her hair began to stand on end, and she even let her eyes glow green with electricity. It made for a fearsome sight.

"Really wish I had those fire powers right about now," said Richie.

"Just stay back and let us handle it."

The wolf that was staring down Richie suddenly leaped into the air. There was a boom and a flash of green and it landed on Richie in a smoldering heap.

"Richie!" shouted Axel. He ran for his friend, but one of the wolves jumped in his path.

Axel slid like he was going for home and stuck his blade straight up. He slid out from underneath the dire wolf just as it collapsed. Axel scrambled to his feet and continued running for Richie.

"Richie, you still with me?" asked Axel.

"I'm fine, just get this stinking bastard off of me."

Axel grabbed the dire wolf and pulled as hard as he could. It nearly flew off of Richie. Axel stumbled back a little bit at the lack of resistance it gave.

"Holy crap, I should go into a circus and do shit like that."

Richie stood up. "Admire yourself later, we're still under attack."

"Right, so you okay?"

"Yeah I'm fine just…owww." Richie doubled over in pain.

"Dude, what's wrong?"

"My stomach. It feels like it's on fire."

"The egg is hatching," Jensen called. "Get him somewhere safe until it's done."

Axel nodded his head and began to shuffle Richie away from the intruders.

The man with the whip started walking after them.

"Oh no you don't," said Clara. She held up her arm, but then a dire wolf landed on top of her. It pinned her arms down with its forepaws and bared its teeth and snarled in her face.

"Big mistake," she said. Clara's entire body glowed green and the dire wolf was launched off of her when a giant bolt erupted from her stomach. It landed in a broken heap a few feet away.

Clara scrambled to her feet and looked around for the man with the whip, but he was nowhere to be found. She heard a whistling noise and jumped out of the way just as the giant's blade smashed into the ground where she had been standing.

"Axel can take care of himself," said Clara getting to her feet. "And I don't want to be next to Richie when that egg hatches. So if you want to fight, bring it on."

She stood back and held out her arms as electricity began to crackle and spark along their length.

The giant hefted his sword out of the ground and began to walk forward. Clara held her arms out in front of her. They were now shining with green sparks.

"Try this asshole." The lightning bolt she released had little distance to travel before it hit the giant. It took him square in the chest and lit up the campsite like it was day.

Clara smiled while the after-images faded from her vision. The smile fell from her face as soon as she could see properly again. The giant stood before her completely unharmed.

"Fucking anti-magic cloaks," she cursed. "Alice I think we need to switch enemies here."

"I'll agree to that," Alice called. She was currently dodging the alpha male as it tried to tackle her to the ground. It leaped for her. She rolled out of the way and came up in a crouch.

The dire wolf snarled at her. It was about to leap again when a tendril of green lightning caught it in the side.

"Hey, sparky," Clara called. "Why don't you try me? I bet I taste better."

It snarled and snapped at her with its gigantic teeth. Clara sent a couple more bolts at it. It cowered and whimpered, then shook itself off and began to slowly stalk towards her.

Jensen meanwhile, was dealing with his own dire wolf. He pulled a dirk from the hidden sheath on his arm.

"I have lived on this planet for almost a millennium. I have killed almost every type of monster. I am not about to die to some insignificant little nothing like a dire wolf."

The dire wolf charged. Jensen reversed his grip on his dirk and teleported onto the back of the wolf. He jabbed the dirk into the spot where the spinal cord met the skull. The blade was magically enchanted to be much stronger and sharper than normal. It easily severed the dire wolf's spine.

Jensen yanked out his weapon and teleported off of the beast as it collapsed to the ground. He walked up to its body and wiped the dirk clean on its fur. He dusted himself off and replaced it in its sheath.

Alice stood before the giant.

"Looks like we get to pick up where we left off last time," she said. "Only this time I'm not worn down."

The giant walked forward with slow deliberate steps.

"See I know your big weakness. Why you need to wear that cloak and your little partner doesn't."

The giant stopped before her. He made a hand gesture for her to keep talking.

"With it you're the strongest, most powerful of the three assassins sent to kill my son. Without it, you're big, slow, and stupid. Clara would have easily killed you there. You are too slow and too big of a target. So your boss has to give you a little something extra just to make you actually work."

The giant swung his sword at her neck. Alice jumped back, then lunged forward and stabbed at the him. He turned sideways and her blade went right by his waist.

Alice jumped back as the great sword smashed into the ground at her feet. She darted forward again and slashed at the giant's leg. It growled as she cut him and he yanked his blade out of the ground.

He stood before her gripping the hilt of the blade with both hands, his feet shoulder width apart, and his muscles tensed to cleave her in half. Then he broke his stance, tucked the blade into his cloak, and started walking away.

Clara sent one more big blast at the Alpha male and it fell to the ground in a steaming pile. She walked over to Alice.

"What a coward."

"I don't think so," said Alice. "That thing is too big and skilled with that sword to be a coward. Something forced him to stop."

"Or someone," said Jensen, appearing out of nowhere.

"Maybe we should go find Richie and Axel," suggested Clara.

"Good idea," agreed Alice.

Chapter 17

Axel laid Richie down next to a tree.

"Why did I do this to myself?" Richie screamed.

"Shh," said Axel. "I know you're in pain but the screaming isn't really necessary."

Richie grabbed the collar of Axel's shirt and dragged him eye-to-eye. "There is a fireball being born in my stomach. If I happen to scream in pain from that you'll just have to excuse me."

He let go of Axel and groaned again.

"Good to know," said Axel straightening the collar of his shirt.

Crack!

Axel whipped around and stood face to face with the whip man.

"Ah, shit," he groaned. This was immediately followed by another groan of pain from Richie.

The whip man glanced at Richie and looked back at Axel. Even though Axel couldn't see his face he could've sworn the man was smiling.

Axel slipped into the fighting stance that had become almost second nature to him now.

"Bring it on, bitch."

The man whipped the lash forward. Axel brought Slik up and deflected it. He rushed forward, but the man brought the whip around and caught him in the side. It then snaked around his leg and jerked his foot out from under him. Axel hit the ground hard.

The whip man unsheathed a knife and stood over Axel. He raised the knife and brought it down to stab the boy.

There was a metallic clang as the knife glanced off of Slik. Axel whipped his sword up at the man's neck. The man sprang back and narrowly avoided getting his head cut off.

Axel got to his feet and held Slik ready.

"I'm not that easy to kill," he said. The man simply spread his whip out behind him in answer.

Axel darted forward and the man jerked the whip into action. Axel casually brushed it aside and got as close as he could to the man. In close range the whip was virtually useless.

But the man wasn't defenseless. His knife was long and serrated the last couple of inches. It may not have been as big as a sword, but it had enough weight to actually block Slik.

The man took a couple of steps back to give himself room for the whip, but Axel closed the distance. He had taken away the man's most potent weapon and he wasn't about to give it back.

Axel lunged forward. The man parried with his knife and slashed back at Axel. Axel blocked and started slashing wildly at the man. He roared in fury and kept up a relentless onslaught. The man blocked every cut and stroke while slowly moving backward the entire time.

Slik thrummed in Axel's hands. This time he wasn't excited about the battle, he was trying to break through Axel's rage. But Axel's focus was completely unbreakable. He was hell-bent on killing the man that had forced him and his friends and family on the run. The man who had tried to kill all of them on several occasions. And he was not going to let him slip through his grasp.

Axel swung at the man's side, but was blocked. He swung around to the other side and again the knife managed to get in the way. But as quickly as he could Axel thrust Slik forward.

This time the man didn't simply block. He used the knife to move Slik off course and throw off Axel's balance. The man punched Axel in the gut with the hand holding the whip. Axel stumbled backward and the whip snaked out once again. Axel's leg was yanked out from under him and he crashed to the ground for a second time. This time however he cracked his head against a large rock and lost consciousness.

The man walked forward and glanced down at Axel. He raised the knife once more. Just before he brought the knife down a rock hit him in the face.

The man whirled around and saw Richie, still on the ground but with another rock ready. He moaned and doubled up in pain, his breath coming in short gasps

He crouched down next to Richie and raised the knife. He held it aloft and prepared to drive it into the boy's heart.

Richie suddenly sat up. He screamed right in the man's face. Fire erupted from his mouth and the man fell backwards as he was engulfed in flames. He screamed in agony as his clothes caught on fire and his skin began to crackle in the heat. Soon the man's struggles ceased and the smell of charred flesh filled Richie's nostrils.

Axel stirred and opened his eyes. He sat up slowly and immediately regretted it. His head beat a painful rhythm on the inside of his skull. He smelled the burning corpse and stared at it shocked. He then looked at Richie who had an equally shocked expression on his face.

"What the hell happened?" asked Axel.

"I think the egg hatched," said Richie. "And I don't know about you but I'm starving."

"Only you could say that while smelling burned human flesh."

"Hey I'm eating for two now and the little guy is hungry. I think he already ate all the food that was in my stomach."

Axel got to his feet. Slik reverted to his normal form. Axel went over and helped Richie up.

"Come on," said Axel. "Let's go find the others."

"And we need to talk about your fighting style," said Slik.

"What do you mean?"

"You just charged the man recklessly," said Slik. "Anger has little place in sword fighting. You must be more calm if you are going to survive."

"We'll work on that later," said Axel. "For now, we have to get moving."

"I couldn't agree more," said Alice. She ran up to the boys, closely followed by Jensen and Clara.

Jensen looked at the smoldering corpse. "Have yourselves a barbecue, boys?"

"You could say that," said Richie. He gave a little cough that was accompanied by a puff of dark smoke.

"Looks like the little frightened rabbit has turned into a dragon," said Clara.

"And just in time too," said Axel. "If that thing hadn't hatched when it did I think we'd both be dead right now."

"We may still be in danger of that if we don't get moving," said Alice.

"Why don't we just keep staying in motels?" asked Axel, flopping down on the bed. "I don't care if they are where desperate douche bags go to have sex with hookers. The beds are still pretty comfy."

"Do we look like we're made of cash?" asked Alice.

"We're using fake and stolen credit cards," said Axel. "I don't think money is one of our problems right now."

"Kid's got a good point," said Jensen.

Alice glared at him.

"You know," said Axel. "I do like not being the only one that has to deal with you."

Alice put her hands on her hips. "Do you now?"

"Yeah," said Axel. "I can always count on someone else distracting you just when you're about to really tear into me."

"You mean like about now?"

"You think that nothing's going to happen," said Axel. "But just wait."

Alice stood there. "I don't see anything."

"Oh, you start yelling at me," said Axel. "You're not going to finish."

"You seem pretty confident in that."

"It has not failed once since we left home."

"There is a first time for everything."

"Would you quit asking," Richie and Clara walked into the room. "I'm not going to breathe fire."

"You know if you really want to get in bed with me, not showing me cool things isn't the way to do it."

Axel laced his fingers together and used them to pillow his head.

"Right on cue,"

"What the hell is going on here?" asked Alice. "There is no use of magic unless we are being attacked or I have you guys training. And you two are certainly not having sex on my watch."

"Hey don't look at me," said Richie. "She's the one trying to get me to breathe fire. And as for the sex thing, you don't have to worry about that. She's just using it to try and get me to go dragon. She has no intention of actually sleeping with me."

"You don't know that," said Clara.

"Fine then," said Richie. "How about now? We're in a motel. We could probably get another room."

"Didn't you hear what I just said!" screamed Alice. "You two are not going to have sex as long as I'm responsible for either of you."

"That a way, Mom," said Axel. "Forbid a couple of impulsive teenagers from doing something. That'll work."

"Axel, shut up."

Axel gave her a salute with a giant grin on his face.

"So, Richie," said Clara, "you should breathe fire."

"No magic," said Alice. "Especially magic that can cause serious property damage."

"I wasn't going to," said Richie. "I've been trying to tell Clara that for the past ten minutes."

"Aw, come on," said Clara, twirling a strand of her hair around her finger and biting her lower lip.

"Uhh," Richie stammered. "Well, maybe just once."

Alice grabbed both of their ears. "Come with me."

She started dragging them out of the room, both of them repeating "Ow" as she did so.

Axel laughed when the door shut. "So glad she's not doing that to me for once."

Jensen chuckled. "Some things never change."

Axel cocked his head. "What do you mean?"

"I mean that my mother used to do that to me when I was a kid."

"Really?" asked Axel.

"If you said even one thing she didn't approve of she'd have your ear in a death grip before you'd draw your next breath."

"So mothers were just as controlling and scary almost a thousand years ago?"

"I still have a few decades before I hit a thousand," said Jensen. "But yeah pretty much."

"Do you think I'll make into triple digits before I die?" asked Axel.

"If you're asking if you have the potential to live that long then I'd have to say definitely." said Jensen. "If you're asking whether you'll be killed by some sadistic sorcerer, I don't know."

"What do you mean you don't know?" asked Axel.

"Normally I'd say if we can get you to the school you'd have a decent chance of making it to your hundredth birthday. But Slik isn't an ordinary Quicksteel. He's much more powerful and for some reason Mordachai has set his sights on him. As long as you have possession of Slik someone is always going to try to get him from you. That particular monster has had a long and bloody history. His wielders are always great and powerful, but they all have a penchant for dying young."

"What do you mean?"

"You've probably heard of a few of his past owners," said Jensen, "Alexander the Great, Perseus, King Arthur."

"I thought King Arthur was just a myth."

"Oh he was real, I can assure you that," said Jensen. "And as for his famous Excalibur…"

"Slik?" asked Axel incredulously.

"The very same," said Jensen. "No matter how many forms Slik has taken he always seems to appear in history as a sword."

"So Slik isn't just some a normal Quicksteel," said Axel. "He is more powerful for some reason."

"I don't know," said Jensen. "But it seems that way."

"But why is he so powerful?"

"I have a theory behind that," said Jensen. "Did your grandfather ever tell you how the Magus stopped the war between humans and monsters?"

"Yeah," said Axel. "He said that they used one of every type of Calla Lutai."

Jensen raised his eyebrows and tilted his head forward.

Axel looked at the pocket of his coat where Slik was sound asleep. "You mean…"

Jensen nodded his head. "I think he was the Quicksteel the Magus used. The story goes that the Magus touched all of the Calla Lutai with their souls. After the blast all of the lesser monsters were changed. It was like they had been touched by gods. Not to mention every other Calla Lutai present. They were all supercharged and much more powerful then they had any right to be. The Magus ordered them to be sealed away and put into hiding."

"But then why is Slik still here. You even said that he's caused a little trouble throughout history."

"That is because of the type of people who end up as his guardians," said Jensen. "They always seem to be the people that are destined to lead armies. But you're right. This one Calla Lutai has stirred up some chaos in the past few millennia. But the Magus were trying to prevent a much larger catastrophe from taking place. If one loose Calla Lutai can cause a few wars, imagine what would happen if you brought them all together."

Axel sat back. "Chaos and destruction the likes of which this world has never seen."

"Pretty much."

"I just have one question."

"Shoot."

"Why me?"

Chapter 18

"On the road again. I just can't wait to get on the road again."

"Shut up Richie!" everybody screamed.

"Jeez, tough car,"

They had been driving for almost ten hours straight. They made it through Illinois and Indiana with out too many problems. Now they were about halfway through Missouri.

"I don't know about you guys but I can't wait to get *off* the road again," said Axel from the driver's seat.

"Only like two and a half more states before we get there," said Clara. Everybody let out an audible groan.

"I hate road-tripping!" Axel complained.

"We could all use a little bit of a break," said Jensen.

"No!" said Richie. "Every time we take a break we end up having to fight off a horde of something. I say we just keep going until we get there."

"What is this school called anyway?" asked Axel.

"Mortimer's Academy of the Supernatural," said Alice. "If it had been up to me we would have gone to the school in Toronto instead."

"There's a magic school in Toronto and we're driving all the way to fucking New Mexico?"

"We would have gone past border patrol, and I don't think any of us have pass ports," said Jensen. "Besides, where better to capture us than at the border. It wouldn't be too hard to get a couple of the patrol guys on their side and just have them arrest us."

"Right, 'cause sorcerers could be anywhere," said Axel dejectedly. "I have to say, this evil sorcerer bullshit is getting pretty old."

"Hey," said Jensen, "one of those sorcerers is my brother. And he was evil from the day he was born. You've had to deal with it for a few days.

I've had a few centuries of this bullshit. When you get to be my age, then you can start complaining."

"Typical old guy answer," said Richie. "We're going through something hard and you've either been doing it longer or have done something harder."

"Boy, you better shut your mouth before I teleport you outside of this car."

"You can do that?" asked Richie.

"He did it to me without even touching me," said Axel. "I'm pretty sure that it wouldn't be hard with him sitting right next to you."

"I can melt the tires before you get too far away," said Richie.

"Then you'd have a car full of mages pissed off because you basically made them sitting ducks for the army of monsters trying to kill them," said Clara.

"Yeah I see your point," said Richie. "So anybody up for a song?"

"I swear to God if you start singing again I'll carve out your still beating heart and make you watch as it stops pumping. Then, just before you actually die, I'll slice your head off so you can go through the agony of that for the few seconds it stays alive," said Axel.

"Holy crap," said Richie, "That was very descriptive. And disturbing."

"Good, that's what I was going for."

"Ah come on," said Richie, "My singing isn't that bad."

"It's like getting a corkscrew shoved in your ear except there isn't the mercy of actually going deaf from it," said Clara.

"Anybody know when the next town is?" asked Axel.

"No why?" asked his mother. The engine started popping and backfiring and the car slowed down and shut off.

"That's why."

"Luckily I bought some gas cans and filled them up at the last station," said Richie.

"Yeah, unfortunately I've already used them all," said Axel. "We are completely out of gas."

"Hey Jensen, we close enough for you to teleport us there?" asked Richie.

"Wouldn't even be able to get to the next town so we could get more gas," said Jensen.

"Well," said Alice, climbing out of the car, "guess we're hoofing it."

"Grab as much food and drinks as you can," said Axel. "I have a feeling we're going to need it."

"But it's really hot out and the sun can really damage my hair," said Clara.

Axel stared at her for a second. "So let's start getting our bags packed. It's going to be a long walk."

"Hey," said Clara. "I just got my hair the way I wanted it."

"Fine," said Axel. "Sit here in the car. But we're still going to take all the food and water so have fun."

"You guys suck," said Clara. "Just because I'm a lady who cares about her appearance."

"Seriously," said Axel. "Stay in the car. It'll be nice not to hear you whining the entire way."

"You're a jackass."

"That may be, but it still doesn't change the fact that I don't give a shit. Now come on, we're leaving." Axel held out a backpack full of supplies after donning his own. The rest of the group were already wearing theirs and were getting a little antsy to get going.

"You do realize it's going to be much easier for them to find and kill us," said Clara.

"It's better to keep moving, even slowly, than to stay in one spot and wait for them to come to us."

Clara gave a defeated sigh. "Damn you and your logic." she said, taking the bag. "Well we better get moving then. The quicker we get to the next town the sooner we can find ourselves a new car."

"That's the spirit," said Richie, "Let's get going."

He walked off whistling a random tune.

"That kid has way too much optimism," said Axel.

"That's not necessarily a bad thing," said Jensen. "It's better than being all whiny and depressed twenty-four-seven."

"And let me guess who the whiny pessimist in our little group is," said Axel.

"If you're thinking you then you already have your answer."

"What the hell is that supposed to mean?"

"If I keep telling you how are you ever supposed to learn?"

Axel adjusted his pack and started walking after Richie.

"You know what? I don't care. Be all confusing. I have a destination and a good group of friends, and that's all I need to know right now."

Jensen chuckled to himself as Axel walked away. "He's not ever going to get to Richie's level, but at least he's learning."

Alice clapped him on the shoulder. "Come on, you old relic, let's get moving."

"Hey, who you calling a relic? I'm just as spry as a four-hundred-year-old."

Alice laughed at him. "Just get a move on, Mr. Millennium."

Jensen scratched his chin as he walked after her. "Mr. Millennium, huh? Has a nice ring to it."

"It was meant to be an insult," said Alice.

"Well too bad, 'cause I like it."

"I'm kind of wondering something," said Axel about forty minutes later.

"What?" asked Alice.

"Spell casters age more slowly than mortals, right?"

"We call them danes, but yes we age more slowly than them."

"Danes?" asked Richie.

"Short for mundanes, kid," said Jensen. "As in normal, every day, boring people."

"Ah," said Richie.

"Right," said Axel. "So if we age so slowly that a spell caster will look like they're tforty when they're nine-hundred, then how old is Grandpa?"

Alice smiled. "Your Grandpa used a glamour to hide his true appearance. In truth he doesn't appear to be much older than me."

"What?" asked Axel. "Why would he do that?"

"Because most people think it's strange that I look like I'm in my early twenties and I have a sixteen-year-old son. Imagine what they would say when they figured out that my father looks like he's in his late twenties. It's kind of weird when your father can pass himself off as your older brother."

"So how old is he really?"

"About four-hundred," said Alice.

Axel shook his head. "So I'm guessing my aging process has started to slow down too?"

"Yep," said Alice. "That happened the moment you bonded with Slik."

Axel nodded his head slowly. "You know, besides the very long nights and the constantly being chased by creatures that inspired nightmares, being a mage isn't really a bad thing."

"There is always an upside to everything," said Jensen. "Nothing bad happens without something good to counteract it."

"That's actually a nice way of looking at things," said Axel.

"Of course that would mean that the opposite is also true," said Clara. "And now it's not."

"You gotta take the bad with the good, kid," said Jensen. "And you have to learn to find the silver lining."

"Blah, blah, blah, morality crap," said Axel. "I have my own way of looking at the world. If you don't like that, then you can suck it."

"Suck what?" asked Slik from Axel's shoulder.

"It's an expression."

"Normally it refers to a guys special organ," said Alice. She slapped Axel in the back of the head. "And don't tell your mother to do that."

"Yes," said Richie. "You can learn to see the world for what it is, or be an ignorant jackass and have your mom go upside your head."

"Shut up Richie," said Axel. "I can see the world for what it is. It's a cold, unforgiving place that will end up killing you."

"Ah, so optimistic," said Clara.

"You were complaining about the sun ruining your hair less than an hour ago," said Axel.

"So," said Clara. "If you hadn't noticed there are a lot of trees around. Which means there's tons of shade. So not only are trees beautiful, but they are wonderful for saving my hair from awful sun damage."

Axel hit his forehead with his palm. "You're kind of annoying, you know that?"

"Clara's right, Axel," said Alice. "It sucks we have to walk but at least we get to enjoy the nice scenery."

"Yeah this isn't so bad," said Richie. "And it's not like things could get worse."

They heard a car drive up behind them. Slik quickly hid back inside Axel's shirt pocket. They turned around just as it began to slow down. It came to a stop right next to them.

"Richie," said Axel.

"Yeah?" asked Richie.

"Never talk. Ever."

"Yeah, that's probably a good idea."

"Can I help you folks," asked the driver rolling down his window.

"Our car ran out of gas awhile back, officer," said Alice. The police man nodded.

"I figured I'd come up on some hiking people after I saw your car parked on the side of the road."

"We are terribly sorry about that," said Alice. "We're just in a bit of a hurry."

"Are you now?"

"Yes," said Alice. "You see, my husband has a job offer in Albuquerque and he can't miss it."

"May I ask why you and your children have come along with him?"

"Just because we're about to lose our house doesn't mean we can't have a vacation. Plus I was trying to give my son and his best friend one last adventure before they have to move away from each other."

"I see," said the officer. "And I suppose grand theft auto makes for one exciting adventure."

"Crap," said Axel.

"Crap is right, son," said the police officer as three more cars pulled up.

"Well look on the bright side," said Richie.

"More bright side crap, really?"

"At least we get a ride into town."

"In the back of a squad car," said Axel. "Not exactly a good thing."

"Drop your bags and put your hands on the car," said the first officer. "You have the right to remain silent. Anything you say can, and will, be held against you in the court of law. You have the right to an attorney. If you cannot afford one, one will be provided for you. Do you understand these rights?"

The group all gave half-hearted affirmatives.

"Then cuff 'em boys," said the officer. Once they had all had their hands cuffed behind their backs, the officers put all of the guys in one car and the two women in another.

"Hey, Jensen?" asked Axel.

"Yeah?"

"You ever go to jail before?"

"Couple times."

"Anything I should know?"

"Yeah," said Jensen. "Don't use the toilet if you don't have to."

"Anything else?"

"Only give them simple yes and no answers. And make it as confusing as possible."

"I thought we would have to do something to make it look like we're innocent," said Richie.

"I think that's a moot point right now."

"And what makes you think that?" asked Axel.

"Shut the hell up back there," screamed the officer in the passenger seat. "Scum doesn't deserve to talk."

"Maybe that," said Jensen.

"Somebody's a little too into his job," said Richie.

"I said shut the hell up."

"Yeah and we heard you," said Axel. "But contrary to popular belief, just because a police officer tells you to do something doesn't mean it's against the law when you disobey."

"You want a bet, boy?"

"Ooh, Mr. Toughguy. Threatening a teenager with his hands cuffed behind his back. You're so scary."

The officer took out his handgun and showed it to them. "How 'bout now?"

"Put that away, damn it," said the officer driving.

"He started it," complained the other officer.

"So what, Rookie. The kid is right. He can talk all he wants and there is not a damn thing you can do to stop him."

Axel laughed. "That's right, *Rookie*, put the damn gun away."

"Boy, you better shut up," said the rookie, pointing his gun right at Axel's chest.

"Or what, you gonna shoot me?" asked Axel with a crazy grin on his face. "Go ahead, do it. I dare you."

The rookie grunted and put his gun away. Axel laughed at him. "This is going to be a fun ride."

Chapter 19

"Three accounts of grand theft auto, two accounts of tampering with private property, multiple accounts of credit card fraud, destruction of federal property, and one account of murder. Also, one of the arresting officers wants me to give him five minutes alone with you and I don't think he wants your autograph. Six days in six states and you have more charges against you than most people get in a lifetime. For the murder alone I could put at least one of you behind bars for the rest of their lives?"

The detective was clearly shocked as he read off the charges he was accusing Axel of.

The detective himself looked remarkably like one of those guys in procedural cop shows. He wore a green button-down shirt tucked into black dress pants with a black suit jacket. He was about six feet tall and had neatly combed black hair. He stared at Axel with piercing blue eyes.

"We know nothing about the murder."

"We have eyewitness reports of a vehicle with a description and license plate number matching the car we found not far from where we picked you up. Now talk, and if you try to tell me some more bullshit about a family trip then I suggest that you get a damn good lawyer."

"My family is kind of unusual," said Axel.

"Kid, this is not a game," said the detective. "Somebody in your little group burned a man to death. Even if that wasn't you, there is enough evidence here put you away for a very long time. I suggest you start talking so that we can work out a little deal."

"Tell you why it would appear as if we have an entire gang's rap sheet against us in less than a week you mean?" asked Axel. "Maybe I should tell you the truth. Chances are you won't believe me anyway. But hell, it would definitely go a long way towards an insanity plea."

"You don't seem crazy to me, kid," said the detective.

"Okay, then," said Axel. "Fair enough. Then can you tell me something detective? Why would a completely sane person travel halfway across America in multiple stolen vehicles, committing murder and a half dozen other felonies along the way for absolutely no reason?"

The detective chuckled. "Touché. Most sane people wouldn't do all of that for no reason. So give me one."

"Five days ago my grandfather gave me a mystical artifact for my sixteenth birthday. Ever since I've been chased by monsters and sorcerers who would do almost anything to get their hands on it. The body you found torched was one of the sorcerer's henchmen. If you were more magically inclined you would have also found the bodies of five dire wolves at the scene. But unless you've actually had magic forced upon you, or were born with the Sight, you would probably see only a pile of rocks or maybe some dead bears. I don't know. I've only recently been able to see monsters. Since I've laid hands on the artifact I mentioned.

The detective sat back in his chair open-mouthed. When Axel finished his story he blinked his eyes and shook his head in amazement.

"That might be some of the craziest bullshit I've ever heard."

"Told you," said Axel.

"You actually think that some magicians…"

"Sorcerers," Axel corrected.

"Right, sorcerers. You think sorcerers are after you because of some birthday present your grandfather gave you."

"That about sums it up," said Axel. "Now do you think I could get away with an insanity plea?"

"I still don't think you're crazy."

"I think that makes you a little crazy," said Axel. "But if you're not screaming for me to be put into the nut-house, then I do know a way to convince you that I'm not lying."

"And what is that?"

Axel reached into his jacket pocket and pulled out Slik.

"Kid, what the hell are you doing?" asked the blob furiously.

"Convincing our detective friend that I'm telling the truth," said Axel. "And even though he won't be able to convince everybody else, he might be more inclined to look the other way when we get out of here."

The detective watched the exchange with an incredulous look on his face.

"What the hell is that?"

"My birthday present," said Axel. "Detective, I'd like you to meet Slik."

"How's it going?" said Slik.

"Fine," said the detective. "I might be going insane, but otherwise pretty good."

"Yeah, I have that effect on people," said Slik.

"So this is what those sorcerers you mentioned are after?"

"Yep," said Axel, nodding his head calmly.

"A talking blob? Really?"

"I'm a little more than that," said Slik. "My body is made of an incredibly durable, extremely flexible, organic, metallic alloy."

"What?" asked the detective, perplexed.

"Slik is a living blob of metal that can change into different weapons," Axel explained. "But they can't be bigger than he is."

"So he can be a sword?" asked the detective.

"And a knife, and a war axe, and a mace," said Slik. "Pretty much any one-handed weapon."

"How about a gun?"

"I still haven't figured out what one of those is," said Slik.

The detective blinked in surprise. "How do you not know what a gun is? Even if you're some magical creature, you have to have seen a gun by now."

"I should clarify," said Axel. "Slik has been in an enchanted sleep for the past seven-hundred years. He has no clue about most modern technology."

"Hey I know a bit about cars and wrenches and those weird portable communication things that paint pictures incredibly fast and receive information from something called the internet."

The detective had a confused look on his face.

"He means cell phones," Axel explained.

"Oh," said the detective. "Your phone gets internet?"

Axel hit his forehead with the heel of his hand. "We're kind of getting off topic right now."

"Right, sorry."

"Slik can not only turn into pretty much any one-handed weapon you can think of," said Axel. "He also gives whoever's wielding him an incredible power boost. He increases the amount of magic available to his wielder, which floods the body and enhances pretty much every cell in that person. I now have dramatically increased strength, speed, and reflexes. Basically, Slik has given me a warrior's perfect body."

"Which is kind of handy to have when you're wielding a living weapon."

"Good, you're catching on," said Axel. "Slik is a Calla Lutai. It roughly translates into lesser monster. Every Calla Lutai has some kind of genetic defect that is normally fatal, or at least makes it hard for them to survive on their own. To compensate they have to bond to a human or other types of monsters. This bonding provides the wielder with an ability that somehow corrects the genetic defect."

The detective shook his head. "Okay now you lost me."

"It's a little complicated at first. I'm just glad that my grandpa told me monster legends as bedtime stories. I am now an expert on things that a week ago I had no idea existed."

"So I guess you weren't lying," said the detective.

Axel cocked his head in confusion.

"Your family is definitely unusual."

Axel grinned. "Tell me about it."

"So now we have a little problem," said the detective.

Axel lifted up his cuffed hands. "You think?"

"In light of new evidence, you're technically innocent. Even the murder could be seen as self defense."

"But…?"

"But," said the detective, "nobody will believe that the evidence exists."

"And you can't tell anyone," said Axel. "It's sort of an 'if everybody figures out that monsters and magic are real, bad stuff will happen' type of thing."

"Like?"

"A potential apocalypse."

"Potential?"

"Well, people and monsters might get along better this time around, or people will freak out and start trying to kill that which they don't understand. And with the way most people act to big life-shattering events, how much are you willing to bet that it will be the latter."

"So by potential, you mean incredibly likely."

"Yep, pretty much," said Axel.

The detective buried his face in his hands. He took a couple of deep breaths and dragged them down his face. "Kid, this is so messed up."

"I'd like to say it gets better from here," said Axel. "But then I'd be lying."

"More bad news?"

"If my friends and I don't get out of here soon, those sorcerers, or at least some of their more unfavorable henchmen, will try and break into the station and steal Slik. Hell, they'll probably come here anyway just because we were here for any length of time."

"Beautiful," said the detective. "And what do you want me to do about it?"

"Nothing," said Axel. "Play ignorant. Chances are they might just send something you can't normally see to check out the place, or one of the sorcerers will come by and ask about us. Just tell him the truth. We escaped and you have no idea how."

"So you're telling me that you're going to escape?" asked the detective. "You do realize it's part of my job to stop you."

"You know that all that I'm guilty of is being chased by homicidal maniacs. And since you can't clear me yourself, just let us escape."

"How do you plan on escaping anyway?"

"I'm not going to tell you," said Axel. "That way you'll actually be telling the truth when people ask how we escaped."

"That is kind of freaky how you're actually planning for little things like that."

"On the bright side, I could always try being a criminal mastermind when this whole saving the world thing is over."

"If you're actually going to steal things then I can't help you."

"It was a joke," said Axel. "You really need to learn to lighten up."

"Well, this line of questioning is over," said the detective. "And you're lucky this is a small town police department. We haven't had a chance to install two way mirrors yet."

"This would be a very different conversation if I had seen mirrors or cameras," said Axel.

"Fair enough," said the detective. "And by the way, the guards change at about seven. Just as a heads up."

Axel smiled. "Thanks Detective…"

"Corsair," said the detective. "Jake Corsair."

"You did not just pull a Bond thing."

"It felt kind of corny even as I was saying it."

Axel shook his head. He picked up Slik and put him back in his pocket.

"See you around, Corsair."

"You better hope not, kid."

"Good point."

Chapter 20

"Stick your hands through the slot."

Axel did as the deputy commanded. There was a gap next to the prison door that he slid his hands through so the deputy could uncuff him. Axel rubbed his sore wrists once they had been freed and sat down on one of the benches in the cell.

All of them had been put in the same holding cell. Richie stood by the door and watched the deputy walk out of the holding area.

"He's gone."

"Everybody still got their respective Calla Lutai?" asked Axel, revealing Slik to assure them that he did indeed have his. Clara took Fared out of her pocket. The tiny fluff ball cooed and crackled. Clip climbed onto Jensen's shoulder and stared at Axel with his TV-static eyes.

"Everyone's present and accounted for," said Jensen.

"Good," said Axel. "Anybody know what time it is?"

"About five," said Richie, reading the clock on the wall opposite the cell.

"Then we better get moving, 'cause the guards switch at seven."

"And how do you know this?" asked Alice.

"The detective told me," replied Axel.

"And why would he tell you the best time to escape?" asked Clara.

"Because the idiot had to take me out while he was being interrogated," said Slik.

"You did what?!" everybody screamed simultaneously.

"Shut up back there!" shouted the deputy from his place at the guard post.

"Axel, what moronic thing did you do now?" asked Alice.

"I told the truth."

"And he believed you?" asked Richie.

"No," said Axel. "But he didn't think I was crazy."

"So you went ahead and proved to him that you're not only crazy, you're insanely stupid too," said Clara.

"He agreed not to come after us when we escape," said Axel. "He also gave me the time when the guards would switch so that we can get out easier."

Alice slapped him on the back of the head. "You never tell a dane, let alone the police, that magic is real. Too many people know and we have mass chaos."

"That's what I told him," said Axel defensively.

"And you trust this guy?" asked Jensen. "You think he'll be able to keep the secret?"

"Yes," said Axel. "I think he will."

"Then there's not much we can do about it now."

"So we're just going to ignore this?" asked Alice.

"Yes," said Jensen. His answer surprised her.

"What?"

"We can't kill the detective, because then we would have even more police on our asses. They just found a burnt body a couple of states away from a stolen car. They assume it was us because our car was seen at around that time, but it could have been anybody. We kill a detective and not only does it confirm the first murder, we get a bunch of police pissed off that we killed one of their own on our tail. I say it's best if we trust Axel's judgment and this cop's integrity and get the hell out of here."

"Finally," said Axel. "Someone's on my side."

"Not quite, kid," said Jensen. "After we get out of here we're going to have a long talk about revealing the Big Secret to danes."

Axel sighed. "Ah, damn it."

"So how are we getting out of here?" asked Richie.

"We need to get our personal possessions back," said Alice.

"What did they do when they found out that you're basically a walking armory?" asked Axel.

"The guards were surprised that I had so many weapons on me and that not one of them was a gun."

"Seriously," said Slik. "What the hell is a gun?"

"Later," said Axel.

"You keep saying that but you never actually show me."

"If shit like this keeps happening, you will definitely see a gun," said Axel.

"I better," said Slik.

"So I have an idea of how to get out of here," said Axel.

"I don't think we need any more of your bright ideas," said Clara.

"Fine then, what's your plan?"

"Simple," said Clara. She held up her pointer finger. Electricity was racing up and down the digit.

"No," said Axel. "We are not frying the cops."

"I meant using it like a taser."

"That's great," said Richie, "How do you propose we get out of the cell then?"

Clara shrugged her shoulders. "I don't know."

"Well I do," said Axel.

We have about an hour before the shift change. Let's do this," said Alice.

"Jensen," said Axel.

The short man nodded and flickered out of existence. Axel took Slik out of his pocket and put his hand through the bars. He held Slik in front of the keyhole. Slik extended a small silvery thread of himself into the lock.

Jensen returned with everybody's things from the evidence locker. He handed Alice all of her blades, which she began to strap onto her body. He gave Clara two daggers and Richie the set of throwing knives that Alice had loaned him. Jensen passed everybody their wallets, then slipped his own into his pocket and belted on his own dirk.

There was a click and the door swung open.

"Got it," said Slik. Axel retracted his hands through the bars and put Slik back into his pocket. They all crept out of the cell as quietly as possible.

Axel peered around the corner. The guard was sitting at his desk watching a basketball game on a small television. Axel motioned for Clara to go forward.

All it took was one small jolt at the base of the unsuspecting guard's neck and he slumped forward onto the desk.

Axel moved forward and checked his pulse. "He seems to be alive."

"Of course he is," said Clara defensively. "He should also be out for a few hours. But I didn't use enough to do any permanent damage. He will wake up with a nasty headache, though."

"Very nice," said Richie. "Now can we get out of here?"

"Just a sec," said Axel, unclipping the guard's keys from his belt. "Now we can go."

They got to the back door and Axel searched for the key to unlock it. After a few unsuccessful tries, Richie stepped forward and pushed him out of the way.

"Let me do it." Richie grabbed the handle, which soon began to glow red. A few seconds later it was a steaming puddle gathering at the base of the door.

"Holy crap," said Axel. "I see you've been working on your powers."

Richie shook bits of molten steel off of his palm. "It's nice to be impervious to heat. And be able to make yourself so hot that you can basically melt yourself out of pretty much anywhere."

"Very impressive Richie," said Alice, "but if you don't mind, we kind of need to get going."

They opened the now handle-less door and entered into a back alley.

"So, where to now?"

"First we need to get a new car." said Axel.

"How about that one?" asked Clara, pointing. They followed her gaze and her outstretched arm to see a police cruiser parked a few feet away.

"No," said Axel. "Police cars have built in trackers in case they are stolen."

"But I always wanted to drive a cop car," Clara whined.

"And you called me stupid."

"'Cause you are."

"Not as stupid as you apparently."

"You want to go?" said Clara, energy sparking from her hands.

"Bring it on," said Axel, the air distorting around his fists.

"Both of you, shut up," said Alice. "We're not taking the cop car, and you're both kind of stupid. Now let's go."

"Your mom's a little uptight," said Clara.

"I heard that."

"She can also kick your ass if she gets pissed off enough. And she has a choice of twenty different blades to help her."

"Good point," said Clara. They all followed Alice out of the alley.

"Is it smart to be walking around in the open like this?" asked Richie.

"Just act natural and nobody will care."

"It kind of annoys me when people say that," said Richie. "How can you act natural? Acting implies that what you are doing is uncommon for your behavior, but natural is what you normally do under a given set of circumstances. Acting natural is a very contradictory statement."

"You done?" asked Axel.

"As a matter of fact...," said Richie his face contorted in anger. He grunted in annoyance, "yes."

"Good, then shut the hell up."

"How's this sound then?" asked Alice. "Act as if we are a normal family out on vacation, and not a bunch of fugitives who broke out of jail thirty seconds ago."

"Better," said Richie.

"So I say we try to find a Ferrari," said Clara.

"We're on the run and trying to stay unnoticed," said Axel.

"That doesn't mean that we can't drive around in style."

Axel drove his palm into his forehead. "It kind of does. We want a nice anonymous car."

"Like the Mustang in New York?"

"No," said Axel. "The exact opposite of the Mustang in New York."

"Well where's the fun in that?"

"You're an idiot."

"Well you're a douche bag."

"Whore,"

"Slut,"

"Bitch,"

"Both of you shut up," said Richie. "Jesus Christ, you guys fight worse than me and my sister."

"Well at least we got the normal family part down," said Jensen.

"I agree," said Slik, poking his head out of Axel's jacket pocket. "You two bicker just like siblings."

"Yes," said Axel. "We are just one perfectly normal family. Except for the talking blob in my pocket, the twenty blades strapped to my mom's body, the lizard in my 'father's' pocket with weird eyes that look like bad TV reception that allows him to teleport, the tiny fluff ball that generates enough electricity to power a few major cities that my 'sister' is carrying, and let's not forget the newly hatched monster in my 'brother's' stomach that lets him breath fire. Yep we are a perfectly normal family."

"Jeez," said Clara. "Is it that time of the month already?"

"Remember, you have to sleep some time. And I have a nice selection of killing methods available."

"Screw the selection; I prefer my own signature style." Clara's eyes flashed green.

"I don't care that we are in a completely public place, you want to do this we'll do this."

Alice grabbed both of their ears. "You may not care, but I do. Now quit your bickering, shut the hell up, and help us pick out a nice car to steal and get away in."

Axel rubbed his ear after she let go of him. "That is the weirdest reprimand I've ever heard."

"Reprimand? Really?" said Clara. "Who the hell talks like that?"

"What did I just say?" shouted Alice.

"Sorry ma'am," said Clara meekly.

"You better be."

"That looks like a nice one," said Jensen. He pointed to a dark green Buick sitting in a crowded parking lot. It wasn't completely new, but it wasn't incredibly old either. It had definitely seen some miles, but was still in good working condition. If things went well, it could definitely make it to New Mexico without many problems. But the past few days had taught Axel exactly how big an if that was.

Still, the car was as good as any other. It looked like thousands of others on the road and would be hard to find once they got away and were able to switch the plates.

"Alright," said Axel. "Let's get this over with."

"And how do you propose we do that?" asked Clara.

"Simple," said Axel. "Slik can unlock the lock, and then you can do that illegal little trick of yours."

"Hey," said Clara. "You've done some illegal things too you know."

"I know," said Axel. "I wasn't trying to shame you. I just want to remind everybody of what we're doing. And that despite what we say, and what I told the detective, we are not model citizens. We may not be the bad guys, but we are not entirely free of guilt."

"Shut up and quite being a sanctimonious bastard," said Clara, walking towards the parking lot. "Let's go. The rest of you keep watch."

Richie went with Alice, while Jensen walked away by himself. They spread out so that it wouldn't look as if they were together and to be able to observe more. Making it easier to spot somebody that might see what Axel and Clara were doing.

Axel bent down next to the lock and took Slik out of his pocket.

"We need your skills one more time, little buddy."

"What would you guys do without me?"

"Hopefully we never have to figure that one out."

Slik chuckled as he extended his tendrils into the lock. He felt around for about thirty seconds. He suddenly made his tendrils solid and turned the lock.

"Got it."

"You are getting really good at that," said Axel.

"Probably a little better than I should be," agreed Slik. "Oh well. Clara, you're up."

"Hey! What are you kids doing?"

"Crap," said Axel. He slid over the top of the hood as Clara got in the driver's seat and hit the unlock button as she closed the door. Axel got into the front passenger seat just as Clara sent a jolt through the dash board. The car roared to life.

"Go, go, go, go," said Axel.

"No really?" asked Clara sarcastically, "I was just going to sit here and do nothing until the car drove itself to New Mexico."

"Just drive before he calls the cops and gets us thrown back in jail."

"Relax," said Clara, pulling out of the parking lot. "We'll be long gone before the cops can get here."

"We just stole a car out of their parking lot," said Axel. "That's a police officer chasing us. He's probably radioing for back up."

"Really?"

"Really."

Clara stopped in front of Alice and Richie. "Get in."

As they were crawling into the back seat, Jensen materialized in the seat behind Clara.

"It is very convenient that you can do that," said Axel.

"Did we just steal a car from the police station parking lot?" asked Richie.

"Yes I believe we did," said Axel. Clara was speeding down the main road. They heard sirens flashing in the distance, but Clara had already turned. She made a few more and hit the highway leading out of town. The sound of the sirens rapidly faded in the distance.

Axel let out a breath he didn't realize he had been holding.

"I think that went better than last time," said Richie.

"And I think that if this is your idea of *better*, than this *better* be the last car that we steal."

"Agreed," said Richie. "Next stop, New Mexico."

Chapter 21

"I'm so glad to be out," said Richie. "It's so cold in the joint."

"What the hell are you talking about?" asked Axel. "We were only in there for four hours. They didn't even have time to feed us."

"I know, and I'm starving."

"You're always starving," said Clara. "We need to save a McDonald's manager's life or something. Get enough free burgers to keep Richie satisfied."

"I doubt even that would work," said Axel. "The dude has a black hole where his stomach should be."

"I've been full before," said Richie.

"When?" asked Axel. "Name one time. I've been to your house for Thanksgiving. You didn't even get full then."

Richie scratched his head. He opened his mouth to say something, but closed it and started muttering to himself.

"Now that you guys mention it," said Jensen, "I am a little hungry myself."

"How much cash do we got?" asked Axel.

"I thought we were paying for everything with credit cards," said Richie.

"Can't," said Axel. "The detective ran all of the credit cards when he thought we were still criminals. Ten bucks says they're monitoring them right now to see if we slip and use them."

"Not to worry," said Jensen. He took out a knife and slit the lining of his shirt. He reached his hand up into it and pulled out another credit card.

"I always keep a spare for situations like this," he explained as he took out a sewing kit and began to repair his shirt.

He handed the card to Axel.

"Dude," said Richie. "I freaking love you."

"Yeah I figured you might."

"So we got cash," said Axel. "Good. Now we can make it to New Mexico."

"So," began Richie. "What's this magic school like?"

"Pretty much a normal school," said Jensen. "except most school's aren't surrounded by a magical barrier, don't have the front gates guarded by gryphons, and don't have explosions occurring on a very frequent basis."

"I'm guessing the subjects are a little bit weird too."

"Just a little bit," said Jensen.

"When's the last time you were there?" asked Axel.

"I try and visit a couple times a year. My sister's the nurse, and I like to keep in touch."

"You have a sister?" asked Axel.

"Lilith," said Jensen. "She's Mordechai's twin, but the exact opposite of him in every way."

"So really nice and likes to help people?" asked Clara.

"Sweetest girl you'll ever meet."

"And by 'girl' you mean nine-hundred-year-old crone," said Richie.

Jensen smacked him in the back of the head. "I mean girl you asshole. Do not disrespect my sister."

"Translation: she's ugly as sin."

"That's it." Jensen put a hand on Richie's shoulder. Richie flickered and disappeared. They heard a thump on the roof half a second later. Then Richie began to scream.

"Holy shit! Get me off of this thing!"

"Apologize for what you said about my sister and I'll consider bringing you back in." Jensen called.

"Axel, help me," screamed Richie.

"I don't think you want me doing that," yelled Axel. "The only way I can get you off involves you flying towards the road at sixty miles an hour."

"You son of a bitch," screamed Richie. "Fine. I'm sorry for what I said about Jensen's sister. Now, please let me down."

"Alright," said Jensen.

"Hold off on that a little bit," said Alice.

"Oh, come on," screamed Richie. "What now?"

"You called Axel a son of a bitch. And since he's my son that means that you called me a bitch. Where's *my* apology?"

"Seriously, you're going to keep me up here for that?"

"Absolutely," said Alice.

"You seriously didn't see that one coming?" asked Axel.

"Yeah," said Clara. "Never insult Alice. You will definitely live to regret it."

"Fine," said Richie. "I'm sorry for calling Axel a son of a bitch, and by extension Alice a bitch. Now please let me back in the car!"

Alice nodded to Jensen.

Richie flickered back into existence in his seat behind Axel.

"Never do that again!"

"It's your own fault, dumbass." said Axel. "Never piss off anyone who has the ability to teleport you. Because they may not always send you where you want to go."

"I didn't want to go anywhere," complained Richie.

"And yet he sent you somewhere," said Axel. "My point is still incredibly valid."

"You know I can burn you alive, right?"

"You know I could have Slik out and stabbed through the seat and your stomach before you let out so much as a puff of smoke."

"I think this car is beginning to get a little too hostile," said Clara.

"And that's really saying something," muttered Richie.

"What was that?"

"Nothing," said Richie quickly.

"Dude never learns," said Axel.

"We need to get out of this car," said Clara. "Or we're going to end up killing each other."

"That's a very mature statement," said Axel. "Who are you and what the hell have you done with Clara?"

"Haha, jackass. Very funny."

Axel laughed. "I see your point though."

"We've already hit Oklahoma," said Alice. "If we keep going we can be to New Mexico before morning."

"But we'll have killed each other before we reach there," said Richie. "I say we at least pull over somewhere and stretch."

"I think there's a larger city coming up," said Axel. "And I think I see a mall."

"A couple of hours?" Clara asked. "Please Alice."

Alice took a deep breath. She looked at the clock in the car. It showed eight o'clock.

"We meet back at the front entrance at ten," she said.

Axel breathed a sigh of relief. "Thank you."

He pulled into the parking lot and quickly found a space. The three teenagers quickly jumped out of the car and sprinted for the entrance.

"Remember, ten o'clock, front entrance."

"Got it," shouted Axel.

"You'd think they'd never seen a mall before," said Alice. "They did grow up in New York."

"They're kids," Jensen reminded her. "They aren't supposed to be living this kind of life."

"I know," said Alice. "Why do you think I tried to hide all of this from Axel? I denied who I was for sixteen years just to keep him safe."

"I can understand that sentiment."

Alice looked at him curiously. "Are you a parent?"

"I was," said Jensen. "A long time ago. Back when I looked more like my age."

"So what happened to your child?"

"Children," Jensen corrected her. "I had three. And a beautiful wife."

"Did they find out that you were a sorcerer or something?"

"Well, yeah," said Jensen. "But they were too, so that didn't really matter much."

"So what happened to them?"

"Mordechai happened."

Jensen's smile and wistful air turned into a look of pure anguish. His eyes, which only a moment before had been shining and happy from a wonderful memory of his family, turned dark and brooding.

"I'm sorry," said Alice.

"I would have killed him right then and there," said Jensen.

"Why didn't you?"

"Because Lilith had thrown herself in front of him."

"Your sister?" asked Alice, shocked. "But why would she do that?"

"Because that's who Lilith is," said Jensen. "No matter how much of a monster Mordechai has become, Lilith will only see the shy, innocent boy he used to be."

"And what do you see when you look at him?" asked Alice. "Do you still see the shy boy underneath all that hate?"

"No," said Jensen simply. "That boy died a long time ago. Mordechai is no longer the child who I smiled at and willingly called my brother. He is a demon, bent on fulfilling his own selfish goals. And that is simply something I cannot allow."

Alice walked beside him in silence.

"So where is Lilith, then?"

"I told you earlier," said Jensen. "She's the nurse at Mortimer's school."

"I know," said Alice. "I just wanted to know more about the woman who would be taking care of my son when he inevitably hurts himself."

Jensen smiled. "She's sweet, caring, and the best healer I've ever met. When Axel does hurt himself, he will be in the best possible hands."

"Well that's good," said Alice. "Now, I don't know about you, but a day at the mall is starting to look like a lot of fun to me."

Chapter 22

Axel breathed in the wonderful smell.

"I'm going to have to agree with Richie here," said Slik. "In a mall full of all kinds of interesting things like video games and sporting equipment, you're a little fruity for going into a flower shop."

"Shut up," said Axel. "I like flowers."

"Yes, but you can see flowers anytime," said Slik. "I've seen thousands that were much more pleasing to look at than any of these. But I have yet to see these things you call video games."

"It's like this," said Axel. "You grew up back when technology was fairly primitive. There were flowers and trees everywhere.

"I on the other hand, grew up in New York City. A place that has so little plant life that we have to actively grow it if we want any."

"So?"

"So," explained Axel, "to you flowers are a dime a dozen, whereas things that are incredibly common to me, like video games, are new and rare. I don't get to see flowers much, but I have a decent collection of games back home. They are nothing new and will be there for generations to come."

"How can you possibly know that?" asked Slik. "They may just be something that entertains this generation, but bores the next."

"Video games are constantly evolving and developing into newer, better versions of themselves. And the ways we use to play them are also changing and improving. Games will be around as long as there are bloodthirsty kids with an incredible urge to gain superpowers and destroy cities."

"Okay, now I absolutely need to see video games. Can you please pick out your flower and let us get out of here?"

"I'm not going for one of the full grown ones," said Axel. "I'm just looking at what type I want. I'm going to buy some seeds so that I can plant my own."

"That sounds like it could take you a while."

"That's the point. I want something to take my mind off things when they get a little hectic. Plus, if I buy a fully grown flower, then chances are that it will somehow get ruined before we even get to New Mexico, let alone the school. The seeds will have a much better chance of survival."

Axel picked out a packet of peace lilies. "I think I'll go with these."

"A fine choice."

Axel turned to the short, young, blond woman standing beside him.

"Peace lilies are a very beautiful and easy to manage type of flower."

"Do you work here?" asked Axel.

"No," said the woman. "But I do have what you would call a bit of a green thumb."

She held up her hand. Her thumb was indeed green.

"Looks like you spend a lot of time in your garden."

"Yes, but then you would too if your home was a tree."

Axel stiffened. "You're a Calla, aren't you?"

The woman nodded. "And you're not as slow as some humans. Yes I am a Calla Bas. Specifically a mandragora."

"A mandrake?" asked Axel. "A plant person?"

"Yes."

"I always thought you were little screaming things," said Axel.

"You should know better than most that that wasn't the only thing Harry Potter got completely wrong. Just like basilisks don't freeze people, or have a deadly stare."

"Yeah, I know," said Axel. "A basilisk just secretes an incredibly powerful poison."

"We mandragora don't scream, that's banshees. We are a mix of plant and animal though. Not entirely one or the other. And we can also change our appearance."

"Right," said Axel, the information resurfacing. "I remember what my grandpa said about you now. You guys are the inspiration for Greek wood-nymphs. You can appear to be beautiful women, or strong young men, but when threatened, you have a tendency to become more plant like and hide. Normally found in forests, and incredibly shy. This has something to do with the fact that your leaves contain incredible magical properties that can be used in most healing spells. That was something Mrs. Rowling did get right."

"You make us sound like cowards."

"Hey, that's just what my grandpa told me. Though at the time I was seven and thought of it more as a bedtime story than a lesson on a magical creature I might one day actually come across."

"So we like to use our camouflage," said the mandrake. "Is that such a bad thing?"

"No," said Axel. "That's using a talent you evolved to survive. Humans have been using that particular trick for a few millennia now. Though they use it to hunt better, you use it so that you are harder to hunt."

The mandrake smiled. "I kind of like you. You seem very well educated and have much better manners than most humans. It's a shame I'm going to have to kill you."

Axel sighed. "How the hell did I guess that?" he asked. "Every time a Calla reveals itself to me it's never to just chat and make friends. Every monster I come across has only one thing in mind. My head on a platter for sorcerers."

The mandrake put a comforting hand on his shoulder. "Don't feel too bad. And don't take it personally. I actually do find you charming. But business is business after all. I can make it quick for you."

Axel gave a half-hearted grin. "If it's all the same to you, I'd rather not die. So instead of just rolling over and letting you kill me I will be fighting back."

"A shame," said the mandrake. "Well, I suppose. I would rather die fighting than to just roll over and accept it."

"Right," said Axel. "Go out with a roar, not a whimper."

The mandrake smiled once more. "Yes, but your not a lion."

"Are you sure?" asked Axel. "'Cause I have some pretty nasty claws."

"Do you now?"

"Yeah," said Axel. "Let me show you."

He brought his hand up faster than even he thought possible. The mandrake's arm fell to the ground while the rest of her staggered back.

She stared at the stump where her arm used to be.

"You're going to pay for that," she spat.

"Look at it this way," said Axel with a cocky grin. "You were going to kill me before. I've just given you a reason."

The mandrake looked at the hand that had sliced off her arm. The back of it was covered with a thin coating of metal that extended to cover all of the fingers. At the tip of every finger was a very short claw like blade whose edge extended over the back of the fingers to the second knuckle. The other side was also sharpened, but only extended to the first knuckle. This intricate design gave Axel the ability to slash in both directions with equal effectiveness.

Axel saw what she was staring at and flexed his fingers as he too admired his new set of claws.

"Slik has certainly outdone himself this time."

"Slik?" asked the mandrake.

"Don't tell me they didn't tell you why they wanted me killed."

"For your Quicksteel."

Axel waggled his fingers, "Well, here he is. You were so busy talking to me you didn't even notice him sliding down my arm."

"I forgot," said the mandrake, "that Quicksteels are shape shifters. They can make themselves into almost any weapon. And because they are so flexible, things like your claws are their specialty. While the design can be copied, it can never be reproduced with such effectiveness. It is really something special."

"You forgot another thing that sets Quicksteels apart from other weapons."

"And what is that?"

Axel pointed to the ground. The blade on his pointer finger extended rapidly and speared the mandrake's crawling hand. "They have a bit more reach than their man-made counter parts."

The mandrake looked at Axel with surprise.

"Did you really think you could distract me like I just did to you?"

"Actually, yes," said the Mandrake. She held up her shorter arm. Tendrils and vines began to sprout from the wound. They wrapped and coiled among themselves. Soon they had taken on the shape of a hand. A coating of bark grew over the vines. Once that completely covered the new limb, it changed and took on the appearance of human skin.

"You were stalling while you gathered the material to regenerate your arm," said Axel. "Neat trick."

"Thank you," said the mandrake. "But I'm still not very happy about you cutting off my other arm."

"If it means that much to you, then you can have it back." He whipped the dismembered limb at its former owner. At the same time he retracted the blade on his pointer finger back to its original length.

A vine sprouted from the mandrake's palm and caught the arm. The mandrake put the arm close to her chest. The limb broke down and was absorbed back into the mandrake's body.

She looked at Axel with a look of pure malice. "I'm going to enjoy this."

Axel smiled and flexed his claws. "We'll see about that."

The mandrake sent a few vines from her arm whipping forward. Axel jumped to the left and rolled out of the way, but the vines simply changed direction.

Axel's right hand came up and the metal on the back flashed in the light. The tips of the vines fell to the floor.

The mandrakes hissed in pain and anger. "Stop cutting off my body."

"Stop attacking me with your body."

The mandrake was losing control of her human form. Her skin reverted back to its natural bark form. Her hair took on the appearance of broad oak leaves. And her clothes looked more like the leaves of a bush than fabric. She would have looked beautiful, except for her eyes. They were two large acorns that glowed with a fierce emerald light. Her face was twisted into a snarl.

Vines began to coil around her body. They grew like the limbs of some mutant octopus, but there were more than just eight and they came in varying thicknesses. A few pushed the mandrake off the ground so it appeared as if she was floating.

"It is time for you to die, mortal."

Vines twisted around Axel's body faster than he could cut through them. The mandrake picked him up and threw him out of the store. People went screaming in all directions.

Axel staggered to his feet.

"We've been here all of ten minutes and already something is trying to kill me. Typical."

The mandrake walked out of the shop on her vines. "You may have some talent, but you are no match for me."

Vines exploded from her body towards Axel.

Chapter 23

"The more I get to know you the hotter you seem to get," said Richie.

"Just because I play video games you think I'm hot?"

"I thought you were hot before, this just makes you hotter."

Clara's character passed Richie's, ramming into it and causing it to spin out.

"It's so cute when I'm kicking your ass."

Richie immediately drove his character into a wall.

"What the hell are you doing?" Clara asked.

"I figured if you thought I was cute when you were beating me this would go a long ways to getting me laid."

"You're an idiot."

"Yes, but I'm an idiot with fire power who thinks you're gorgeous."

"Aww, that's so creepy."

"Ouch."

Clara laughed as she crossed the finish line. (In first of course.)

As they walked out of the store Richie pulled out a pack of cigarettes and put one in his mouth. He snapped his fingers and lit his thumb on fire. He was about to light the cigarette when Clara grabbed his arm.

"What are you doing?"

"Having a cigarette."

"Don't you know how bad they are for you?"

"Actually, since I'm bonded to a Brimflare, they really aren't that bad for me. One part of the Gift that Brimflares give is that they allow their wielder to breathe smoke and toxins with no negative side effects, in fact we actually seem to thrive off of them. Smoking this is like having a breath of fresh air."

"And who told you that?" asked Clara critically.

"Jensen," Richie explained. "We were the first two done with our interviews, so he helped me figure out my powers while you guys were away."

"How are you able to control your powers?" asked Clara. "When I first got Farad I couldn't really control his Gift until my magic was fully awakened. I had enough control to keep him alive and that was it. You seem to have amazing control after a day."

"Jensen had a theory about that. He said that when someone undergoes a traumatic experience that it could awaken their magic. He said that having a Brimflare hatch inside my stomach along with the stress of the past few days might have tipped me over the edge. After that it was just a matter of learning to control the heat being generated by my little friend." He patted his stomach affectionately.

"So what do you want to do now?" asked Clara.

"I don't know about you but I'm starving."

"You're always starving."

"Yes, but now I'm starving for two."

Clara laughed. "Now that you mention it I am kind of hungry."

They walked to the food court which was packed even for the time of day and the size of the town. After they got their food they grabbed a table and started eating. Richie had gotten five double bacon cheeseburgers, three orders of fries, two strawberry milkshakes and a large Mountain Dew. Clara had three slices of pizza, two chocolate milkshakes, an order of bread sticks, and a large Diet-Coke.

Richie cocked his head at her order.

"What?" asked Clara with a piece of pizza halfway to her mouth.

"I don't think I've ever seen a woman who eats as much as I do."

"I'm not eating as much as you." she pointed out. "And are you calling me fat?"

"No," said Richie hurriedly. "I just think its impressive that someone like you could eat that much."

"Someone like me," said Clara with open hostility in her voice.

"I meant someone that's skinny and beautiful and why are you smiling?"

Clara's mouth had been twitching as she was trying to hide her amusement, but now she burst out laughing.

"What's so funny?"

"You," she said and started laughing harder.

"Okay now I'm confused."

"I'm fucking with you," Clara explained. "I know what you meant."

"That's a little mean."

"I'm sorry, I just couldn't resist."

"Actually it's kind of hot."

Clara shook her head. "You are so weird."

Richie looked a little downcast. "Weird, huh?"

"Don't worry," Clara said, leaning in close. Richie's eyes grew wide at her proximity.

"I like weird," she said.

"Really?" said Richie leaning in a little closer.

"Really," said Clara leaning in even farther.

Their lips drew closer. Richie closed his eyes. He hung there for what seemed like an eternity. He finally opened his eyes. Clara's deep brown ones stared at him.

"I'm sorry I thought I was picking up on something there."

Clara bit her lip and drew back. She shook her head. "It's not your fault. It's just that you deserve someone better than me."

Richie reached across the table and took her hand. "I can't think of anyone better."

Clara smiled and took her hand out of his. "Richie, there's things you don't know about me. Things that would make you stop looking at me the way you do."

"Looking at you like what?"

"Like I'm the most interesting person in the world. Like I'm worthy of your time."

"Clara, to me you *are* the most interesting person in the world. You are smart, and beautiful, and courageous, and so much different than any other girl I've met. Normally when I'm around beautiful women I get tongue tied and nervous and try to be someone else. Someone I think they might like. When I'm around you I feel like I can be myself. Why would I ever even consider anyone else."

"Richie you've known me for about a week. And I'm not that courageous."

"Really, you could have fooled me."

"Would someone who's courageous run away when their parent's are getting killed."

"What?" asked Richie completely caught off-guard.

"My parents were mages. My entire life I've known about magic and monsters. My parents started training me to harness the energy inside of me as soon as they were sure I had the gift. I remember getting Farad's egg for my fifth birthday. By the time I was six I was shooting lightning at everything. That was when they started to teach me to use it responsibly. They told me that not everybody knew about magic and that it must be kept a secret. It was frustrating at school getting picked on by kids and knowing that I could fry them any second, but that my parents would be more upset about me using magic than getting beat up. When I was ten I remember arguing with my parents to let me use Farad in a talent show to make all of the other kids like me."

She smiled a sad smile and slowly shook her head. "Now I realize how stupid of an idea that was, but at the time I thought it would work. I wouldn't let it drop until my dad was screaming at me that I needed to grow up. The last words he probably remembers me saying to him were 'I hate you'.

"They came that night. Evil wizards. You see, there are some wizards who want to use magic to control the world. Manipulate peoples minds, destroy armies, take anything they want for themselves. My parents were part of the Bureau of the Mythical, Abnormal, Supernatural and Weird."

"What the hell?" asked Richie.

"It's a super secret government agency that's responsible for making sure the magical world stays secret. They capture or kill any rampaging monsters with below-sentient intelligence, arrest and prosecute mages and monsters with sentient intelligence who misuse their magic, help humanoid monsters find jobs, stuff like that."

Richie shook his head. "So what happened that night?"

"They were everywhere," said Clara. "They kicked in the door and smashed in the windows. My dad's battle-ax shot to his hand before they even took a step inside."

"So your dad had telepathy?"

"No. My entire family was bonded to Stormpuffs. My dad used his electricity to magnetize his ax to himself. My mom did the same to her bow and quiver. They fought like demons. They must have killed at least twenty of them, but they just kept coming. My dad yelled at me to run, but I was too scared. One of the wizards grabbed my arm, but I let out as much energy as I could. I was a knee-jerk reaction. The guy dropped dead without a scream. That was the motivation I needed. I ran out of our house. A few of the wizards chased after me, but I managed to lose them in the streets. I hid out in an alley for a while. After I lost the wizards I finally realized that I had left my parents behind. I snuck back to my house and watched from a distance. The wizards were clearing out. I could see one of them, who I assumed was their leader, yelling and waving around my dad's battle-ax. He was huge and had fiery red hair, and a thick black beard. He sounded like he had a thick accent, Irish I think or maybe Scottish. I couldn't tell. One of the wizards walked up to him and said something, the big guy obviously didn't like it because he shouted and the guy went flying."

"How the hell did he do that?"

"I wasn't sure until I saw the Vibraclaw on his shoulder. It's a type of Calla Lutai that looks like a cross between a bat and a rat. It had large leathery ears and thick gray fur with a pink, hairless tail. It's mouth was very long but instead of being pointy like a rat's, it was smashed at the end like a bat's. Two leathery wings extended from it's elbows. Vibraclaw's can produce sonic energy. They literally vibrate the air around them until it starts producing miniature sonic booms, but if they try to release the energy they normally end up exploding themselves. So they allow their wielder to direct the energy. By vibrating a very specific area, very hard, very fast, they can actually displace enough air to move objects. I've even seen a few Vibraclaw wielders smash through solid brick walls by displacing the air next to it.

"After all of the men had left I snuck into the house. I found my parents' bodies in the living room. They had taken the bodies of all the wizards who my parents had killed, but left my parents to rot. My dad had been stabbed through the chest and my mom's throat had been slit. I crouched down next to my father. I laid my head across his chest and cried. Then I felt something brushing my hair. I looked up to see my father staring at me. He was barely alive. I took his hand and begged him not to die. He managed to gasp out two words. He said 'Key, Safe' and then he took a key on a leather cord from under his shirt, tore it off his neck and put it in my hand. I told him I would keep it safe as I sobbed over him. He nodded, smiled, and died. Ever since I've been hopping from place to place staying with friends of my parents."

"Wow," said Richie. "That's one hell of a childhood."

"That's an understatement."

Richie reached across and took her hand again. "I still think you're courageous."

"I ran away," said Clara.

"You were ten and frightened. And you came back."

"I shouldn't have run in the first place. I should have stayed and fought alongside them."

"And then you'd be dead too," said Richie. "And we wouldn't be here right now. Hell we probably wouldn't have made it this far without you."

"I haven't done anything worthwhile."

"Clara, without you we wouldn't have made it out of New York. We wouldn't have escaped from prison and we sure as hell wouldn't have got away from the harpy swarm."

"Axel was the one who got us away from the harpies," Clara pointed out.

"If you hadn't done your super bolt, Axel wouldn't have had enough time to have been awakened and we would have died."

"You don't know that."

"I don't care," said Richie. "You can't change the past. And, personally, I don't want to."

"So you're happy my parents died?"

"Of course not," said Richie. "But I am glad that you're here now. Whether you had stayed or not, your parents would be dead. You said yourself that they were vastly outnumbered. But if you had stayed then you wouldn't be here now helping us get to the school. And now you have a chance to avenge them."

"What do you mean."

"I mean that you have to make sure that they didn't die for nothing. Whoever sent those men has to be stopped. And do you still have that key?"

Clara pulled it out of her shirt. "Right here." It was a large ornate brass key. The end was a diamond shape that had been twisted into a spiral pattern. The other end was a cross shape with uneven protrusions coming from each of the arms."

"Then you have at least done what your father asked so far and kept it safe."

"Small consolation."

"Listen Clara," began Richie. "You are the most..."

Clara waited. "The most what?"

Richie didn't answer. He was staring at something over her shoulder. She turned around to see what he was watching. There was a man having an argument over at a pizza restaurant.

"What do you mean you're out of sausage?" he yelled. "Why don't I tear you apart and use you as a topping, how does that sound?"

"Does that guy sound familiar to you?" asked Richie.

"Vaguely, but I can't place him."

"I want to speak to your manager," the man yelled. "Maybe he has enough intelligence to get me what I want."

"Oh shit," Richie cursed. He stood up and dragged Clara after him. "We have to go now."

"Why?"

The man stopped his tirade in mid-sentence and started sniffing the air.

"Because I know where we've seen that guy before."

"Where?"

"He was our cabbie in New York."

"You mean the cabbie who ended up being..."

The man turned and stared directly at them. His eyes glowed blood-red.

"Yeah, that one. We should run."

Clara almost yanked his arm out of the socket.

"Way ahead of you."

They took off running just as a deafening roar filled the food court. People started screaming and running in every direction. Richie turned back just as the werewolf finished it's transformation. He started running faster.

"Shit, shit, shit!"

He could hear the beast as it pounded closer.

"Let me try something," said Richie. He turned around and started running backwards. He snapped his fingers and lit his thumbs on fire. The flame expanded and his hands were covered in fire balls. He threw one straight into the werewolf's face. The next one hit it's chest. The monster simply bounded through it.

"That didn't work," said Richie, turning around and continuing his head-long dash.

"You dumbass," screamed Clara. "Remember in New York when I hit it with a super-charged bolt and all I did was stagger it and singe it's fur."

"Vaguely."

"Dumbass."

"So how do we kill a werewolf?" asked Richie.

"Got any silver?"

"Do I look rich?"

"Then we need to cut it's head off."

"Got any blades on you?"

"None that could go through its neck," said Clara.

"We are so fucked," said Richie. "We need to find Alice."

"Where would she be?"

"How should I know?"

"You know her a lot better than I do."

"And apparently most of the things I knew about her were wrong."

"Follow me," said Clara. She took a sharp turn right. Richie almost fell as he tried to follow her. The werewolf almost bounded past them. It's paws skidded on the linoleum as it tried to gain traction. By the time it was able to follow them they had extended their lead by a few yards.

Richie saw a banister up ahead and his face grew pale.

"Clara, please tell me you're not planning what I think you're planning."

"Remember to roll before you hit the bottom." She took a flying leap and sailed over the banister.

"This crazy bitch is going to get me killed." Richie took a glance back and saw the werewolf a few feet behind him. "Fuck it. Falling is probably a better form of death than being torn apart anyway."

He sailed after Clara. The werewolf was not far behind. Normally, jumping seems like a bad idea. Being caught by a werewolf in mid-air is a real possibility. But physics is a tricky bitch. Since the werewolf was traveling much faster, weighed a lot more, and, being much stronger, was able to launch himself with more force, he ended up having much more momentum than the two teenagers. As a result, Richie began to fall just before the werewolf caught him. As a matter of fact the werewolf had so much momentum that he flew over the banister on the opposite side and smashed himself into the wall behind it, actually burying his head into the concrete.

Clara rolled just as she hit the ground and popped right back to her feet. Richie landed on his back a moment later.

"That hurt," he groaned.

"Dumbass, you were supposed to roll right before you hit the ground."

"I did, I flipped right before I landed."

"They idea is to roll away your momentum on the ground so that you don't hurt yourself."

"Well it didn't work."

"Dumbass."

"Would you quite calling me a dumbass, you bitch."

"Dick."

"Quite calling me names," Richie yelled as he scrambled to his feet.

"Aw, you're no fun, Axel would have called me a worse name."

"Wait you guys do that on purpose?"

The werewolf yanked it's head out of the wall and shook itself off. Then, it let out a bone-chilling howl and jumped down.

"Let's talk about that later," said Clara, grabbing Richie's arm and dragging him along.

The werewolf let out another roar and leaped in front of them.

"Guess it was tired of chasing us."

"We are so screwed," said Clara.

The werewolf started taking slow menacing steps towards them.

"Clara, if we die, I just wanted you to know something."

"And what's that?"

"I'm really glad I got to know you."

"Me too," said Clara taking his hand. "But we're not dead yet."

The werewolf lunged.

Chapter 24

"So how do you think this one looks?"

Alice held a green shirt with a low neck in front of herself.

"I don't know," said Jensen. "Maybe you should try it on."

Alice looked at the shirt critically. "Maybe," she thought out loud. She looked at the price tag.

"Not even if I was a millionaire."

Jensen chuckled. "This is a pricey store," he pointed out. "You're not going to find anything cheap in here."

"Maybe we could find you something though."

The smile dropped from his face. "What's wrong with what I'm wearing?"

"You look like you're homeless."

"I am homeless."

"By choice, that doesn't mean you can't wear nice things."

Jensen looked down at what he was wearing. She did have a point. His clothes were covered in dirt and had scorch marks scattered all over them. His shirt had food stains on it and since he wasn't wearing any shoes his feet were almost black with dirt.

"I like the way I look," he said.

"Why would anyone choose to look homeless."

"Alice, I'm a transient person by nature. I get around by being unseen. Who pays attention to a homeless person?"

"What do you mean transient by nature? Not all wizards are transient."

"No, but a good portion of them are. Plus you know how being bonded affects somebody."

"It changes their magic," said Alice.

"Right, but what is magic?"

Alice cocked her head. "I don't follow."

"A person's magic is the thing that gives them life. It is in a sense like their soul. When a person becomes bonded to a Calla Lutai their magic isn't the only thing that changes. It can change them physically too. Look at Axel, he's now much stronger than the normal human and Clara is immune to electric shocks. But more than that being bonded also makes some changes to your personality. What would be the point of having a person who can teleport who never wants to leave home. Being bonded to Clip gives me the natural tendency to want to move, to be everywhere I can, to go anywhere I can. He makes me unhappy with staying in one place for too long. Even now I'm starting to get the itch to get going, get moving."

Alice nodded her head. "I suppose I can understand that."

"Do you mind if I ask you a question?" Jensen asked.

"Yes and I'll even let you ask another one," said Alice with a grin.

"So I told you something about my past when we talked about my family right?"

"Right?" said Alice skeptically.

"So let me ask you a personal question."

Alice took a deep breath. "Listen, Jensen..."

The older man held up his hand. "I can understand not wanting to share your past, but you said you wanted to know more about my sister because she will be taking care of Axel. Well, before I let him into a school full of children who barely know how to defend themselves I need to know something about him."

Alice's mouth hung open. "What the hell are you talking about? You know Axel. He wouldn't hurt anyone. He's not a danger to the children."

"Not directly, but you've seen what he can do. I get you come from a long line of mages, which is going to give him a lot of natural power, but that in and of itself doesn't explain where he gets it all from. The kind of power he displayed was unlike any other I've ever witnessed. So I need to ask. Who is Axel's father?"

Alice gaped at him. "What?"

"Who is Axel's father?"

"He doesn't have one," said Alice sternly. She gave him a look that told him to drop it. And Jensen did what every man has the innate ability to do perfectly. He played stupid and pretended not to notice.

"I get that Axel's father isn't in the picture, but unless you're trying to tell me he's the second coming of Jesus and you're the Virgin Mary herself, biology states that he has to have a father."

"Jensen drop it."

"No," said Jensen bluntly. "Like I said, most of the kids at this school don't now how to properly defend themselves yet. If he's the son of a powerful wizard whose going to assault the school to get at Axel I need to know."

"And what if he is?" asked Alice acidly. "Are you going to not allow him in? Are you going to let him fend for himself and die?"

"Of course not," said Jensen calmly. "I would never let an innocent child die if I could prevent it. Whoever his father is and whatever his sins, Axel should not be punished for the conditions of his birth. Unfortunately for some of us we don't get to choose who's DNA we end up sharing. But Mortimer may have to take special precautions. He will accept Axel, of that I have no doubt. But, Axel won't be the only young person under his protection. I'm just thinking of some other children I've helped reach that school in the past few years. So I'll ask you one more time, what can you tell me about Axel's father?"

Alice took a deep sigh. "Not much. I told Axel that I got pregnant with my high school boyfriend, and that once he found out he skipped."

"But due to the fact that you are much older than you appear, when you would have been high school aged, your boyfriend at the time would have probably been fighting in Germany."

"It seemed like a good lie at the time. Axel didn't know my true age and since I never figured out his father's last name I had no idea of knowing if he was dead or not, so I didn't want to tell Axel he was dead in case he decided to check in on his son at some point."

"Smart," said Jensen. "Also the fact that you don't know his last name suggests a rather quick relationship."

"You can say that again," said Alice. "About seventeen years ago I was in Chicago. This was way back when I worked for the Bureau. There was a rash of bogart occurrences in the area and they sent me to deal with them. After killing all twenty of the shifty bastards I thought I deserved a few days off. Fortunately the Bureau agreed."

Jensen was impressed. Bogarts were shape-shifters. The could look like anything. A mouse, a cockroach, a dog, even inanimate objects like chairs and lamps were common disguises. They tended to be the cause of most ghost stories. They were very territorial and once they moved in to a place they almost never left. Nor did they like when anything else living tried to enter. They normally just bumped around and whispered in peoples ears until they left, but if that didn't work they could easily become violent. One bogart would have been hard enough, twenty was a nightmare Jensen couldn't imagine.

"So I'm guessing something happened during those few days off."

A small smile touched Alice's lips. "You could say that. I was touring the city, enjoying myself. Shopping, clubbing, just having fun, you know."

Well, one day I'm standing in a martial arts studio that sold authentic fighting equipment. And not just sparring gi's, they also had a nice selection of weapons. Throwing knives, shuriken, nunchaku, you name it. So I'm looking at their selection of katanas when this guy walks up. You know what he says to me? 'It is so rare to see a woman with good tastes these days.'"

Jensen chuckled. "So what did you do?"

"I turned to him and said 'Well apparently it's less rare than a man with good tastes. Any swordsman worth their salt can tell these wouldn't do shit in a real fight.'

"He bursts out laughing. We started talking. First about weapons, then fighting styles, then just random things. We ended up at a bar and danced for a while and got drunk. I remember going back to my hotel room and some things after."

"What kind of things?" asked Jensen.

Alice gave him a mysterious look. "Seriously, two drunk adults do things in a hotel room and you have to ask what?"

Jensen shrugged his shoulders. "I was assuming *that* happened. I was just kind of looking for specifics."

Alice shook her head. "Why are all men such perverts?"

Jensen shrugged again. "I dunno, genetics."

Alice rolled her eyes.

"So then what happened after those...'things'?"

"Nothing, woke up the next morning and the man was gone. And a couple weeks later I found out I was pregnant. I haven't heard from him sense. Of course thinking back it was kind of obvious that the guy was a mage."

"So basically you had a one-night-stand about seventeen years ago where you probably only figured out the guy's first name, which may also have been bogus, and never saw him again."

"I tried to find him, but like you said I only got his first name and I'm pretty sure it was fake, I know the name I gave was."

"So now he can't track you down."

"Nope."

Jensen ran his hand through his hair. "That really doesn't help us. Especially since we haven't exactly been the most anonymous of people on our little road trip. If this guy is as powerful as I think he is, he's bound to have heard something about Axel by now."

"Look that's all I know," said Alice

"It'll have to do," said Jensen. "I've got some contacts all over the place. I'll see what I can dig up."

"You're going to track down a guy I had a one-night-stand with seventeen years ago and do what?"

"Well once I find him, I'll just keep an eye on him and see if he has any plans of finding his son. Judging by your story he probably doesn't even know he has one."

"But he's going to have heard about a kid being chased by wizards with enough power to take out one of the largest harpy flocks ever heard of single handed," Alice pointed out. "He starts digging and finds out who I am it wouldn't take a genius to figure out his real relation to Axel."

"That's what I'm worried about," said Jensen.

"Oh dear, that shirt would look amazing on you."

They turned to see one of the employees from the store standing behind them. Her hair was done in a towering style that was probably in fashion when she was young enough to be shopping at stores like this one. Her hair was light brown with wide bands of platinum. She was wearing a light pink blouse tucked into a magenta skirt and towering black heels on her pantyhose covered feet. Her face was covered in more than a few layers of makeup in a vain attempt to cover up her many wrinkles.

Alice looked at the shirt still in her hands. "I do too," she said. "But I think it's just a little too pricey for my taste."

"Come now, deary. What'sss money really good for? And don't you want to look good for your death?"

"What did you just say?" asked Jensen.

"I said we all sssshould look nice when we go," said the clerk. "And with your time coming so soon and all I just figured."

"Don't look at her eyes," said Jensen. "She's a gorgon."

"Clever boy," said the clerk. "But sssince you've figured me out there'ss no ssssensssse in continuing to ussse thiss rediculousss dissguissse."

Her skin began peeling off revealing the diamond-shaped scales underneath. Her hair began to writhe like a nest of snakes. The strands began to mold together, growing scales and unwinding themselves from each other. A small triangular head poked itself out. It's beady eyes locked onto Jensen and Alice and a forked tongue slithered from it's mouth.

The woman's legs bulged, ripping the pantyhose and the skirt as they fused together. Muscles rippled along her entire body as she began to grow. Her clothes becoming shredded tatters on her reptilian body.

Jensen grabbed Alice and teleported them outside of the store.

"We have to run," he said.

"How come you didn't get us farther away? We're right outside the entrance."

"This was as far as I could get us. Now let's use the little bit of a lead it bought us."

The gorgon smashed through the clothing racks in the store and burst out of the entrance. She hissed and snarled. Her eyes locked onto the two of them and her face broke into a sneer.

"Come now, you can't run from me for forever."

"We need to go now," said Jensen.

"Ya think?" shouted Alice, who was already thirty feet away in a dead sprint. Jensen teleported himself next to her and started running alongside of her.

"What's our plan?" he huffed.

"Are you already out of breath?" asked Alice.

"I'm old...okay," he said between gasps. "I'm also...not used...to running."

Alice shook her head. She risked a glance back at the gorgon. The monster was slithering along after them. People started screaming and trying to run from the hideous snake woman. A few unlucky souls accidentally looked into her eyes as they glanced back and were now screaming as their bodies quickly turned to stone. More than a few of the statues were crushed by the gorgon or shattered by her tail as she snaked past.

"Got any ideas?" she asked Jensen as she turned back around.

His eyes darted around the mall. He grinned at something up ahead. "I think so, but it's a bit of a long shot."

"If it gets us out of this alive I'm open to anything."

"You see that antique store ahead of us on our left?"

Alice narrowed her eyes and spotted it maybe fifty yards ahead. "Yeah."

"You remember the story of Perseus and Medusa?"

"Vaguely."

"Just give me about five minutes and then steer her into that store," said Jensen. His form flickered and he was gone.

Alice stared at the space where he had been with her mouth open.

"You did not just leave me to fight a gorgon by myself!" she shouted.

"Looksss like your little friend isss a bit of a coward, deary."

Alice spun around and whipped out her swords.

The gorgon laughed and stopped about ten feet from her. She ducked her head in an effort to catch Alice's eyes, but they were closed.

"Closing your eyesss may prevent you from turning to ssstone, but they won't ssstop me from killing you."

Alice took slow even breaths. She couldn't fight her opponent with her eyes open, so she had to use her other senses. She could smell the musty odor of snake all around her. She listened to the muscles of her opponent as they tensed and relaxed. She could feel the heat and the movement of the air. She used another sense too. One only available to people who can use magic and that she had trained years to hone and perfect. She sensed the magic coming from the gorgon, seeing the creature's aura in her mind's eye.

"You can't defeat me, little one. Far greater warriorsss than you have tried."

Alice's blade moved before her senses had even registered the attack. She sliced the gorgon's arm and rolled away from her claws. She came up near her body and sliced through her abdomen. Before Alice could move again, however, the gorgon's tail smashed into her flicking her away. Alice hit a wall hard. She stood up and shook her head to clear it. She opened her eyes to take in her position. She was right outside the store Jensen had pointed out.

"Hope you've had enough time, old man," Alice muttered to herself. She ducked inside the store with the gorgon close behind her. The store was full of antique mirrors. She glanced around at a hundred different versions

155

of herself. Jensen flickered into being right next to her and grabbed her arm. Next thing she knew she was at the back of the store.

"Here take this," he said. He handed her a small mirror about two feet across and three feet tall. It had two bungee cords going around it about a third of the way from the top and a third of the way from the bottom.

"What's this?" she asked.

"A mirror shield."

"What good does that do?" asked Alice incredulously. "She can't turn herself to stone. What are we going to show her her own reflection and hope she dies of fright?"

"Perseus and Medusa," said Jensen.

And suddenly it clicked. Perseus was a Greek warrior who killed Medusa, the queen of the gorgons. He used a polished shield to defeat her. By looking at the shield he could tell when she was behind him and since the gorgon's ability didn't work from a reflected image, he was able to cut her head off using the position of her reflection as a guide.

Alice put one of her swords away and slipped her left arm through the bungee cords, grabbing the top one and letting the bottom one come to rest at her elbow. The shield was positioned so the mirror side was facing her.

"Where did you get the cords from?"

"Hardware store across from this one."

"Jensen you are a genius."

The older man smiled. "I know."

"Where are you deariesss," the snake woman hissed.

"One of us will distract her and the other one will attack. When she shifts her attention the first one hits her again. We'll keep going back and forth like that until we can kill her."

Alice nodded.

"I'll go first," said Jensen. And with that he teleported right in front of the gorgon.

"You know," he said, "I had heard gorgons were ugly, but holy shit."

The gorgon hissed and lashed her tail at him. She suddenly screeched as a burning pain exploded into her back. She twisted around to find Alice stabbing her repeatedly.

"Little witch!"

Alice dived off just as the gorgon swiped her claws at her. She hissed again as Jensen stabbed her in the stomach.

"Very clever," she said. "Ussing the mirrorsss to avoid my eyesss. But that isss a problem that is eassily remedied."

She lashed her gargantuan tail at all the mirrors in the store, shattering them. She added her claws and teeth and in a few minutes the entire store's inventory was reduced to a pile of glass shards on the floor.

With the destruction of the mirrors Jensen and Alice were left horribly exposed.

"Any other bright ideas?"

"Yeah. Run."

The rushed towards the entrance. But before they could make it the gorgon's thick reptilian tail smashed in front of them blocking their path.

"Going ssssomewhere?"

"Jensen, I need you to do me a favor."

"And what would that be?"

"Find Axel. I'll hold her off for as long as I can. But you need to get my son and the others and get them to the school."

"There is no way I'm leaving you..."

"You have to. I need to know that my son is okay."

"And you will. We are far from done."

"Jensen, I thank you for your concern and for all that you've done for us. But you're just going to have to go on without me."

Jensen placed a hand on her shoulder. "I will not see another of my friends die. Not today. Not alone."

Alice smiled gratefully at him.

"Then what are we going to do?"

"You are going to die!" shouted the gorgon. Baring her fangs, she struck.

Chapter 25

The vines exploded towards Axel. He raised his hand and closed his eyes, expecting the worst. Right before they hit, Slik burst apart into a shock wave of tiny razor-sharp fragments that tore through the mandragora. The plant creature screamed in agony.

The pieces of Slik slid across the floor and melted back together next to Axel's hand.

Slik shook himself off. "You have no idea how weird that feels."

Axel scooped him up and scrambled to his feet. "Nice job, little buddy. Now let's get the hell out of here."

He took off running as fast as he could. Slik peered over Axel's shoulder. The mandrake had just reabsorbed the scattered pieces of herself and was rushing after them.

"You might want to run faster."

"Alright but I have a question," said Axel as he dug his heels in and put on a burst of speed.

"Do you really think now is the right time?"

"Might not get a chance later," Axel pointed out.

"Fair enough. Okay, shoot."

"If you can do shit like you just did, then how come you need to be bonded to me?"

"I can only do that shit while I'm bonded."

"Okay, I'm officially confused."

"You know how you're faster and stronger while you're bonded to me?"

"And apparently have amazing stamina too."

"Right, well part of that is adrenaline, I would focus more on running than how long and fast you've been running."

A vine smashed down directly behind them.

"Though a little faster would be nice."

"Preaching to the choir." said Axel as fear and adrenaline pushed him to even greater speed.

"Well, just like I make you more physically capable, you make me able to harden my body. Without you I'm just a talking puddle of metal."

"Interesting, so you can't shape shift unbonded?"

"Not like I can now. When a Calla Lutai bonds to a human they trade pieces of themselves. We Quicksteels rely on this trade to survive."

Axel came to a three-way intersection and turned right. Wooden darts the size of small knives embedded themselves into the wall behind him.

"Now I suggest we talk more later. For now, run!"

"Probably a good idea."

"You got any plans?" asked Slik.

"Try and find the others and see if we can't take her out together," said Axel. "I hope they're having a better time at the mall than I am."

Richie barreled into Clara as the wolf lunged. He wrapped his arms around her and turned as they smashed into the wall, taking most of the force himself.

"So much for a good time at the mall," he said as the wolf sailed past them.

"Run!" shouted Clara.

They sprinted away from the werewolf as fast as they could.

"Is there any time limit to how long he can be all furry?" asked Richie.

"I've heard that lycanthropes can stay in beast form for up to an hour without any problems."

"So maybe we just have to wait until he changes back and then kill him."

"Richie, I don't know about you, but I'm already starting to get tired and he's only been chasing us for about ten minutes."

"So, yeah, got any other ideas?"

"Working on it."

They skidded around a corner with the beast right on their heels. The werewolf couldn't get any traction on the linoleum and smashed into the wall. After about a second's pause it was tearing after them again.

"I got an idea," said Richie, "but you're going to have to trust me."

"I'm up for anything."

"When I say now, turn around and start running the other way. Run around the werewolf."

"Are you insane?"

"Just trust me."

Richie took a glance back. The animal was almost breathing down their necks.

"Now!"

They both turned and started sprinting the other way. They ran around the werewolf in opposite directions. The wolf attempted to stop, but again couldn't get any traction. It turned and took a swipe at Richie who reflexively ducked. He heard the gigantic claws whistle millimeters above his head. It took a little bit for the wolf to get enough friction to start running after them.

"We need to head towards the center of the mall and see if we can't figure out a place to barricade ourselves in until he changes back."

"What about the others?" asked Clara.

"Hopefully they'll hear the sounds of people screaming and the wolf trying to eat us and come and help."

"That sounds like a brilliant plan."

"You got a better one?"

"Unfortunately no. Let's go."

"Where the hell is Alice when you need her?" asked Richie in exasperation. "Or Jensen for that matter."

Jensen grabbed Alice as the gorgon attacked. Her fangs closed on thin air.

"Run!" shouted Jensen. He had teleported them just outside the mirror shop. They took off running as the gorgon slithered out. Alice threw the mirror shield away as she ran. It only weighed her down and threw off her balance.

"Got any plans?"

"Yeah," he said. "We need to find the kids. Where do you think they'd be?"

"Richie's with Clara."

"What makes you so sure?"

"Are you telling me you haven't noticed how close those two are getting lately?"

"Not really, no."

Alice shook her head. "Men."

"Alright so where would two teenagers go in a mall."

"Clothing stores and game shops."

"I think I saw a few clothing stores towards the center of the mall. So we just need to find Axel and head towards there."

"I don't think we have to worry about Axel."

"Why not?"

"Because a gorgon appearing in the middle of a mall is going to draw a lot of attention. And knowing my son, he'll assume one or more of us are in danger and come try to help out."

"Sounds brave."

"No, it sounds stupid. He has no training, can barely use his powers, and has no subtlety whatsoever. He'll rush in and get himself killed."

"Then we had better get there first."

They ran as fast as they could towards the center of the mall with the gorgon directly behind them.

"We'll never make it before she catches us," said Alice. "You find the kids and I'll try and hold her off."

"Quit trying to be a hero," said Jensen. His form flickered and he was gone. Alice turned around just in time to see him land on the gorgon's back and then she too was gone. Jensen rematerialized right next to her a moment later.

"Let's go."

"How come you didn't just do that in the first place?"

"'Cause I was only able to teleport her about ten feet into the nearest store. It won't take her long to figure it out and be after us again."

They continued to sprint towards the center of the mall.

Richie looked over his shoulder as he and Clara reached the mall's center. The wolf was almost within clawing distance.

"Over there," said Clara. Richie looked at where she was pointing. He saw a hardware store that looked like it was deserted.

"Perfect, lets get inside and close the grate.

"You close the grate, I'm going to need to do a little something that is going to take a few seconds."

"A few seconds we don't have."

"So make them."

As they ran up to the store Richie jumped up and grabbed the grate pulling it down behind them. The wolf smashed into it but it held.

Clara spun around and chanted a few words in a language Richie didn't recognize. The wolf was suddenly flung back as if he'd been zapped.

"I thought electricity didn't work on him."

"It doesn't," said Clara. "But other types of magic do. I set up a barrier, but it won't keep him out for long."

"So basically we're still fucked."

"We at least have time to think and hope that the others will get here."

"Well they had better get here fast."

Jensen and Alice ran into the center of the mall and froze at the sight they saw. A werewolf was prowling outside of a hardware store with a closed grate. Jensen looked closer and saw a barrier shimmering over the metal.

"Now you're mine."

The gorgon's hissing broke them out of their stupor. They jumped out of the way as her teeth smashed into the ground.

"What do you want to bet that thing is after the kids?" Jensen asked.

"But which ones?"

Wooden darts smashed off the barrier.

"I'm guessing Richie and Clara."

"What makes you say that?"

"Because that mandragora is chasing Axel."

The boy sprinted in with the plant woman right on his heels.

"Mom! Jensen! What the hell is going on!"

"I think it might have something to do with that," said Jensen pointing towards the other side of the room. The others looked at where he was pointing and both cursed simultaneously. Looking over the scene like a dark statue, silent as a shadow, was a huge cloaked figure with the hilt of a massive sword sticking over it's shoulder.

All three monsters began to move in closer.

"I think we should join Richie and Clara now," said Jensen. He grabbed Axel and Alice by the shoulders just as the Calla lunged.

Richie jumped in surprise as they appeared behind them. His hands burst into flames.

"Holy hell, am I glad to see you guys," he said, extinguishing his fire balls.

"I hope you don't mind," said Axel. "But we brought a few guests to the party."

"I can see that," said Richie. "Oh by the way, have you heard that me and Clara adopted a dog."

"Yeah, about that. I think you guys might want to rethink that decision. He just tried to bite me."

They both laughed and gave each other a hug.

"I have no idea what you guys think is so funny or why you're laughing," said Clara. "But we have three Calla Bas outside that want to rip our faces off."

"Make that four," said Jensen. "Our rather large, sword-wielding friend is out there too."

"So basically, we're fucked." said Slik.

"In so many ways," said Axel.

Chapter 26

"So anybody got any ideas?" asked Richie.

"No clue," said Alice. "I can't get close to that slithery old hag without her trying to turn me into a lawn ornament. And If I can't look at an opponent I have a tough time trying to predict their moves."

"Really?" asked Richie, perplexed. "You kind of struck me as someone who would be able to do some blind swordsman crap and slice twenty guys apart with your eyes closed."

Alice smacked him in the back of the head. "Shut up, smartass. I'm good, but I'm not that good."

Richie rubbed the back of his head. "You really need to learn how to take a joke. But I know what you mean, though. Apparently werewolves aren't really affected by fire or electricity."

"Yeah, and every time I cut off a piece of that plant bitch it just grows back and she can reabsorb the parts I cut off." said Axel. "I mean it seems to hurt her, but then she just seems to get really pissed off."

"And let's not forget about that behemoth either," said Jensen. "He's a tough nut to crack just by himself."

"Well this barrier I put up isn't going to last forever," said Clara. "We need to find a way out of here. Is there a back door we could go through?"

"Already checked," said Richie. "The only way in or out is through that grate."

"It looks like our only choice is to fight," said Slik.

"So basically, we sit in here until the barrier goes down and the monsters rush in and kill us." said Richie. "Or we try to fight our way through four very powerful enemies that seem specifically chosen to make each of our particular fighting styles and abilities useless. Fantastic."

Axel cocked his head. Slik looked at him curiously.

"What's up?"

"Not sure?" said Axel. "Richie say that last part again."

"Fantastic?"

"No before that."

"Sit in here until the barrier goes down and die?"

"After that."

"Monsters specifically chosen to kill us?"

Axel drove his head into his palm "Idiot."

"Hey, that was the only part left."

"Not you," said Axel. "Me. Why the hell didn't we see this before. Richie you're a genius."

"Thank you," said Richie with a smile on his face. "Why?"

"Okay just hear me out. You just said each of these monsters was chosen specifically for taking out members of our group, right?"

"Yeah," said Richie slowly.

"You and Clara were given a werewolf because they are incredibly resistant to fire and lightning. Mom and Jensen got a gorgon because both of them need to get close to kill and when you get close to a gorgon you run a severe risk of getting turned to stone. They sent me a mandragora because no matter how much you cut them they can just grow back."

"You got a point here kid?" asked Jensen.

"Yes," said Axel, "As a matter of fact I do. What if we just switch monsters?"

They all looked at him, dumbfounded.

"How the hell will that work?" asked Clara.

"Think about it," said Axel. "If you take the gorgon you won't have the same problem as Jensen and Mom. You don't need to get close to kill, and as I recall you can still electrocute a snake to death."

Clara opened her mouth to argue, but closed it. She tilted her head to the side and stared at Axel curiously.

"That might work."

"Okay, then I'm still taking on a werewolf whose resistant to fire by myself," said Richie.

"Actually, Richie, I think you should take out the mandragora. If years of playing Pokemon games have taught me anything it's that fire has a huge advantage over grass. I wonder if she can regenerate after she's been turned to ash. And as for the werewolf, Mom won't have the same problem as with the gorgon, and with me helping I think we can manage."

"And where does that leave me, kid?"

"That giant is big, slow, and stupid," said Axel. "Who better to fight him than a guy who can be everywhere at once. He can't block everything."

"This can't be that simple," said Richie.

"It's not going to be simple," said Axel. "But we're dead if we keep trying to fight the monsters they picked for us, this way we at least stand a chance."

"If it gets us out of here alive I say we should do it," said Clara.

"We got nothing to lose," said Alice. "But they're not going to switch just because we want to."

"And that's our biggest advantage," said Axel. "They aren't going to expect us to change things up and it'll give us an element of surprise."

"So how are we going to do this?" asked Jensen. "You can't expect us to just run out there and in the chaos that ensues hope we find the right targets."

"Okay, listen close," said Axel.

"This is boring," said the mandrake.

"Patiencccce," hissed the gorgon. "The barrier will go down eventually."

"Who put you in charge," said the werewolf.

"Well sssombody has to be."

"Oh my god that hissing is so annoying," complained the mandrake. "I was told this mission was supposed to be easy and that we wouldn't actually have to interact with each other."

"Well we wouldn't if you had jussst been able to take care of one single untrained child."

"Like you're one to talk. How come your marks are still alive, huh?" the werewolf pointed out.

"Unlike you mine could actually damage me. What's your excuse."

"She has a good point," said the mandrake. "Mine could slice off pieces of me, but yours were essentially defenseless against you. How the hell are they not already dead?"

"I'm normally not a vegetarian, but I feel like I should make an exception in your case."

"Hey we're not sssuppossssed to be fighting each other."

"Stay out of this you dried-up, old hag."

"I sssee what you mean about becoming a vegetarian, at least temporarily."

"Oh my god, your voice actually hurts my ears. I think I'll make it a snake salad."

"Not getting along too well I see."

They all turned towards the new voice. Axel and Alice stood behind them.

"But, how?"

"I don't care, I could use a snack." the werewolf started advancing forward.

"Hey, he's mine."

"And the woman isss my victim."

The monsters all faced each other. Just as they were about to start they're apocalyptic brawl the giant's sword smashed into the ground between them. The shadowy figure slowly shook his head and pointed towards the two humans.

"Fine," hissed the gorgon. "We'll kill them, then each other."

"Sounds good to me."

"But you really think it's going to be that easy?" Jensen flickered into being and grabbed the giant. "I think you and I should have a little talk. Let's let the kiddies play, shall we?"

Their forms shimmered and they were gone.

"Two of them against three of us?" asked the werewolf.

"I like those odds." said the mandrake.

A fire ball hit her in the back. She screamed in agony as the searing heat caused a few of her leaves to wither.

"Hey, I want in on this." Richie stood at the entrance to the store they had barricaded themselves in.

The gorgon, who was closest, started for him. "You will make a beautiful sssstatue."

Before she struck, her body tensed and she let out a screech of pain as green electricity crawled over her.

"Why do people always forget about me?" asked Clara. She stood in the doorway of another store with Farad on her shoulder and static running up and down her arms.

"I don't know," said Richie. "You're a gorgeous girl with red steaks in her hair that can shoot lightning, not exactly forgettable."

"Richie, as much as I appreciate being called gorgeous, now is not the time for you to be flirting with me."

"Hey, we could possibly die here, I think now is the perfect time."

"Will you two shut up?" growled the werewolf. "All this lovey-dovey crap is going to give me serious indigestion while I'm trying to eat you."

He suddenly howled in pain as a throwing knife sprouted from his back.

"Silver plated blades, got to love them," said Alice.

"Okay, I vote we change targets," said the beast, yanking the knife out of his back.

"Agreed," said the other two in unison."

Jensen and the giant appeared on the upper floors of the mall. Jensen immediately teleported again. The giant looked around in confusion.

"You know that kid has a good mind for strategy," Jensen said. He was leaning against the banister looking down on the fight taking place below them. Richie was throwing fire balls at the mandrake who was simply making holes in herself so they would miss her, but Jensen could tell that even though they weren't hitting, the projectiles were taking their toll. The heat was drying her out and slowing her down. And every time she attacked the boy, he would simply burn her vines, or wooden knives, or whatever part of her she sent at him.

Clara was having fun zapping different parts of the Gorgon so they would seize in mid-strike throwing off the snake woman's balance and causing her to miss. The girl twirled and spun as she shot off lighting bolts in a maniacally beautiful dance. The gorgon didn't stand a chance.

As for Axel and Alice, the wolf was having a very tough time dealing with them, especially since Quicksteels naturally had bits of silver in their bodies and Alice liked to coat her blades with it due to its effectiveness against so many supernatural beings. It turned and snapped at both of them, but as soon as it focused on one, the other would be there to slice or stab at it.

"He even saw a use for an old man like me."

Jensen turned towards the giant. "Most people look at you and see your size as a huge, daunting advantage for you in a fight. But Axel saw it as your greatest weakness. I have seen how you move. Your size slows you down."

Jensen disappeared. The giant grunted as he felt a searing pain in his back. He swung around and his sword cleaved through thin air. He grunted again as his leg collapsed from under him.

Jensen appeared before him. "And what little mobility you actually possessed is now gone." He held up his dirk for the giant to see. It was coated crimson. The sticky liquid slowly rolled down the blade. "How well can you fight while hamstrung I wonder."

The giant swung his sword.

The fire ball whizzed through the mandragora.

"You're not very accurate," she breathed.

Richie laughed. He could tell that he was still doing damage. The heat from his fireballs was causing the mandrake to wither. Already her hair-leaves were turning brown like a tree in autumn.

"It doesn't seem to matter if you dodge if the flames still get close to you, besides you can't actually touch me."

"Oh yeah?" She sent out a fan of wooden knives. Richie threw up a wall of flames that reduced them to ash before they were able to hit him.

"Yeah I don't think you actually can."

Vines exploded through the wall. They wrapped themselves around Richie and started crushing him. He gasped for breath as one squeezed his wind pipe. The wall of flames quickly died.

"What's the matter?" asked the plant woman. "You were so talkative before. Cat got your tongue? Or in this case I guess it would be 'Vine got your throat?' Guess you can't light me on fire when I'm actually touching you, huh? Don't want to risk burning yourself."

The vines began to smolder. She screeched in pain and quickly withdrew them.

Richie coughed and greedily sucked in lung-fulls of air. His coughs quickly became laughs. "You really are stupid aren't you? What kind of pyromancer would I be if I couldn't withstand my own flames? By the way, you might want to put out your vines."

The mandragora looked down at her still smoking vines. They still had live embers on them which suddenly burst into flames. She quickly made more vines with blades on them and cut off her burning limbs which quickly disintegrated.

"This has been fun but I think it's time to end this," said Richie.

"And how are you planning on doing that?" asked the mandrake.

"Simple," said Richie. "You see I'm incubating a Brimflare in my stomach. They generate massive amounts of heat but can't actually get rid of it. So that's where I come in. I can take the extra energy and prevent it from overheating. Normally I would just disperse it through the air, I might raise the temperature of a room a little bit, but nothing majorly bad would happen. But if I were to concentrate it enough I can actually set the air on fire. This is how I make fire balls or that wall of fire. What most people don't seem to realize about pyromancers is that I don't actually have to be near where I'm concentrating the heat, there just has to be enough heat in the surrounding area for me to do what I want. See I was just keeping you distracted long enough to disperse as much heat as I could through this room. It's actually risen about ten degrees since we started fighting. Now what do you think would happen if I were to suddenly concentrate all this heat into a very small area? Like where you're standing?

The mandragora felt the temperature of the air around her rise. In a few seconds it was sweltering. The water in her body was literally boiling out of her. By the time she had the thought to move, her body was as dry as kindling. She looked at Richie fearfully and managed a strangled gasp before she burst into flames.

A smile broke out on Richie's face. "Pokemon, huh? Well Axel, apparently I'm a friggen' Charizard."

The gorgon struck. A bolt of lighting hit her mid leap and all of her muscles tensed, causing her to fall flat on her face.

"Quit that," she snarled. Clara laughed maniacally

"What, and let you eat me? Not a chance in hell."

"You're jusssst prolonging the inevitable. I can't be killed by lighting."

"Fair enough," said Clara. "Then it's time I try out something I've been wanting to do for awhile." She reached up under the back of her shirt and took out two daggers. "My parents were also electromancers. But they didn't rely on just electricity like I do. My father had a battle-ax and my mother used a bow and arrow. To see them use their weapons was nothing short of amazing. See they had this trick. They could channel electricity into the metal, and by controlling the electricity they could move the weapon without actually touching it."

Green sparks began to race up and down her daggers. "So I may not be able to kill you with electric shocks, but how about electrified blades?"

She let go of the daggers, but instead of falling to the ground they stayed floating in midair. Clara concentrated and the blades began to spin. Shooting off sparks of electricity.

Clara's eyes glowed green. "This is going to be so much fun."

She gestured with her hands and the blades shot forward. The snake managed to get out of the way, but Clara gestured again and one of the blades changed course and managed to slice through her.

The gorgon screamed. Clara smiled.

She began to dance. Twirling and twisting a beautiful dance of death. The blades followed her movements and began to dart and spin all around the gorgon. The snake-woman was fast though, she managed to dodge most of the slashes, but every once in a while one would hit and send jolts of electricity through her veins. And she was getting tired. She knew she couldn't keep this up for long.

She glanced at Clara and knew she only had one chance.

She leaped onto the girl, pinning her to the ground with her arms above her head. "If you can't move your arms then you can't direct those blades. Your mine girl."

Clara's eyes were screwed shut, but her face split into a grin. "Now who told you that?"

The gorgon tilted her head in confusion. *THUNK! THUNK!* The gorgon looked at Clara shocked as she heard the thuds and felt two objects bury themselves in her back. Her demonic eyes slid back in her skull and she collapsed on top of Clara.

The girl tried lifting the corpse off of herself, but the gorgon was mostly muscle and easily weighed a few hundred pounds.

Clara sighed laid back and concentrated. Her entire body began to glow green. The energy erupted from her body and blew the gorgon off.

She stood over the smoking corpse and smiled.

"Fried snake anybody?"

Farad crawled onto her shoulder and cooed.

"You're right. She would probably taste awful. Now let's go help the others."

The werewolf backed away holding his paw to his head. He could feel the place where his ear had been. He looked at the blood in his hands. He glared at Alice and snarled.

"I fucking hate silver."

Alice smiled holding up the top half of his left ear. "Looks like I did find a nice souvenir at the mall after all."

"Mom, that is so gross."

The wolf snarled again. "I'm done playing games. Momma always said don't play with your food. You'll live to regret it."

"I suppose when your a rampaging monster and your food wants to kill you that's a good philosophy." said Axel. "But what happens when your food refuses to be eaten."

Axel swung Slik forward. As he did the Quicksteel extended his blade and made it much more thin and flexible. The metal whip flashed towards the lycanthrope's neck. The werewolf became a blur of movement that Axel's eyes could not follow.

There was a crash and a thud next to him and he was knocked off his feet.

Axel scrambled up and looked around in confusion. He felt a vice squeeze his heart.

His mother was pinned under the werewolf. Her swords were laying out of her reach and the wolf was aiming his teeth towards her throat.

Anger and fear surged through Axel as only one thought tore through his mind.

"GET! OFF! MY! MOM!"

A blast of energy flew out of Axel with each word. The werewolf looked up in confusion as the first one slammed into him, throwing him off of Alice. He was pushed back even further by the next two. But as the fourth and strongest one hit him he flew into the wall with enough force to leave a rather large but shallow hole.

The werewolf shook his head and extracted himself from the wall.

"Annoying little whelp."

Axel was looking down but the werewolf could still see his face twist in rage. "Don't you ever touch my mother again."

The werewolf was surprised at the cold tingle that went down his his spine. Was he actually afraid of this human. He shook himself off. Humans were food. You couldn't be afraid of your food. The wolf roared and charged at the boy.

Axel raised his eyes just before the werewolf struck. The wolf hesitated. It wasn't more than a split second pause, but it was his worst mistake.

Axel's arm flickered and the wolf plowed into him. The boy dug his feet in and managed to halt the beast's momentum.

The wolf stared at Axel in surprise. He could see the blood flowing freely down the human's arm. *His* blood.

Axel jabbed Slik deeper into the wolf's throat. Suddenly another blade scraped alongside Axel's as it was stabbed through the wolf from behind. Axel looked over the wolf's shoulder to see his mother perched on it's back.

"Good job, son."

"He's not dead yet."

"On three?"

"Three."

They jerked their blades in opposite directions and the wolf's head went soaring into the air. The body stood motionless for a couple of seconds then fell forward.

"And this is why you never mess with my family."

Alice smiled. "We may be a little messed up..."

"A little?" Axel asked with a grin.

"But when somebody pisses us off, they better run like hell."

Axel looked at the headless body of the werewolf. "Or die trying."

The giant laid his sword across his back as Jensen's form flickered. He grunted as the shorter man stabbed him in the stomach.

"You learn fast. Maybe you aren't as dumb as you look. But one thing you should know about old men is that they always have a trick up their sleeve."

Jensen teleported just before the handle of the claymore crushed his skull.

He appeared on the huge man's back.

"Let's go for a ride."

The next thing the giant knew he was falling. Jensen had teleported him just under the roof in the center of the mall. The man flailed as he began to fall three stories.

"Look out below!" Jensen called as he let go of the man. The others glanced up and scattered.

Just before the giant hit the ground Jensen appeared right next to him and drove his foot into the man's stomach. When the dust had settled the giant was lying in the middle of a three-foot-deep crater.

Alice, Axel, Clara, and Richie all gathered around it. Jensen flickered right next to them.

"It's about damn time this guy died. He was getting kind of annoying."

Axel cocked his head and looked at the body curiously.

"What's wrong?" asked Slik.

"I thought I saw his hand twitch."

"But he's dead," said Richie.

Axel watched closely. The giant's finger twitched again. If he hadn't been watching he would have missed it.

"Everybody back up."

Confused they all did as he said. Just as Alice was going to ask Axel what was going on, the giant sat up. He stood and cracked his neck.

"Why won't this asshole just fucking die?" asked Richie.

"I'm so sick of this shit," said Jensen. His form flickered and he appeared on the back of the giant. He raised his dirk high and drove it into the giant's skull. The giant finally made use of his vocal cords as he howled in pain. It was the howl of a wild animal and Axel was surprised a human was capable of such a sound.

Jensen sent a pulse of energy through the blade of his knife and into the giant's brain. The man's head visibly bulged under his cowl. Jensen yanked his dirk free and teleported just as the body fell.

"Now I'm sure he's dead this time. Kind of hard to function without a brain."

"Glad that's over," said Richie.

"Yeah," agreed Axel. "I can't believe that crazy, half-assed plan actually worked. I kind of thought we were all going to die there."

"That would have been good to know before we all went ahead with it," said Clara.

"If you thought it would fail you guys wouldn't have tried so hard to make it work. I was trying to be confident and give us just a bit of hope were there was none. And it worked, so we're good."

"What if it hadn't?" asked Richie.

"Then you all would have died and I would have ended up in the hands of the enemy," said Slik. "Which is what would have happened if you hadn't tried it in the first place."

"Hey, sorry to break up all the whining," said Alice, "but we need to get out of here now. We can all bitch at Axel for being a manipulative dick later."

"Hey," said Axel. "It worked didn't it?"

"Not the point, but no time to discuss it right now. A mall full of people just saw four monsters trying to kill five people with abnormal abilities. The police will be here very soon and they are going to ask some questions we won't have good answers for. Let's go."

That spurred them all into action. They all fled the mall as fast as they could.

"Next stop, New Mexico," said Axel, with a relieved smile on his face.

Chapter 27

The sign for New Mexico flashed past.

"How much farther?" asked Axel.

"Not much," said Alice. "About fifty miles."

Axel glanced at the speedometer over her shoulder. They were going about eighty. At that rate it would take them a little over half an hour to get there. A little over half an hour and he could breathe easily.

"What's to stop them from getting into the school?" asked Richie.

"You mean besides the most powerful magical barrier in existence?" asked Jensen.

"Well, yeah," said Richie.

"Oh, just some of the most skilled living mages, who also happen to be the teachers, a flock of overly protective griffins, some the most well crafted golems currently known, and a fifty-foot high wall that's about twenty feet thick and made of magically enchanted stone. Sound good to you?"

"Yeah, yeah, that sounds like it could stop an army."

"Let's hope we don't have to put those words to the test," said Jensen.

"Look out!" screamed Clara.

A black wall enveloped the windshield. Alice immediately slammed on the breaks. Axel leaped out the door with Slik (in sword form) already in hand. The others weren't very far behind. They scanned the road behind them but saw nothing.

"What the hell was that?" asked Richie.

"'That', my dear boy, was me."

They all turned around to see a well dressed man standing behind them. He was tall with a black button-down shirt tucked into black dress pants.

"Mordechai," Jensen growled. "Should have known."

"Ah, dear brother. It's been far too long."

"Not long enough if you ask me."

"Ooh. Still angry about that little incident with your wife. What was her name now? Sally I believe."

"Her name was Sarah." said Jensen softly. He looked at his brother with pure malice.

"Wait, that's your brother?" asked Richie.

"Unfortunately."

"Ah, Richard. How have you been? Taking good care of that little present I gave you?"

Axel stared at Richie. "You know him?"

"Uh, yeah." said Richie. "You remember how I told you I found the Brimflare egg."

"Yeah..." said Axel slowly.

"Well I didn't exactly find it."

Jensen whirled and caught Richie by the collar of his shirt. "Of all the stupid things. You took a Brimflare egg from him? And what did he ask in return. And don't you dare tell me nothing."

Richie reached into his pocket and dug out a gold coin. "He asked me to hold onto this."

Jensen snatched the coin from his hand. He studied it for a few seconds then he said a few words in the same magical language Clara had used to set up her barrier. The coin melted and released a puff of black smoke.

"It had a tracking spell placed on it. That's how they always knew where we were. You fucking idiot."

Jensen whirled, his fist flying towards Richie's face. Richie flinched. But the blow never came. The boy opened his eyes to see Alice holding Jensen's fist and staring him down.

"Calm down."

"But he could have gotten us all killed."

"I know," said Alice. "And I'm just as angry and disappointed as you are, probably more so. But clocking Richie isn't going to change anything. He fucked up. And he's probably very sorry. Right, Richie?"

"I am." said Richie. "I've been thinking of a way to tell you. I should have told you as soon as I brought the egg back, but I was afraid you'd take it away. And I didn't want to lose it, or the power. And then things kept going wrong and then it hatched and, and...I'm so sorry."

Jensen took a deep breath. "It's alright." His eyes softened. "Magus know I've done my fair share of stupid shit. But next time you think about making a deal with someone who's obviously evil, please don't."

"Fair enough."

"I hate to break up this touching little moment," said Mordechai, "but I have far better things to do and quite frankly It's making me want to vomit."

Jensen turned back to his brother, the hate instantly returning to his eyes.

"I think it's time we ended our little family feud. Don't you?"

"As much as I'd love to, dear brother, I have not come to talk about our petty squabbles." He held up a finger and pointed it straight at Axel. "I am far more interested in the boy and what he possesses."

"You'll never get Slik," the boy spat.

"Is that a fact?" said Mordechai with a condescending sneer. "I tend to get what I want."

"Over my dead body."

"As you wish." Mordechai held up his hand and a ball of dark energy burst from his palm.

Before the blast could touch Axel, however, Jensen jumped in its path. He gasped as his insides turned to ice.

"Run," he growled.

"But..."

"I said get out of here!" Axel could almost feel the rage rolling off of the man.

"Everyone in the car," he said.

"Hell no," said Clara. "I'm not leaving you, Jensen."

Jensen looked at her. "Girl, this isn't the time to get all noble. I know you hate running, but this is between me and my brother."

"But...?"

"GO!"

Axel placed his hand on Clara's shoulder. "Clara we need to go."

"NO!"

"We really don't have time for this." Axel picked up Clara and threw her over his shoulder. She beat her fists on his back as he walked her to the car. He opened the door and threw her inside.

Axel looked at Richie. "Let's go man."

Richie stared at Jensen. "I can't. This is all my fault."

"Is that right?" asked Jensen. "Then I guess I have to thank you for this opportunity. I finally have a chance to kill this madman. Now go. You may have fucked up, but this is my fight."

177

Alice placed a hand on his shoulder. "He needs to do this himself, and we need to get to the school."

Richie nodded and got in the car. Alice opened the driver's door. She paused. "We'll meet you at the school."

Jensen waved without turning around. Alice got in the car and drove away.

"I hope you realize my associates are waiting for them."

"They can take care of themselves."

"That's what you thought about your son. Admittedly he did put up a good fight. But he still died begging for mercy. And that is what will happen to your new little protege. He'll go out on his knees begging for a few more minutes. For kindness that will never come. Oh how I'll take my time and make him suffer.

Jensen screamed in rage and teleported himself in front of his brother and drove his fist into Mordechai's face. His form flickered as his brother staggered back right into Jensen's roundhouse kick. As Mordechai stumbled forward Jensen flickered again. Mordechai held his hand out to the right and sent out a blast of dark energy. Jensen froze as it drilled through his stomach.

"Always so predictable. Two-hundred years since we last met and you still use the same patterns. Keep this up and I'll throw enough death energy into you that by the time this fight is over you'll be a withered husk."

Jensen straightened. "Necromancers. Always thinking they are so amazing just because they have the tiniest control over death. Just because you can control some rotting corpses doesn't mean your a god."

Mordechai laughed. "I'm better than most necromancers. They control the death energy in a corpse to work it like a puppet. I, on the other hand, actually absorb it. The little bit of life energy left inside of the body after it dies is then enough to allow the corpse to actually move on its own. Of course they now have free will, but when the corpse is someone as loyal as my three henchmen that really isn't a problem."

Jensen stared at him in horror. "You're actually bringing the dead back to life. You fucking maniac. Who are you to decide who lives and who dies?"

"Why, dear brother, you said it yourself. I'm a god. I have mastered the most powerful force in existence. I have taken the only absolute in this world and turned it into a mere suggestion. I have truly mastered death."

Jensen shook his head. "You can't master death. The best you can hope for is to keep it at bay. One day even you will die." Jensen drew his dirk. "And I plan on making today be that day."

He flickered again. Mordechai sent a pulse in front of him, but Jensen teleported again as soon as he reappeared. Mordechai sent a blast behind him, again Jensen jumped before it could hit. Mordechai sent a blast to his right. Jensen's form flickered again.

"So predictable. And now you'll come from above." He looked up just as Jensen's fist clocked him in the right side of his face. Instead of teleporting above his brother as Mordechai though he would, Jensen had teleported to a spot so close to where he actually was that it might as well have been the same. The effect was that it appeared he had teleported, when in fact he didn't.

"You were saying." Jensen pressed his advantage. Punching Mordechai twice in the gut, teleporting and kicking him in the back of his knee. Flickering again and slicing his hamstring. He teleported and kicked his brother in the back, sending him sprawling.

"You're not the only one whose learned a thing or two."

Mordechai scrambled to his feet. "You are going to pay for that."

An electronic jingle sang through the air. "One moment," said Mordechai, taking his cell phone out of his pocket.

"This had better be important," He snarled into the phone, turning to spit out some blood. The look of anger was replaced by confusion, which slowly became manic glee. "I'm on my way. And good work."

He returned the phone to his pocket. "Well, dear brother," he said, straightening his hair and shirt, "I would love to stay and finish our little chat, but something extremely important has just come up. I suppose we'll just have to take care of this some other time."

"Or we'll take care of it now," said Jensen. "You are not walking away from me."

Mordechai stared at him. "We both have somewhere more important to be. I wasn't lying about my associates. You might want to hurry. Until next time brother."

He turned and was enveloped in a cloud of dark energy. When it cleared he was gone.

Jensen screamed in rage. "This isn't over you coward."

Clip crawled onto his shoulder and burbled something into his ear. "I know, little buddy, I know. Let's go help the others and hope we aren't too late."

Chapter 28

"We need to go back," screamed Clara.

"No," said Axel. "He needs to fight his brother by himself."

"What if he dies?"

"That's the risk he took," Alice pointed out. "He knew what he was getting himself into, probably more than any of us. He wants to fight his brother for closure."

"That's stupid."

"Clara, what would happen if you found the guy who killed your parents and one of us killed him instead of you? How would you feel?" asked Richie.

"That bastard is mine and if we do find him you are all to back the fuck off."

"That's how Jensen feels," said Slik. "Except it's worse do to the fact that this is his brother who he loved and trusted until Mordechai betrayed him in one of the worst ways possible. Even if he dies from this, if we were to interfere in any way he would hate us and himself forever."

"Besides," said Axel, "We have a more important matter to deal with. Right Richie?"

"How many times do I have to say I'm sorry?"

"You mean for selling us out to a crazy bastard who's been hunting us? And just for something as pointless as power?"

"Okay, that's it." Richie turned around. "Yes, I'm sorry I made a deal with Mordechai. But let's get something straight. I'm not sorry I made the deal, just who I made it with. Ever since you got Slik you've done nothing but bitch and moan. 'Oh no, there's monsters and sorcerers after me. Let's all forget that for some reason that even without my talking blob of metal that turns me into Superman I have enough magical energy to completely obliterate like thousands of harpies. Or that all of this probably would have happened anyway. But I just can't stand that my perfect life as the school's best football player and guy that every girl I meet wants to lose her virginity to is over. Suddenly with all this amazing power I'm less attractive. Oh wait...I'm not.' Do you seriously not hear yourself?

"I've had to watch as you do things people would give everything they have to be able to do. I had to watch as an amazing, beautiful, smart, funny, albeit slightly crazy, girl walked up to you and started hitting on you while completely ignoring me. And I got to watch as your seemingly normal mother, whose half my size by the way, changed from the strict but kind woman who basically treated me like her son, but also looked like she was going to collapse from stress, into some bad-ass sword-wielding monster slayer. All the while I had to sit there and attempt to not die. I was baggage and you guys know it. But since I've made the deal you all look at me differently. I'm now one of you. I actually belong. So don't give me any shit cause I know in a heart-beat, no matter what you say, that if any of you was my position you would have done the same thing."

They all stared at him speechless. Axel finally recovered enough to close his mouth. He ran his hand through his hair and shook his head. "Richie, I had no idea."

"Of course you didn't. You were too busy thinking about yourself."

Axel took a deep breath. "I'm sorry. And you're wrong. I wouldn't have done the same thing. I probably would have curled up in the fetal position and gotten killed by some monster, before I ever had the chance to make the deal."

Richie shook his head and laughed. "You're probably right."

Clara snorted. "Probably? He would have been so busy bitching he wouldn't have even noticed as the werewolf tore him in half."

"Shut up, Bitch."

"Asshole"

"Skank"

"Whore"

"Dumb-ass"

"Douche"

"Shut up!" Alice glanced at them in the rear-view mirror. "Now is not the time for you all to be fighting."

"No, it's okay," said Richie. "They actually do it on purpose. I think it's their way of saying I love you."

"Richie are you saying that the girl you're interested in is in love with your best friend?" asked Clara.

"I meant in a completely platonic way. Like a brother and sister. Besides Axel said your so crazy he'd never have sex with you in a million years."

"I never said that."

Slik cleared his throat. "You said and I quote 'Richie, if you try this, when, and this is a when not an if, when Clara goes ballistic, I will not help you. I'm going to laugh my ass off while hiding in a bush saying I told you so and praying to any deity I can think of to not let her find me."

Clara stared at Axel with her eyebrow cocked and a feigned smile on her face. "Really, you think I'm that bad, huh."

"Richie I'm going to kill you." Silence met his statement. His brow furrowed. Richie was never one to let someone else get the last word. "Richie?" he turned to his best friend who was staring open-mouthed and wide-eyed out the back window. All color had completely drained from his face.

"Richie?" He snapped his fingers in front of his friend's face. "Richie! What are you even sta-..."

He turned to look at what the other boy was staring at. "Holy fuck!"

"What?" said Alice turning around. "Oh you got to be fucking kidding me!" she exclaimed as she saw what the others were staring at."

"Not again," groaned Slik. Roaring down the street after them on motorcycles were three very familiar figures wearing black cloaks.

"What do you mean 'Not again?'" asked Axel.

"You are not the first people to have killed these men."

"Are you sure of that?" asked Richie.

"Positive. The last man I know for sure who killed them was my previous wielder, Jason."

"I thought you were in that box for seven-hundred years," said Clara.

"I was."

"How the hell are they behind us then?" asked Axel.

"My guess, they have a necromancer on their pay-role."

Richie furrowed his eyebrows. "Death magic? That actually exists?"

Axel gave him a quizzical look.

"What? I'm a huge sci-fi and fantasy nerd. Of course I know what necromancy is."

Axel shrugged. "Fair enough."

"To answer you question," said Alice. "Yes, necromancy exists. There is a type of Calla Lutai called a Necroarachna or Death Spider. When living things are born they have a set amount of life energy, as they age it is converted to death energy. This process can be accelerated or slowed down by many things, but basically the more life energy you have the more likely you are to stay alive, the more death energy the more likely you are to die. Necroarachnas have an incredibly accelerated life to death process, basically they make death energy very quickly. Their wielders can control death energy, by doing so they can harmlessly dissipate the energy into their environment."

"Or inject it into a corpse and control it like a rotting meat puppet," Clara added.

"Or blast it into someone else until they become so full of death energy they actually die." said Axel.

An arrow slammed into the rear windshield.

"Maybe we should talk about this later," said Slik.

"How much farther," said Axel.

"About ten minutes." said Alice as another arrow hit the window sending spider webs across the glass.

The whip man rode up beside them swinging his lash. He brought it down on the hood, leaving a dent across it's length. He brought it down again, this time it sliced through the middle of the car. Axel and Clara brought their legs up just before it would have sliced them off.

The rear windshield exploded as another arrow smashed through it embedding itself in the dashboard. Alice swerved at the whip man, narrowly missing him. Fortunately, he did slow down enough that they were able to pull out of his range.

"That's it," Clara snarled. She pulled out her daggers and sent electricity through them. She hurled them out the shattered window. The men easily maneuvered their bikes out of their path, but Clara just pulled them back. They headed straight for the archer who had another arrow knocked and ready to fire. Just before they buried themselves in his back, a claymore appeared and they bounced harmlessly off. The giant calmly returned his sword to its sheath.

The archer loosed his arrow straight for Clara's head. She covered her face with her arms. A searing heat whooshed past her face. She opened her eyes to see the arrow burning on the road behind them. She turned around to see Richie holding out his hand.

"You okay?" he shouted above the roaring of the wind. She numbly nodded her head.

The giant gunned the throttle on his bike and cruised up beside them. He unsheathed his sword and jammed it into the front tire.

The car spun and flipped, coming to a rest in the ditch beside the road. Thankfully it had landed right side up.

Axel sat up and shook his head. He looked down at himself. Nothing felt broken, in fact besides a few cuts, scrapes, and bruises, not to mention a killer headache, he was completely unharmed.

"Wow that was lucky. Everybody okay?"

None of them answered. He looked around in panic. Clara seemed to be breathing, and Richie was moaning faintly in the front, but his mother wasn't moving. He reached forward and felt her neck and was relieved to feel a pulse. He tried opening his door but it wouldn't budge.

"Hey Slik, you alright little buddy?"

Tiny drops of silvery fluid gathered on his knee. Slik's head emerged from the resultant puddle and he shook himself off. "I'll live."

"Great, can you make yourself into a sword? I need to cut through this door."

"Sure thing." Axel jammed Slik into the door and jerked upward. It came away with a screech and fell to the ground. Axel climbed out and cautiously surveyed his surroundings. The three men sat on their motorcycles nearby. Slik returned to his normal form.

"We are in quite bind here, Kid."

"Tell me about it." Axel looked down the road. He watched as what he thought were mountains slowly resolved into a massive black wall with the tops of tall, medieval style buildings peeking over it. A transparent blue haze seemed to form a dome over all of them.

"We were so close."

"If you run you might be able to make it."

"I wouldn't be able to take two steps before I got shot with an arrow. Besides, even if I did manage to get away, I can't just leave the others here. These guys will probably kill them out of spite."

"So what are you going to do?"

Axel looked at him. It was so hard to believe that all of this started over something so tiny.

"Well as I see it I have three options. Option One, run like a little bitch. We've already discussed that and pointed out all the major flaws.

Option Two, I hand you over to them in exchange for allowing the rest of us to live."

Slik looked at him. "I'm actually glad you suggested it, because that sounds like our best option right now."

"Hey we still have Option Three."

"Which is?"

"We fight."

"Axel the others are kind of out of it right now. The odds are heavily against you walking away from that."

"Hey, they get you either way. At least this way, I might buy they others enough time to recover enough to defend themselves. And who knows, I might be able to take one of them with me."

"You are untrained. And they are much bigger and stronger than you are. We are outnumbered and outmatched. And you still want to fight them?"

"Slik everything you just said is true and has been true this entire time. By all rights I should be dead ten times over by now, but I'm not. I have no idea how, but I've managed to survive this long. And I'm not giving up when I'm this close. Not without a fight."

The men revved their engines.

"Well then I guess we're fighting. Let's get this over with."

Axel stared at the three men in cloaks who had chased him across the country and attempted to murder him and his friends. All for the tiny metal blob in his hands who was so terrified that Axel could actually feel him quivering.

"Slik I just want to say I'm sorry for being a whiny bitch this entire time. Truth be told, I regret nothing. I am honored that you have allowed me to be your wielder."

"And I am honored to be your partner. Now let's kick some ass."

Chapter 29

Axel ducked under the great sword, sliced the arrow aimed at his neck in half and deflected a blow from the whip flying toward his side. He whirled around to take a swipe at the whip's owner who had driven too close, but was sent flying when the giant's fist crashed into his face. He staggered to his feet and spit out a mouthful of blood.

"We need a plan."

"Do you think it's too late to run?" said Slik, returning to blob-form.

"Not helping!"

"Sorry," said Slik. Axel dived and rolled out of the way as the lash-bearer tried to run him down. A line of arrows followed him, one grazed the back of his calf. It was a very shallow wound, but it stung like fire.

"Any advice that doesn't make me look like a coward?"

"Well since you've had a combined total of about five hours of sword lessens, and only about five minutes of that involved you actually fighting someone, I'd say we're kind of boned here if you keep trying to go at them with a weapon that they have probably dealt with a thousand times before and that you barely know how to use."

"That's encouraging," said Axel, jumping out of the way as the giant swung his claymore at Axel's head. Axel landed in the dirt. He looked up to see the archer taking aim at his head.

"Slik! Shield! Now!"

Slik expanded into a two-foot diameter disc just in time to stop the arrow from punching a hole into Axel's brain.

"Thanks man."

Slik's eyes appeared on the back of the shield. "No problem."

Axel got to his feet and picked up the metal disc. He heard the whistling and moved before he even saw the whip. It bounced harmlessly off of the shield.

Axel stared at it as a plan began to form in his head.

"Slik, can you give me a handle or a strap or something so that I can put you on my arm?"

The disc boiled as a band grew out of the shield on the side with Slik's eyes. Axel placed his right arm inside of it and it tightened until it was snug. Axel brought the shield up and blocked two more arrows aimed for his head and neck.

Axel started running. "This is great," he said. "Now can you make the edge as sharp as you possibly can and maybe curve yourself a little bit?" Small ripples moved over the shield as Slik did as Axel asked. Just as Slik's shape solidified, the whip-man rode his bike right into Axel's path. He twirled his whip above his head and gunned the throttle.

Instead of jumping or rolling out of the way, Axel started running as fast as he could toward the man. Just before impact, Axel jumped at him in a flying tackle with the shield up in front of his body. He connected with the lash-bearer and tore him from his seat. Axel rolled off of him as he landed and ended up on his feet. He turned around in time to see the whip-man's bike crash into the giant. He was now wrapped up in a pile of twisted metal.

The whip-man was lying dazed on the ground. Before he had a chance to recover, Axel rushed over and drove the edge of the shield into the man's chest. He jerked it out and stood up straight, looking at his new weapon with satisfaction.

"I can't believe that actually worked so well. First the mall and now this. I really need to start half-assing my plans more often."

"Yeah, yeah," said Slik. "Be proud of yourself later. Here comes another one."

"Right," said Axel, whipping up his shield to block the flurry of arrows. As the archer got closer Axel jumped out of his path, turning in mid air so that the shield was parallel with the ground right in front of the motorcycle's front wheel.

The force almost took Axel's arm off and sent him spinning and rolling along the ground. The shield had sliced through the front tire, which caused the bike to vault the archer twenty feet to land heavily on his back. He was able to get to his feet, nocking and drawing an arrow as he did so. As he turned to fire, a silver flash sliced though his bowstring and embedded itself in his chest. Axel yanked Slik out of the man's body the Quicksteel reverting to blob-form.

"I'm just a living weapon so my opinion probably doesn't matter much here, but I don't think you're supposed to throw a shield like a discus."

"It worked didn't it?"

"Not the point."

"Why are you complaining, we actually won."

A groaning screech filled the air as the giant wrestled himself out of the twisted pile of scrap metal that was the remains of the two motorcycles.

"You were saying."

"Two out of three isn't bad," said Axel. "I thought for sure I was going to die like five seconds into this fight."

"This isn't one of those two-out-of-three moments, Kid. We have to kill them all or it means nothing."

Axel glanced towards the car. There was still no movement from inside.

He looked back towards the giant with his jaw set. He had to do this. He felt the adrenaline rush he got before any big football game, but this time it was amplified. Before he just had to worry about letting his team down, but if they lost they shook their heads, showered off, and practiced for the next game. Now it wasn't a game. If he lost he, his mother, and his friends would die.

"Slik, I'm going to need some advice for this one."

"Remember what you told Jensen? You are much faster and more agile than he is. Just keep moving and get in cuts where you can. Even if each individual injury is small, they will get big fast. Even if you have to keep fighting until he bleeds out then so be it. Just hit him more times than he can hit you."

The giant grabbed the ruined carcass of one of the motorcycles.

"Slik I need a sword."

The Quicksteel glittered as it sliced through the bike. The two halves tumbled down the road.

The giant had closed the distance between them with surprising speed. He swung the blade in a horizontal slash. Axel ducked and side stepped and slashed at the man's stomach. The giant's sword met Slik and Axel felt the vibration's numb his arm.

Axel leaped back. The giant leveled his sword at him and charged. Axel spun and slashed at the man's leg. The giant turned at caught the blow. Axel spun to the left and slashed at the man's kidney. As the giant brought his sword up Axel spun to the left and sliced his left leg just above the knee.

Axel could feel the energy from Slik mixing with his own. The Quicksteel felt like he was just an extension of Axel's arm, like he had been in Axel's hand for his entire life.

As he stared at the giant the world began to flicker. Day turned to night. Asphalt became dirt. Trees flourished where before there had been only desert. The giant charged again. Axel felt his body move of it's own volition, as if someone was jerking him around like a puppet.

He took two steps, jumped as the giant slashed at him, drove his sword into the ground and pushed off with his arm. He spun in the air and drove his foot into the giant's chest, landing behind Slik in a crouch.

The world snapped back to normal. The giant staggered back, but remained upright. Axel could still see the other place in his mind. It felt like a memory, but one he knew wasn't his own. As the giant moved towards him again, he saw how it had happened before, saw the sword bite into his side. Defeat even in victory.

Axel grabbed Slik and rolled away from the slash that would have cut him in two. He could still feel the energy from the Quicksteel flowing into him, helping guide his movements. The world seemed to come into focus. And not just his vision. He could hear the soft shift of the giant's muscles, smell the sweat and decay from the man, feel the heat rolling off of him.

The man moved toward him with exaggerated slowness. Axel moved. He slipped around the blade and slashed though the man's stomach. Twirled around the man, spinning Slik so fast he looked like a saw. He slashed the man's kidney, swung up and sliced under his arm, taking out the brachial artery. Spun and crouched taking the man's hamstring and moving lighting fast to sever the femoral artery on the other leg. He rolled behind the giant and stabbed Slik into his back, sliding him in between the man's ribs and turning his lung to hamburger.

In a span of about three seconds, Axel had delivered multiple fatal wounds. He jumped back, but the giant managed to stay on his feet. Still moving when any normal person would be dead. He brought up his sword.

Axel gritted his teeth, almost positive now this man was a monster. He saw the car sitting behind the man. His loved ones were counting on him. Axel looked into the shadow of the hood that hid the man's face. All of the pain, desperation, and fear of the last few days swelled up inside of him. This man had put him through hell.

Axel screamed in rage, all of the emotions over the last few weeks finally boiling over. In his mind Slik screamed with him. Their souls mixing and fusing. Axel charged the man, bringing his sword high above his head. The giant managed to get his sword up just in time.

But it didn't matter. The energy flowed out of Slik in a blast, shearing through the Claymore as if it were a piece of paper. Slik slammed into the man's chest. Axel yanked him out and sliced through the giant's neck.

There was a thud as the giant's head hit the ground. His body followed a couple of seconds later with a crash.

Axel stood panting. He had done it. His family was safe.

Slik returned to his original form. The metal blob was also gasping for breath. "Good job, kid. I have no idea how you did it, but you won."

"At the risk of sounding overly cliché, *we* won."

Slik nodded. "We should go check on the others."

"In a minute," said Axel. "I'm still a little dizzy."

Axel shook his head. "I just need to lie down for a bit."

Darkness began to encroach on the edges of his vision. The world seemed to drift away. The last thing he heard was Slik screaming his name.

Chapter 30

The world was slow to come into focus. Axel blinked his eyes uncertainly. He was lying in a large feather bed with criminally soft sheets. A large window to his right allowed him a view of clear blue sky.

Axel looked around and saw nine other beds like his, all empty. Curtains stood open around all of the beds, but could be closed for some semblance of privacy if desired. He scratched at an itch on his arm and found a plastic tube that lead up to an IV bag.

Slik was asleep on his chest, curled into a ball and snoring softly.

"Wow, I never thought a blob of metal could actually look cute."

"And I never thought I'd hear you use the word 'cute,'" said Slik opening his eyes.

Axel chuckled softly. "Where are we?"

"Mortimer's Academy for the Supernatural."

"So we made it?"

"We made it."

"Where are the others?"

"Probably eating."

Axel's stomach growled. "Speaking of which..."

Now it was Slik's turn to chuckle.

"So, how long have I been out."

"About two days."

"Two days!"

"Calm down," said Slik. "You used a lot of energy in that fight. You also have a broken rib and a bunch of scratches and bruises. The one on the back of your calf looked particularly nasty. The woman who healed you said it was lucky she caught it. Apparently the archer likes to coat his arrows with poison."

"You are not helping me remain calm."

"Don't worry. The healer took care of everything. You'll be off trying to get yourself killed in a few days."

Axel thought back to the fight. "Hey Slik?"

"Yeah?"

"During the fight, I saw images of someone else who had fought the giant. They felt like memories. Do you know anything about that?"

Slik sighed. "They were from Jason, my last wielder. He died defeating those men so that he could get me to a safe house. Someplace where I could remain hidden."

"It felt like he was moving my body, fighting for me."

"That's very possible," said Slik. Axel furrowed his brow and tilted his head. "I told you before that Calla Lutai trade bits of their souls with their wielders. Part of Jason's soul resides in me, just as part of yours does. We were very strongly connected during that fight. The part of Jason's soul inside me must of thought you needed some help."

"I'm glad he did," said Axel. "I would have probably died if it weren't for him."

"Well it looks like you're finally awake."

Axel looked in the direction of the voice to find the nurse had walked in. She appeared to be in her mid-twenties, with long flowing blond hair that cascaded down past her shoulders. She had beautiful dark-blue eyes and a warm smile. She wore a white lab coat over a long black dress that ended about mid calf. Her feet were sheathed by a set of black heels that added to her height. It was hard to tell from the position he was in, but Axel guessed she was about five-nine. A small white snake rested on her shoulders.

Axel sat up slowly. "And you must be the healer that saved my life. Thank you."

Her smile grew wider. "Don't mention it. Besides, I heard you saved my brother's life a few times so consider us even."

"Your brother?"

She laughed. "I should probably introduce myself. My name is Lilith." She extended her hand toward him.

Axel stared at her in awe. *She* was Mordechai's twin sister? He shook his head to clear it and took her hand. "You are not what I was expecting."

"Oh?"

"I thought you would look more like your twin."

A light clicked behind her eyes. "Ah, I see you've met Mordechai then."

"I have. It was actually his men that are responsible for me being here."

"Then for that I would have to apologize. You see, when we were little, we were each given a Calla Lutai. Jensen got Clip, I was lucky enough to get Vitae here," she reached up and gently stroked the snake, "and Mordechai got Mortis."

"Mortis?"

"I'm assuming you've met Clip."

Axel nodded.

"Well, Vitae here is a Thuergalserpentae, a Life Viper. Through her I can control life energy. It's what makes me such a good healer."

"Also explains why you are a nurse at a school for magic. I've seen some of the side effects of misusing it."

"You haven't seen anything yet. Anyway, Mortis is a Necroarachna. He gives Mordechai power over death energy. But he has also twisted and polluted my brother's mind. He is now obsessed with power and will do anything to get it."

"Yeah, I know. His henchmen chased me here from New York. It has been one hell of a week."

"You can say that again," said Richie walking into the room. Clara, Alice and Jensen were close behind them.

Alice rushed over and hugged her son. He gave out a gasp of pain as she attempted to break more of his ribs.

"Mom, I love you too, but that kind of hurts."

"Sorry," said Alice releasing him. "I'm so glad you're okay."

Her hand snaked out and smacked the back of his head. "Don't you ever scare me like that again. I mean, what were you thinking? Taking on those three by yourself? I swear you are just trying to give me an ulcer."

Axel laughed and immediately regretted it. Having a broken rib really sucked.

"Leave the boy alone, Alice," said Jensen. "He did fine."

"No thanks to you," said Lilith, rounding on her brother. "Why on Earth would you ever teach an untrained novice how to merge souls with his Calla Lutai?"

"I didn't," said Jensen. "He did that by himself."

Lilith looked shocked. "But how? That takes an incredible amount of energy and control."

"I have no idea how he did it," said Richie, "But whatever he did, I'm glad he did it. Dude you totally saved out asses back there."

Clara snorted. "It was no big deal."

"What do you mean no big deal?"

Axel looked at her critically and asked, "Clara, are you mad because you didn't get to help kill them?"

"Maybe."

"Well, if you had gotten off your lazy ass and joined me I would have been glad for the help."

"Hey, it's not my fault I was knocked unconscious, Douche."

"Bitch."

"Asshole."

"Dumbass."

"Slut."

"Whore."

"Not again," said Richie. "You two have no idea how annoying that is."

"Shut up, Dick!" they both screamed together. They looked at each other and started laughing.

Lilith took Jensen aside. "We have to keep an eye on him."

Jensen looked at the three teenagers laughing and joking with each other. "We have to keep an eye on all three of them. But, let's let them have a few days of rest. They have definitely earned it."

Lilith looked him in the eye. "We are not done here, not by a long shot."

"So what do we do now?" asked Axel.

"Well, for now," said Alice, "I've enrolled you in this school. So starting tomorrow you'll be training."

"What kind of training?"

"Well," said Lilith, "we have normal classes, like history, math, and science. But we also have classes for magic, learning the ancient language, and, of course, weapons specialty classes."

"Sweet," said Axel. "I'll take as many of the weapons classes as I can."

"That's great," said Alice. "And you're in luck because they just got a new Battle Arts teacher."

"Are they really good or famous or something?" asked Axel.

Alice smiled at him evilly. "Not just good, the best."

"Mom, please don't tell me it's you."

"You got it."

"Crap."

Epilogue

"Get out of my site!"

Mordechai shut the door behind him as the glass shattered against it. Lady Nyphon had a notorious temper and didn't tolerate failure very well. As the Magus of Revenge and Hatred it was to be expected. Though he suspected she wouldn't be mad for very long. He may not have been able to get the Quicksteel as she asked, but the prize he gave her was far more valuable.

"She sounds pissed," said Alexei, falling in step with the necromancer.

"She will get over it soon enough," replied Mordechai smoothly.

"Maybe, but you have to be smarting. I mean losing to a boy, you are getting sloppy in your old age."

"His power was unprecedented. I will not underestimate him again."

"'Unprecedented' is putting it mildly. I've never known of one so young to be able to form a complete soul meld. And so soon after awakening his magic. Your brother always had an eye for talent."

"I wouldn't say that. He trained you didn't he?"

Alexei chuckled. "I said he had an eye for talent, I didn't say that the talent always listened."

Mordechai glanced at the ice mage. "What exactly is it that you want?"

"I thought that maybe you could use a little help."

"Why would I need help?"

"You're right, you have this totally under control. Tell me, How badly were your little puppets damaged? I heard the big one in particular was in a very sorry state."

"The boy is very resourceful."

"Again, putting it mildly."

"Even if I did agree to your help, what exactly do you get out of this?"

195

Alexei smiled. "You let me worry about that. Now come on, we could both use a bit of a win here."

"I don't like you and I don't trust you."

"And the feeling is mutual. But why does it matter? Who cares who delivers the Quicksteel? If we deliver it together, Lady Nyphon will be just as pleased as if only one of us does. We both have our methods and resources. We could make a powerful team."

"What exactly did you have in mind?"

"The boy has power. More than can be explained by a Calla Lutai, even one such as that."

"He is John Matson's grandson. That means he comes from a long line of powerful mages."

"That might explain it. Except I've met John, and I know of his daughter. Both are very skilled and very powerful, but I don't feel as if that would account for all of his potential."

"What are you getting at?"

"Do we know anything about the boy's father?"

Mordechai paused. "Do you know something?"

"I have my suspicions. And if they are correct, we could be in very big trouble if daddy dearest decides to enter the picture."

"Whoever he is he's no match for me."

"Because you've proven yourself to be invincible," said Alexei, his voice dripping with sarcasm.

"Even if the boy's father can beat me, nothing can destroy Lady Nyphon," Mordechai pointed out.

"Correct," said Alexei. "Nothing can kill a Magus. Well almost nothing."

"What are you suggesting."

"I'm just saying that maybe we should keep an open mind," said Alexei. "I will do some digging and see what come's up. In the meantime, I think it would be in everybody's best interests to keep an eye on him."

"And are you going to do that?" asked Mordechai with a sneer. "Because I think you're a little old to be going to school."

Alexei laughed. "I wouldn't make it through the door. Neither would you for that matter. We would both be killed on site."

"Then it's a good thing that I don't plan on going to the Academy myself."

"Oh, but you do have someone in mind?" asked Alexei with a sly grin. "I knew I could count on you, you sneaky devil."

"Yes, I have agents everywhere, even in the school. I may be old, but I assure you that I have not lost my touch, despite what you might think."

"Let's hope not, my friend. For both out sakes."

Printed in the United States
By Bookmasters